MURDER IN AN IRISH PUB

Siobhan climbed the ladder while Eoin held it. When she reached the window and saw layers of grime, she wished she had gloves. She used her sleeve to wipe a patch clear and peered in. Expecting to see a lad laid out on the floor, she was thrown when she saw something suspense in midair. *Is that a sack?* Even as her mind was searching for reasonable explanations, her body was already reacting to the horror.

It's a man. Suspended from the ceiling . . .

Books by Carlene O'Connor

Irish Village Mysteries

MURDER IN AN IRISH VILLAGE

MURDER AT AN IRSH WEDDING

MURDER IN AN IRISH CHURCHYARD

MURDER IN AN IRISH PUB

MURDER IN AN IRISH COTTAGE

A Home to Ireland Mystery

MURDER IN GALWAY

Published by Kensington Publishing Corporation

Murder in an Irish Pub

CARLENE O'CONNOR

KENSINGTON BOOKS
www.kensingtonbooks.com

KENSINGTON BOOKS are published by

Kensington Publishing Corp.
119 West 40th Street
New York, NY 10018

All Kensington titles, imprints, and distributed lines are available at special quantity discounts for bulk purchases for sales promotion, premiums, fund-raising, educational, or institutional use. Special book excerpts or customized printings can also be created to fit specific needs. For details, write or phone the office of the Kensington Special Sales Manager: Attn. Special Sales Department. Kensington Publishing Corp, 119 West 40th Street, New York, NY 10018. Phone: 1-800-221-2647.

Kensington and the K logo Reg. U.S. Pat. & TM Off.

ISBN-13: 978-1-4967-1907-2
ISBN-10: 1-4967-1907-7
First Kensington Hardcover Edition: March 2019
First Kensington Mass Market Edition: February 2020

ISBN-13: 978-1-4967-1910-2 (e-book)
ISBN-10: 1-4967-1910-7 (e-book)

10 9 8 7 6 5 4 3 2 1

Printed in the United States of America

Acknowledgments

Thank you to my agent, Evan Marshall, my editor, John Scognamiglio, and all the staff at Kensington Publishing, who work tirelessly behind the scenes on every book. Thank you to my friends and family, especially my mother Pat Carter, whose endless well of ideas keeps me inspired and challenged. I hadn't intended on writing a locked-room mystery until she believed I could do it. Thank you for that. Thank you to fellow writer and friend Tracy Clark for your support; thank you to Kevin Collins, Seamus Collins, and Bridget Quinn for all my random questions; and last, but never least, thank you, dear readers, for reading.

Chapter 1

Siobhán O'Sullivan dimmed the lights in Naomi's Bistro, tucked falling strands of her auburn locks into her garda cap, and smoothed down the coat of her uniform as if she was going on a date instead of reporting for duty. What luck. Getting paid to attend the opening rounds of the International Poker Tournament. The good folks of Kilbane were stunned it was being held in their medieval village. Imagine, Eamon Foley, the best poker player in all of Ireland, just a few doors down in O'Rourke's Pub. A tinker out of Dublin, he won so often that people surmised he had eight hands under the table, earning him the nickname: "the Octopus."

Perhaps the moniker had nothing to do with his mad card skills, and his wandering eyes were to blame. Siobhán wasn't a gambler, but she'd bet his pregnant wife wasn't happy about that.

Siobhán stepped out into the fresh spring night,

locked the door to the bistro, and flipped on the light above their sign. NAOMI'S BISTRO was carved on a wooden plank, written in black script and outlined in her favorite color, robin's egg blue. Looking at it always gave her a rush of pride, that comforting feeling she was home. Like many families who ran businesses in Kilbane, Siobhán and her siblings lived in a flat above the bistro, melting the lines between work and home like a hearty ham-and-cheese toastie.

She stepped onto the footpath and took in the white tents being erected up and down Sarsfield Street. This weekend would deliver a double dose of excitement, coupling the poker tournament with the annual Arts and Music Festival. Starting tomorrow, the place would be alive with paintings, and carvings, and Irish dancing, and handmade wares, and musicians staked out on corners, making heads bob and feet tap.

There was something so delicious about closing a street to traffic, and ambling down it without fear of being mowed over by a lad with a twitchy foot. Twilight was descending, injecting purple and red streaks into the Irish skies. The sound of hooves caught her attention. Sixteen-year-old Amanda Moore was leading her prized racehorse, Midnight, down the street, holding the rope gently, her father striding proudly beside her. Only two years old, he'd already won the Cork Races and was favored to win many more. He was all shiny black and sinewy muscle. Gorgeous. Siobhán wished she had time to stop and nuzzle the horse, but the games were about to begin.

She felt a tad guilty as she passed the tent for Naomi's Bistro, imagining her brother James hard at work, until she spotted him sparring with Ciarán, the runt of the O'Sullivan Six litter. They held their tent poles aloft, thrusting and slicing through the air, locked in a deadly duel. James gave her a nod and a wink, while she resisted the urge to warn them about losing an eye.

Just ahead, a line snaked out of O'Rourke's Pub, and lads itching to part with their wages clustered around the betting shops. The air was thick with the smell of curried chips and easy money. Piles and piles of money. The winning purse was a quarter of a million euro. Not to mention all the side bets that were being made, deals done in the shops, and deals done on the footpath, and deals done in the dark. She shuddered to think of the men who would bet it all, feverish with hope, only to end up losing everything but the shirts on their back, and sometimes they lost that too. If only it was hyperbole. Betting could spike a fever in some men, and those stricken with the worst of it had lost tractors, and cars, and houses, and cattle, and eventually wives.

Across the way, Sheila Mahoney was puffing on a cigarette outside of her hair salon, platinum blond hair streaked with green, spy glasses perched over her ample bosom, as if she planned on peering in on the games from a distance. She spotted Siobhán, held up a strand of her hair, and mimicked hacking it off. It had been ages since Siobhán had paid her a visit. She absentmindedly touched her cap as she stared at Sheila's new black-and-white sign: CURL UP AND DYE.

Siobhán turned her attention to the pub, and her heart sank when she saw the line. There were so many people they crowded out the front window sporting Declan's collection of Laurel and Hardy memorabilia. O'Rourke's was an institution in Kilbane, as it well should be. Declan had been serving pints, and holding court, and hearing confessions longer than Father Kearney. He was as respected as he was feared, which was why his pub was chosen to host the games. If lads got too riled up, one could count on Declan O'Rourke to settle them down. Menace and knacks would not be tolerated, not in his pub.

Garda or not, this crowd looked as if they'd toss you into the street for cutting ahead of the line. Siobhán was relieved when she saw Maria's pretty face pop up in the window and gesture to the patio. By the time she reached it, Maria was waiting to usher her in through the back. Tonight it paid to have dear friends who worked in the pub. "Hurry. Round one will be starting, so." They pushed their way through the sea of bodies until they could duck behind the counter. Siobhán loved the long polished oak bar with its scratches and dents, initials, and dates, secrets embedded like fossils in the water-marked swirls.

Maria plunked down a pair of wooden crates so they could stand on them and see over the heads to the poker tables. What Maria lacked in height, she made up for with her big personality. She was not one to miss out, and she'd have your head if you dared exclude her.

Siobhán scanned the room for Macdara Flannery, not sure if she was looking for her detective sergeant or her lover, feeling foolish when she spotted him in plain clothes. Their eyes locked and her heart gave a squeeze. That tall man, that messy hair, those blue eyes, and that lopsided grin he flashed like a weapon. She worried once again if any of them had seen her sneaking out of his flat in the early hours of the morning. He was her superior, and romance was forbidden. Yet they persisted.

She looked away first, heat crawling up her neck. She hated to admit it, but ever since their romance had become clandestine, it had added an undeniable excitement, a rush that fueled her days with an extra spark. It was hard enough to prove oneself as a female guard, and not a day went by when she didn't berate herself for the risk they were taking. For the first time in her life, she could relate to drug addicts. The inability to stop. The insatiable craving for more.

Why didn't he tell her the uniform wasn't required? Her eyes flicked around the room, clocking the other guards. Not a single one had put on his or her uniform. She was like that lone eejit at a party who passed over a pretty cocktail dress for a rabbit costume. Three months as a guard and Siobhán was still making rookie mistakes. She took off her cap, letting her auburn hair cascade down, and unbuttoned the top few buttons on her starched white shirt.

"Thatta girl," Maria said, letting out a wolf whistle. Siobhán laughed, and was trying to think of a retort, when her thoughts were interrupted by Rory Mack, who was hurricaning his way through the crowd.

"Hold the games." Rory's deep voice carried above the din. He was a former rugby player and still looked every bit of it. Well into his sixties, he'd maintained his bulk and swagger. His face sported the ruddy complexion of a man who drank as many pints as he served. Siobhán stole a glance at Declan O'Rourke, whose pale face showed no such tinge of red. He'd managed to serve his product instead of guzzling it, and for a second she felt a strange flush of pride. "I propose we move the poker games to Sharkey's." Rory was the owner of the rowdy pub just outside the town walls. A big fan of Sinatra's version of "Mack the Knife" (and given his surname was Mack), he, in turn, named his pub Sharkey's. (Others teased the name was meant to draw predators to his pub, with all the blood in the water from lads drinking and fighting.) It was *that* kind of pub, and given that it was housed in an old stone building that Siobhán adored, and they always had a good turf fire going, she wished it was more of a respectable establishment. It certainly used to be when Mikey Finnegan owned it. But three years ago Mikey retired to the hills of Donegal, and Rory Mack swooped up the old stone pub, changing its name and reputation forever.

"We've been through this," Macdara said. "We're not debating it again, Rory."

Rory pivoted to Declan, extending a meaty hand. "Sharkey's is far enough away from the festival that if the crowd gets unruly, we're better equipped to handle it." His hand flexed as if his fists were the equipment he had in mind.

Macdara didn't flinch. "It's not going to get unruly."

"You're a fool if you t'ink dat."

"That's 'Garda Fool' to you," someone called out.

Macdara had to shout to speak over the laughter. "Not another word, Rory. You'll get plenty of lads in for a pint when the night rolls on."

"You're going to regret it." Rory shook his head and threaded his way out of the pub, the door slamming behind him. From the small stage in the corner, a microphone screeched. There stood a middle-aged man, with a protruding belly and shock of white hair. He wore a navy blazer and white shirt. Siobhán recognized his referee uniform from watching poker tournaments on telly. If she judged him on his face alone, she'd be tempted to call him a silver fox, but his body had gone the way of a lazy dog. He stepped forward, and pointed to the three round tables with ten chairs each. "Let the games begin." Whoops and hollers rained down as pint glasses were hoisted up. "Ranked third place, first out the gate is Shane Ross. Or as some like to call him, 'the Shane of Spades.' Known for his ability to bluff.

Keep your eye on dat one. A dark horse, but my money's on him."

Applause rang out as a slouched man in his twenties, with floppy brown hair, raised his hand, acknowledging the crowds as he ambled to his seat. His face was stripped of all emotion as if he'd drained them at the door. *A bluffer.* Siobhán felt excitement bubbling in her. What would it feel like to be a card shark? Would she be a bluffer? Who was she kidding, her face turned scarlet at every turn. Would that be an asset? Or a tell? She wanted to believe it would be an asset, but she knew it would be a tell.

"Ranked number two, hailing from London, England, Miss 'Queen of Hearts,' the lovely Clementine Hart." A stunning black woman, garbed in a bold red dress with a plunging neckline, lipstick to match, and knee-high black boots, strolled out, waving to the crowd. This was not a woman wishing to blend in with the men, and Siobhán started the applause. Clementine took her time pulling out her seat, then lowered herself into it as if she knew all eyes were on her, before crossing her legs and folding her hands delicately on top of her knee. Siobhán had an instant girl crush and couldn't take her eyes off her.

"Imagine the life she has," Maria said, her voice a mixture of awe and jealousy. Siobhán was doing just that. Fancy restaurants, piles of bags from Marks and Spencer, a lovely flat with a view of Big Ben, and a sporty little car dragging a string of admirers from her hubcaps.

"And now, the moment you've been waiting for, the number-one-ranked player in all Ireland. The lad needs no introduction, outta Dublin, please welcome Eamon Foley."

His nickname went unsaid, but Siobhán could feel it bouncing around the room as Eamon Foley strode out. *The Octopus.* Handsome was an understatement. He had that thing they called star power. Tall, with wavy dark hair, and a vicious smile, he strode to his table in a black leather jacket and mirrored sunglasses. The glasses were forbidden during the games, and Siobhán had a feeling that's exactly why he was wearing them. The intimidation factor. She made a mental note to buy herself a pair. She could wear them when interrogating her siblings. Once he sat, he took off the glasses and tucked them in the pocket of his jacket. His eyes were a startling green, and for a hot second they locked with Siobhán's. He saluted her.

"Oh, my God," Maria crooned beside her. "You lucky duck." She reached over and pinched Siobhán on the back of her arm. Siobhán swatted her with the back of her hand, and didn't dare look in Macdara's direction, although she could feel his eyes on her too. In fact, everyone was suddenly looking at her, the lone eejit in uniform spraying out pheromones.

The Octopus dropped his salute and grinned at Siobhán, and she wanted to grin back, but she'd lost all feelings in her lips. And then the moment was gone. His eyes left hers and traveled through the crowd, as if they were all his competition and he was sizing them up.

Dealers dressed in black materialized with stacks of chips and tidy decks of cards, holding them aloft by the tables, waiting for word to set them down.

Maria leaned in, her breath hot on Siobhán's neck. "How do you play this game again?"

Declan, who had been standing at the end of the bar keeping an eagle eye on his establishment, was suddenly by their side. He delighted in educating people. He began explaining the game of poker and its endless

variations. Texas Hold'em. Five-card draw. Five-Card
Stud. Seven-Card Stud. Lowball, highball, wild card,
kill game. "Sometimes," he said, his eyes sparking, "a
joker is added."

Siobhán's gaze traveled over the players. "Or several."

There was a rhythm to the games as sure and steady
as music. The swish and smack of the cards. The clink
of the chips. A gasp or moan as each hand was revealed. Pint glasses piled up, along with anticipation,
as players were eliminated, one by one. Some of the
losers were good sports, bowing out with a friendly
wave, while others had to be dragged from the tables
raging and cursing. Before they knew it, round one
had whittled down to the favored three: Shane Ross,
Clementine Hart, and Eamon Foley.

The coordinator appeared at the microphone. "Those
were some games. Boy ya, boy ya! Ladies and gentle-
men, we're down to the final three of round one. They'll
play each other in one last game this evening, to reestab-
lish their rank for the start of the morning rounds." He
leaned in with a wide grin. "A fresh round of victims,
that is."

Laughter and cheers ensued as the top three gathered at the center table. A petite waitress with a water-
fall of blond hair fawned over the Octopus, offering
him a bottle of water. It was obvious she was taking
her time, twirling the bottle as if it were a baton in a
one-woman parade. Her skirt was short and her legs
were long. Clementine stared daggers into the poor girl
until she retreated. Siobhán glanced over to the stools
by the windows, where a very pregnant Rose Foley
was perched. If she was jealous of the waitress fawn-
ing all over her husband, she didn't show it. Her focus
was out the window as if she was counting the seconds

until she could escape. She looked weeks past her due date, and Siobhán found herself thinking they'd better hurry up and finish this hand before the wee thing popped out.

Rose wore a yellow maternity dress and her soft brown hair was piled in a messy bun. It painted the picture of a sweet lass, which was why it was so jarring that her mouth was set in a thin line. When she turned her gaze back into the room, her eyes looked as hard as two black stones. Perhaps she was unconsciously imitating her husband's poker face, but once again Siobhán got the feeling Rose Foley would rather be anywhere but here. Feet up, mug of tea, baby born already. Siobhán hoped that was the case, for the black cloud above her head couldn't be good for the little soul.

The last cards of the night were dealt. Anticipation hovered in the air until Shane Ross pushed a few chips into the center. Clementine did the same, using her long red fingernail. The Octopus hesitated, then bulldozed his entire mound of chips into the center. "All in!" Declan exclaimed. The crowd tilted forward, eager to see what Shane and Clementine would do.

Shane went all in.

Clementine stared. She uncrossed her legs and leaned on the table, for the first time blending in with the boys. Hearts suspended in the throats of those who watched and waited, but she paid them no mind. Then she leaned back with a sigh and shoved her remaining chips into the pile.

Shane laid down his cards. The coordinator hovered by the table, announcing the verdict. "Two pairs. Sevens and fours."

Clementine smiled, then gently fanned hers out. "My milkshake brings all the boys to the yard."

Maria elbowed Siobhán. "I love her."

"Three jacks," the coordinator bellowed. The crowd hummed. Three jacks. *"All the boys" indeed.* Siobhán found herself digging for the rules of poker. *Three of a kind beats two pairs.*

All heads swiveled to the Octopus. He broke out in a grin, sending goose bumps up Siobhán's spine. He slammed his cards down with a satisfying smack. A gasp was heard, and then two. Even the coordinator seemed too stunned to call it. Maria shoved Siobhán off her crate.

"Hey."

"You're a giant, get over yourself." Siobhán was tall, but a giant? She resisted the urge to shove Maria, who was feverishly piling Siobhán's crate onto her own and climbing on top. "Declan. Binoculars," she barked like a surgeon.

Declan tossed a pair to Maria, who held them up like a pirate spotting treasure on a distant shore. She called out the hand: "The ace of spades, ace of clubs, eight of spades, eight of clubs, and a joker."

This time Declan gasped, a sound Siobhán had never heard in her life. "What?"

Declan crossed himself, and when he finally spoke, his voice was gruff. "Dat's 'the Dead Man's Hand.' "

" 'The Dead Man's Hand'?" Siobhán had never heard of it.

Clementine Hart shot out of her chair. "Impossible." She pointed at Eamon. "Cheater!"

"Joker's wild," the Octopus sang. "Would you look at that! I've got the Dead Man's Hand, but I'm still alive. And jokers are wild, so that's a full house, if I do say so m'self."

Shane Ross looked as if he wanted to overturn the table. He had emotions after all. "I smell a cheat."

Eamon screeched his chair back and folded his arms across his chest. "You really think I wanted the Dead Man's Hand?" He shook his head. "I've had enough bad luck in me life." He glanced at his wife.

Siobhán poked Declan. "The Dead Man's Hand?"

Declan crossed his arms. "It's a legend in poker. Black aces and black eights, with a hole card."

"A hole card?" He might as well have been speaking a foreign language.

Declan waved his hand. "It means it doesn't matter what the last card is. But this time it does. It's a joker. Jokers are wild, so he can pair it with the aces for a full house."

Siobhán was still lost. "Is it bad luck or good luck?" *The Dead Man's Hand. Definitely doesn't sound good.*

Declan's eyes lit up. "Legend has it 'Wild Bill' Hickok was holding that exact hand when he was murdered."

Wild Bill Hickok. Another thing for her to Google on a long list of things she was never going to Google. Clementine and Eamon shot to their feet, shouting as they circled each other.

"Look!" Shane Ross pointed at Eamon's chair. The crowd moved in.

"What is it?" Siobhán asked Maria.

"There's a deck of cards sitting on Eamon's seat," Maria narrated.

"A cold deck," Shane said. "He switched them out."

Eamon whirled around and looked at the deck of cards on the seat. "That's not mine." He held his hands up as if that proved his innocence. Was it an act? Was he bluffing? Siobhán couldn't tell.

"That blond tart," Clementine said. "Was she the one who slipped you the cold deck?"

Heads swiveled. The blondie waitress was nowhere to be seen. The one-woman parade had vanished.

Eamon's face was now scrunched in rage. So much for his poker face. "I'm being set up!"

The coordinator stepped forward, clutching the lapel of his blazer. Clementine bulldozed his path. "You're the referee."

"Coordinator is my official title," he said with a grin. Then he tapped his chest. "Nathan Doyle." He bowed.

Clementine didn't seem to care about his name. She was on a mission. "You must immediately disqualify Eamon Foley for cheating. He switched the decks."

"Prove it," Eamon said. He pointed at Clementine. "She set me up."

"Me?" Clementine was indignant. "If I was going to set someone up with a good hand, I would have chosen me."

"Someone did." He looked at his seat as if it had betrayed him. "Would I have jumped up if I was hiding a cold deck under me leg?"

He had a point there. Nathan Doyle appeared terrified of angering either player. He threw a desperate look to Macdara.

Macdara stepped out from his post in the corner. "Everyone sit down. Sit down and calm down."

Clementine stormed to the table. She pointed to the cards on the table, then held up the cold deck. "They're identical. This was a switch operation."

"I had nothing to do with that," Eamon said.

"The Dead Man's Hand?" Clementine said. "You expect us to believe that?"

"Someone might be taking the piss, alright, but it isn't me." Eamon held his arms up and began to bounce like a boxer celebrating his knockout victory. "The jokes on them—or the Joker's on them, I might say—because I'm still number one!" Patrons cheered and fists pounded on tables.

"Why don't we compromise," Nathan said, attacking his eyeglasses with his handkerchief. "Let's throw out the results of this game. You can replay it in the morning." He placed his glasses back on, blinked, and looked around for confirmation.

"Count the cold deck," Clementine said. "If he cheated, it will be five cards short."

Eamon whirled on her. "If you're setting me up, it will be five cards short."

She put her hands on her hips. "You were caught red-handed."

The Octopus let out a howl. "I was set up!" He picked up his chair as if it were a projectile.

"Hey," Declan said. He stepped toward the Octopus. "Put that down."

"I'll review the video!" Nathan tried to shout above the boisterous crowd. "Announce me decision in the morning."

Declan had arranged all cameras in the pub so they were aimed at the playing tables. There was too much money in these games to leave it to chance. One bad call and there would be mutiny.

"Review the tape now!" Eamon demanded.

Nathan threw yet another desperate look to Macdara, who shook his head. Siobhán suddenly understood. If the Octopus was to be kicked out of the tournament, they weren't going to announce it to an oversized crowd drunk on pints and greed. Macdara asserted himself. "As stated, the coordinator will review the tapes this evening and render his decision first thing in the morning."

When, hopefully, the angry mob would be sleeping it off . . .

That didn't sit well with Eamon Foley. He lifted the chair again and this time hurled it across the room. Heads ducked as it flew overhead. It struck the back wall, knocking down one of Declan's beloved Laurel and Hardy posters. The sound of glass breaking mingled with splintering wood.

"Me favorite poster," Declan bellowed, fist raised. "You'll pay for dat."

"He should be disqualified," Clementine added. "He's a danger to us all."

"Don't you dare talk about me husband like dat." Rose Foley was off her stool and looked ready to go to the mat.

Declan lunged for the Octopus, stopping short of touching him. "This is your only warning. If you so much as knock over your pint, you will be tossed out on your ear for good."

Eamon Foley pinned his beautiful green eyes on Declan.

"Don't test him," Siobhán said under her breath.

"Don't test him," Macdara echoed for all to hear.

Eamon swiped up another chair from the table.

"Don't you dare," Declan said, jabbing at the air with his index finger. "Don't. You. Dare."

Eamon hurled the chair at the wall. It bounced off *The Quiet Man* poster and struck Declan in the chest before crashing to the floor. The crowd erupted, boos and cheers in equal measures.

"That's it!" Declan said, bending down to pick up his chair. "Out of me pub now."

"You wouldn't dare," Eamon said. "I'm the reason all these people are here."

"Out!" Declan's voice thundered through the pub.

Macdara moved in with other guards, wrestling Eamon's hands behind his back before Declan could get to him.

"Don't touch him," Rose Foley said, pushing forward with her belly. "I'll sue!"

"Let's all calm down." Nathan Doyle's voice barely rose above the din. Not a single person acknowledged him. The man was in the wrong job. He'd be better suited to help stray sheep cross the street.

"We're done for tonight," Macdara said as they marched Eamon through the crowd. "Nathan Doyle will review the tapes and announce his decision in the morning."

"Yikes," Maria said, throwing a glance at the coordinator. "Wouldn't want to be *him*."

Neither would Siobhán. The Octopus was beloved. Disqualifying him would take nerves of steel. Men had received death threats for less.

"What did I tell ye?"

Siobhán's head pivoted to the male voice. Rory Mack had returned, looking triumphant. *Is this somehow his doing?*

"You can have the lot of 'em," Declan said. "Eamon Foley is not allowed back in me pub."

Rory Mack pumped his fist in the air. "The tournament will resume bright and early at Sharkey's!" He beamed. "Tonight we celebrate. First pint is on me. Everyone. Let's go to Sharkey's!"

A whoop ran through the crowd as they began to spill out of O'Rourke's.

Macdara joined Siobhán at Declan's side. "I'll need all the tapes pulled from the cameras."

Declan delegated his staff and they began tending to the cameras. Siobhán took out her notepad. "Will you be pressing charges?"

Declan shook his head. "No, luv. I just want him gone." He glanced at Nathan Doyle, who wore the expression of an animal caught in a trap. What a dreadful mess. The clear winner tonight was Rory Mack. Siobhán had a strange feeling he was going to live to regret it.

Chapter 2

Siobhán was up just before the sun; it was the best time to ride her pink Vespa without worrying about cars speeding around the curves. The air was crisp and clean, and the morning birds were singing. If Siobhán kept her gaze up, the world would look serene. But the iron street lamps that dotted Kilbane revealed the ugly truth, the underbelly of the night before. Empty bottles were strewn on the normally pristine footpaths, along with food wrappers, mineral cans, and busted balloons. The downside of festivals. Like tinsel off a tree after Christmas—they'd be cleaning long after the crowds were gone. She resisted the urge to stop and clean up. It would be fruitless until the tourists were back home. Besides, she wanted to be at Sharkey's before any of the players arrived. She was dying to hear Nathan Doyle's decision. Hopefully, the camera tapes would show if the blond waitress slipped Eamon a new deck, and whatever the verdict, it would be accepted by all.

By the time she was pulling up to the old stone pub just outside the town walls, the sun was rising, glinting off yet more bottles of ale abandoned in the field alongside the pub. The neon-blue shark with "Sharkey's" played across his belly was still lit. Probably like most of the folks who had partied the night away. Empty packets of crisps, cigarette butts, and boot prints continued to tell the story of a wild night. She, for one, had been asleep the minute she tucked the young ones into bed and hit the pillow. Much to her chagrin Gráinne and Eoin set off to join the crowd at Sharkey's. James spent the evening at Elise's; although he'd been in alcohol recovery for years, he knew not to put himself into tempting situations. Siobhán always thought her moderate approach to drinking had been formed by her brother's struggles. *"There but for the grace of God go I . . ."*

Still, there was a part of her that felt as if she had missed out on a fun night. It seemed as if everyone in town had zoomed over to Sharkey's after Declan tossed Eamon out. She hopped off her scooter, taking in the morning dew on the field and the birds singing away. Siobhán was prepared to sit and wait for the arrival of Rory Mack. She had just started to stretch out her legs, when she noticed the front door of the pub was ajar. Was he here already? Perhaps he'd never gone home. She approached and pulled on the door.

Inside, the darkness was choked with the smell of ale and smoke. Siobhán opened the door wider and waited for her eyes to adjust. "Hello?" Tables had been pushed to the side, their tops still littered with pint glasses. Multiple shoe prints were visible on the floor.

The evening had no doubt ended in dancing. Playing cards were strewn on multiple tabletops.

"Rory? It's Garda O'Sullivan." For all she knew he was asleep behind the bar, or in the storage room, or under the pool table.

The place was a ghost town, the floor sticky. She shone her torch, but there were no stray lads sleeping under the tables. She would much rather wait outside in the fresh air.

She was on her way out, when the beam of her torch caught a stream of liquid snaking out from beneath a closed door in the back corner of the pub. The storage room. Over the years she'd seen Rory Mack ferry in and out of it, carrying napkins and pint glasses. She'd heard tale of lads sleeping it off in there. She glanced at the liquid again. She wanted to think it was water—some kind of leak—but the smell of urine was too obvious to ignore. Making great pains not to step in it, she pounded on the door. "It's the guards. Open up." There was no sound, not even a creak of a floorboard. She tried the door. It was locked tight. Some yoke was in there, most likely passed out. If his little accident didn't wake him, he might be in danger of alcohol poisoning. She had to check it out.

She stepped back and kicked the door with the heel of her boot. It didn't budge. She thought of the patio directly behind the pub. If memory served, there was a small window on the back wall of the pub, situated up high. It was in the right position to at least see inside the storage room—not a window big enough to climb into, most likely designed to vent the air. But if she could reach it, she could at least peer inside. She didn't want to call in the cavalry unless it was absolutely necessary—every guard would be on duty all weekend and sleep was a precious commodity.

The door to the patio was several feet from the storage room. It swung open and Siobhán stepped out, noting with disgust the overflowing buckets of cigarette butts and empty bottles just tossed on the ground. Rory Mack and his crew should have stayed behind to clean. She sighed and looked up to the window. There it was, just below the roof, a narrow window, about the size of a bread box. She was going to need a ladder. Ironically, there was probably one tucked away in the storage room. The patio housed a wobbly picnic table. She wasn't in a mood to try and drag it underneath the window. Besides, it might not be high enough. The window was a good fifteen feet in the air. A ladder was the smart way to go. Would Liam's hardware store be open this early?

The only phone number she had for Rory Mack was the number for the pub. Even if she called information and tracked down his home number, chances were good that he was dead to the world. She would call home and see if one of the lads could hurry over with their ladder.

Her brother Eoin showed up on the patio fifteen minutes later, ladder held aloft. His head was topped with the usual: a Yankees baseball cap turned backward. If he'd spent all night at Sharkey's, he didn't look any worse for the wear. She breathed a sigh of relief that unlike James he'd dodged the alcoholism bullet.

"That was fast."

Eoin grinned. "I hitched a ride."

Siobhán frowned. Normally, this was the type of village where one could feel safe climbing into their neighbors' vehicles. But with all the strangers in town, she didn't like it.

"From who?"

"Mike."

Relief settled on her shoulders. Their family friend Mike and down-the-road neighbor was good for more than selling fruit and veg; he and his pickup truck had been a real friend over the years. "Did he ask why you were hitching a ride with a ladder so early in the morning?"

"He did indeed." Eoin's eyes glowed with mischief.

"And you said?"

"'I would tell you, but then I'd have to kill you.'" A grin spread over his face. He'd been holding on to that one.

She shook her head. "Tell me you're joking."

"He loved it. Never heard him laugh so hard."

Siobhán laughed at the thought of it. "Good man."

Eoin glanced around the patio. "Why do you need it?"

"Tell me about last night."

Eoin shrugged. "It was jammers. A lot of drinking. A bit of brawling."

"Brawling?"

"I'd say a few of the games got out of hand." He sighed. "Yer man nearly came to fisty-cuffs with the other player."

"Eamon Foley?" Eoin nodded. "He almost hit Clementine?" It was a guess. Clementine had been convinced Eamon was cheating, and Siobhán had a feeling she wasn't going to let up.

Eoin gave her an appraising nod. "He might have done. If Shane Ross hadn't stepped up to protect her."

So much for sportsmanship. Perhaps they should think twice the next time a poker tournament wanted to come to town. Siobhán pointed to the wall below the window. Eoin maneuvered the ladder right where she wanted it. "What's the story?"

"I think someone is passed out in the storage room."

He glanced at the window. "You'll never fit through dat."

"I don't need to fit through it, I just need to look in."

"Right, right. Can I do it?"

"No."

"But I carried the ladder."

"This is police business."

"Dealing with drunks. Was garda college worth it?"

"Hold the ladder, will you?"

"Hurry up. I have to get started on brekkie."

"I know." With the festival, it was all hands on deck at the bistro. Eoin had turned out to be a great chef, and once in a while admitted he was considering going to cookery school after he passed his leaving certs. Maybe he would become a famous chef and one day they would all live in a mansion on a cliff, overlooking the ocean.

She climbed the ladder while Eoin held it. When she reached the window and saw layers of grime, she wished she had gloves. She used her sleeve to wipe a patch clear and peered in. Expecting to see a lad laid out on the floor, she was thrown when she saw something suspended in midair. *Is that a sack?* Even as her mind searched for reasonable explanations, her body was already reacting to the horror. *It's a man. Suspended from the ceiling.*

Leather jacket, denims. Wavy black hair, head tilted to the side like a broken doll, face bloated, eyes bulging. Green eyes, which were so alive last night. Eyes that had landed on her. Hands that hurled two chairs across the room. Slotted to win a quarter of a million euro. A rope encircled Eamon Foley's neck, and she followed it up to the wood beam where it was tied off. Beneath him a chair lay on its side. She gasped and the ladder tipped back. "Eoin!" Eoin immediately shoved the ladder forward, smashing her face into the window.

He'd put the heart in her crossways. She concentrated on her breath to calm the drumbeat in her chest.

"Sorry, sorry," Eoin called. "What is it?" She waited for the thumping in her heart to slow enough to peer in again. It was him. The Octopus. Dead. There was no doubt he was dead. "What is it?"

Heaven help him. "I'm coming down." Her hands and legs shook as she descended. The minute she hit the ground, she took out her mobile. She glanced at Eoin, who was staring wide-eyed, waiting to hear what she'd say. She held up her finger and shook her head before hurrying out of the patio and out of earshot. She was grateful to have Macdara on speed dial.

"He's dead," she said the minute Macdara answered. "The Octopus is dead."

Chapter 3

Macdara arrived with a team of guards and equipment. Paper aprons, gloves, face masks, crime scene tape, and a chain saw, in case they needed to cut the door open. For a brief second Siobhán felt nostalgia for the time when her work tools were sugar, tea, buttermilk, and oats. After photographing and noting that the door to the storage room was indeed locked tight and could not be busted down, a guard began to use the chain saw around the doorknob. Given that the door was thick wood, and there wasn't enough space underneath to slip any kind of tool to open it, this was the only way they were getting in.

One of the younger guards agreed to drop Eoin back home. Siobhán finally told him that a man was hanging in the storeroom, but explained she couldn't yet tell him any more, and was grateful when he quickly assured her he would keep it to himself. He was a lad of his word and it gave Siobhán a small bit of comfort. Rory Mack had been summoned from what looked like anything but a good night's sleep. He tumbled out of his truck and stumbled toward them. Taking in the guards and the crime scene tape, he took out a pack of fags.

"What's the story? Was I robbed?" He stuck a cigarette in his mouth and let it dangle.

Macdara took the lead. "How would a person lock himself inside your storage room?"

Rory raised his eyebrow. "Is Eamon passed out?"

"You knew he was in your storage room?"

"Aye. He needed to sleep it off. Couldn't go home to the missus in that state."

"How could he have locked himself in?"

"There's a dead bolt on the inside."

"Why?"

"It was the only way to guarantee a bit of peace." His look said it all. He'd probably taken a number of "naps" in there himself over the years. She did not want to know. "Why don't you just bang on the door, get him to open it for ye?"

Macdara told him to stay put and stay quiet until they were ready to talk to him. He began to pace and smoke alongside his truck.

"Didn't you used to have a ladder?" Siobhán asked Rory.

He looked up, squinted. "Aye. It's in the storage room."

Siobhán returned to the storage room and scanned for the ladder as crime scene photographs were snapped. She could not see a ladder, nor were there any places someone could hide a ladder. The room was approximately two hundred square feet, with enough space for shelves on either side, and enough room in the middle to fit a cot. The door was directly across from the venting window, and she gauged the distance at ten feet.

She took in the chair lying on its side; then her eyes followed the rope up to the wood beam, where it was looped and tied off. Siobhán wasn't versed in the variations of knot tying, but even a layman could see that this one was sturdy and looked practiced. Did all lads know how to tie knots? The guards took in the body with a moment of silence.

"There were a lot of shenanigans last night," one said. "But I never imagined it would come to this."

Macdara began delegating. The rest of the storage room looked as if it hadn't been touched. Shelves lined the sidewalls, stocked with cans of beans, pint glasses, and paper products. A thick layer of dust covered the tops of everything on the shelves. No one had touched them recently. The dead bolt was rusty but sturdy and it had been firmly locked in place. They would not be able to go through Eamon's pockets or do anything with the body until the state pathologist arrived. If she was in Dublin, it could take days for her to arrive. Siobhán lamented the fact out loud.

"A bit of luck then," Macdara said. Siobhán lifted an eyebrow. "Turns out Jeanie Brady is a poker fan." Macdara nodded to the body. "She's already in town."

"That is a bit of good luck."

"Rumor has it she was here last night. And she isn't a morning person in the best of times." He took out his mobile and handed it to Siobhán.

She frowned. "You want me to call her?"

He winked. "Being the boss has to have some perks."

* * *

After the rope was photographed, including a close-up on the knot, guards measured the position of the body. Eamon Foley's feet were hanging twenty-four inches from the ground. It didn't take more than that to asphyxiate. It looked consistent with a man standing on the chair, and then knocking it out from underneath. She couldn't imagine what went through a person's mind in that moment. Suicide was such a cruel way to go, and disrupted the mourning process as loved ones were left to struggle with a haunting, relentless question: *Why? Why? Why?*

Jeanie Brady arrived in a timely manner. She was an inquisitive woman with bright hazel eyes and an extra layer of fat around her short body, but she had a quick and graceful way about moving, which made Siobhán wonder if she used to be a dancer. She spent some time examining the body, the marks on his neck, the bulging of his eyes, the bloat in his face, taking notes and double-checking their photographs. Once she was satisfied, she called for the rope to be cut so they could take him down.

Siobhán felt a strange sense of relief once Eamon Foley was laid out on the floor. Jeanie Brady fell to her haunches, and with gloved hands she started through his pockets. She narrated each of her moves.

"We've got a note," she said, holding it up. It was white-lined notebook paper and looked as if it had been torn from the book by hand.

Macdara nudged forward. "What does it say?"

Jeanie frowned, moving the note away from her eyes, then close-up, then away, driving Siobhán mad with anticipation. "'Can't beat the Dead Man's Hand.' With his signature underneath."

A chill ran up Siobhán's spine. "What?"

Jeanie seemed eager to explain. "Ace of spades, ace of clubs, eight of—"

"I know what the hand is," Siobhán said. "Wild Bilcock or some such." She was messing up the name. How was she supposed to keep such facts in her head? "I'm just shocked that's what the note says."

Jeanie didn't look happy to be interrupted and a quick glare from Macdara confirmed Siobhán should have kept her gob shut. Jeanie turned the handwritten note around to reveal large, looping black letters:

Can't beat the Dead Man's Hand
Eamon Foley

Jeanie cocked her head as she studied Siobhán's expression. "Why the reaction to the note? Does it mean something else to you?"

Macdara edged in. "Were you at the games Friday night?"

Jeanie shook her head. "I wanted a bit of supper. By the time I finished, everyone was storming out of O'Rourke's."

"Eamon Foley was dealt the Dead Man's Hand Friday night," Macdara said. "That's what started the accusation of cheating."

"I miss everything!" Jeanie said. "I have the worst luck." She glanced at the body and her full cheeks reddened. "Perhaps not the worst." She looked up, her eyes sparkling. "Do you know the legend of the Dead Man's Hand?"

"Yes," Siobhán said. "Black aces, black eights, and a hole card. Supposedly, it's the hand Wild Bill Whatever was holding when he was murdered." Macdara started chuckling. "Bilcock?"

"Hickok," Macdara said. "America. The Old West. Worked the frontier. Purported wagon master, lawman, gunfighter, gambler, spy—"

"Nobody can be all those things." Siobhán was pretty sure.

"He could stretch the truth, it seems," Macdara said with a wink.

"Right, so." Siobhán shrugged and turned to Jeanie. "Americans."

Jeanie jerked her thumb at Siobhán and Macdara. "Would ya look at Gardaí Wikipedia over here," she said, clearly unhappy about it.

"Either way," Macdara said, "he was supposedly murdered shortly after he was dealt that hand. The Dead Man's Hand."

"He was murdered," Siobhán echoed.

Macdara held up his hand. "Don't go reading in-to it."

"How can I not?" Siobhán wished she could touch the note. "That can't be all it says."

"And yet . . ." Jeanie made a point of staring at Siobhán. "That's all it says."

"What kind of suicide note is that?" Aside from the signature it read more like a taunt from a killer.

Jeanie studied the note again. "I'd say it's a clever ren-dition of 'Good-bye, Cruel World.' " Her hands plunged into his pockets again. "What's this?" Her hand emerged and she held up something brass and shiny.

Macdara moved in closer. "Brass knuckles?"

"A bit odd," Jeanie said, dropping it into a plastic bag. "Then again he was a scrapper, wasn't he?"

"Don't scrappers just use their fists?" Siobhán said. Why would he need brass knuckles in Kilbane?

"Why don't you check *Scrappers for Dummies*," Jeanie retorted. Macdara was right. Jeanie Brady was not a morning person at all and Siobhán was clearly on her bad side.

Macdara took the bag and stared at the knuckles. "He didn't make friends easily."

Jeanie's hands went back to rummaging. "This is interesting." She plucked two playing cards out of his shirt pocket. The queen of hearts and the jack of spades, but that wasn't the bit that had them all staring. Someone had taken a black marker and marred them. The heart of the queen was now a gaping black hole, and the same treatment had been given to the mouth of the jack.

"Clementine Hart and Shane Ross," Siobhán whispered. *Black heart, black mouth . . . heartless . . . keep your mouth shut?*

"Why did you mention them?" Macdara said.

"They call Clementine the Queen of Hearts, and Shane the Shane of Spades."

Jeanie looked at the cards again, her head cocked. "Wouldn't it make more sense if his name was Jack?"

Siobhán cut in. "Clementine's hand in that round was three jacks."

"Her milkshake," Macdara said.

"Her what?" Jeanie did not like being left out.

"It's an R and B song. Kelis. 'Milkshake.' Clementine quoted from it when she got the three jacks."

"Why don't you sing us a few bars there, boss?" Macdara's grin said it all.

"I could use a milkshake," Jeanie said with a sigh.

Macdara wiggled his eyebrows at Siobhán. She knew the song wasn't about milkshakes and that's why he was making fun. Jeanie didn't need to be bogged down in the details.

"Chocolate," Jeanie said. "No. Strawberry." She put her finger on her chin. "I wonder what they would taste like mixed? Choc-straw. Or should it be straw-choc?"

Macdara brought the conversation back to the cards. "Why would Eamon black out the heart and the mouth? A parting shot at his rivals?"

"I don't know," Siobhán said. "Maybe it's a message."

"Go on," Macdara said. "What's the message?"

Shoot. Is he testing me? She looked at the cards. "You're heartless, and . . . keep your mouth shut?"

Macdara studied the cards again. He pointed to the queen. "Brokenhearted?" He shifted to the jack. "Mute?"

Siobhán shrugged. She liked her interpretations better, but sometimes the secret to maintaining relationships was not to overshare. "Eamon—or *someone*—is trying to tell us *something*."

Jeanie stood. "That's everything out of his pockets." She sounded disappointed.

"Keys? Billfold?" Siobhán asked. "Mirrored sunglasses? Coins? Mobile phone? Wads of cash?" If they played poker here last night, the Octopus would have cleaned up.

"No," Jeanie said. "No keys. No wallet. No cash. No coins. No mobile phone." She looked at them. "Did he smoke?"

"I'm not sure," Siobhán said.

"Either way. No pack of fags. No lighter or matches." She laughed. "I guess we'd be here all day if I kept listing the items I *didn't* find in his pockets."

"Keys, cash, and mobile," Siobhán said. "Those definitely should have been on him."

Jeanie nodded. "'Tis a bit odd, isn't it?"

"Just ask Wild Bill," Siobhán said.

Jeanie perked up. "What?"

"Murder," Siobhán explained. "It's not odd if it's murder."

Chapter 4

"Murder?" Macdara gently pulled Siobhán into the corner of the storage room. "How do you make that leap?"

"No cash, let alone wallet, mobile phone, or keys. The brass knuckles and strange note—"

"—signed by him—"

"—the marred playing cards. And the fact that if he had just waited *two days,* he might be a quarter of a million euro richer."

"The door was bolted from the *inside,*" Macdara said. "We had to get in using a chain saw." Macdara nodded to the venting window. "And you know yourself, you wouldn't be able to squeeze more than an arm through dat."

Siobhán eyed the window as if it were an enemy.

"Why have we no footprints?" Jeanie said, looking

at the floor. Unlike the dusty window and shelves, the cement floor was shiny.

Macdara stared at it. "Someone mopped this floor recently."

He was right. With the exception of the trail of urine across the floor, the rest of it was spotless.

"Some publicans like to keep things tidy," Jeanie pointed out.

"The rest of the place is disgraceful," Siobhán said. "Why would Rory Mack only clean this one room?"

Macdara joined her train of thought. "It's quite obvious someone mopped this room before Eamon hanged himself or was hanged."

"Of course. I think we can conclude the room was mopped *before* he was hanged." Siobhán hoped it hadn't come out as sarcastic, but the look Macdara gave her was evidence to the contrary.

Macdara shrugged. "Maybe it *was* Rory. Keeping it clean for his guest of honor."

"How did Rory know in advance that Eamon would end up here?"

Jeanie grinned at Macdara and jerked her head to Siobhán. "She's quite the pistol this morning." Her gaze returned to the body. "It could have been the deceased."

"You think a dead man mopped the floor?" Macdara blurted out.

When Jeanie glared at him, Siobhán breathed a sigh of relief that he said it before she did. Jeanie waited for her look to sink in, then resumed. "When it gets right down to it, it's not easy to take your own life. Maybe he was wrestling with the decision. Cleaning can be calming." Her eyes traveled up the rope. "Or compulsive."

Siobhán surveyed the storage room for what felt like the hundredth time. "I don't see a mop. Do ye?"

Macdara and Jeanie began searching the room like they were playing a game of hide-the-mop. It didn't take long to realize nobody was going to be a winner.

"Why are you worrying about a mop?" Macdara said. "We have to figure out if there's any other way to get in or out of this room besides a door with a dead bolt."

Total sore loser.

Siobhán looked at the ceiling. Above wood-beam rafters was a solid roof. A quick glance showed no disturbance.

"I think we're looking at a straightforward suicide," Jeanie said. "What a shame."

Siobhán could no longer control her frustration. "There is nothing straightforward about this crime scene."

"Don't jump down my throat."

"Sorry, sorry."

Macdara stepped in and offered Jeanie one of his lopsided grins. "'Pistol' is right. Siobhán gets worked up over puzzles."

I do not. Maybe she did. That sounded condescending, but given that Jeanie Brady looked as if she wanted to toss Siobhán out of her crime scene, she was grateful for the save. When she resumed speaking, she tried to imagine they were all having a cup of tea, chatting about the weather. "He was ranked number one. Just days away from winning. Why would he kill himself?"

Macdara considered it. "Maybe Nathan Doyle announced his decision. Maybe Eamon knew he was out of the tournament."

Siobhán shook her head. "Nathan Doyle wasn't supposed to announce anything until this morning."

"And people always do what they're supposed to?" Macdara quipped.

Jeanie took a bag of pistachios out of her coat pocket and dove into them. "I was here last night."

This was news. "Here?" Siobhán said. "You?" Macdara nudged her from behind.

Jeanie narrowed her eyes. "Yes. Me. Here."

She just couldn't win this morning. "I don't mean anything negative. You're from out of town, so how would you know?"

"How would I know what?"

"Sharkey's has a bit of a reputation," Macdara said. "It can be a rough-and-tumble pub."

"Was Nathan Doyle here?" Siobhán asked. Had he announced that Eamon was out of the games? She hoped not, that was certainly a recipe for disaster.

Jeanie turned. "You're talking about the official with the glasses and the belly?"

"Yes," Macdara said. "That's the one."

"Is he single?" Jeanie said. "I'm asking for a friend."

"No idea," Macdara said.

"Get rid of that belly with some brisk morning walks and he'd be a handsome enough devil, I'd say." She looked to Macdara and Siobhán to see if they agreed.

"A right handsome devil," Siobhán said.

Macdara cleared his throat. "I gather he was here."

"Yes. He was here." Jeanie held up her finger as if it were an antenna she was raising to get a clearer picture. "The female card player was pressuring him to announce his decision, but he stood his guard. Real manly, don't you know. He said he'd have his decision at half ten in the morning." She smiled. "I bet he's punctual too."

Siobhán's ears perked up. "*Pressuring* him?"

Jeanie nodded. "She has some fire in her, that one."

Siobhán glanced again at the chair, and then the rope hanging from the wood beam. "Putting the dead bolt aside for a moment, how difficult would it be to hang another man?"

Macdara took a moment to think about it. "Murder by hanging is extremely rare."

"Thanks be to the heavens," Siobhán said. "I'm sure there are easier ways to kill a man."

"Siobhán!" Macdara said.

"Or woman?" Siobhán added.

"That's your argument?" Macdara said.

"No. It's terrible. I wish we lived in a peaceful world. In the meantime we have a job to do. And hanging, as you say, is a rare way to murder a man. . . ." Macdara and Jeanie waited, their full attention pinned on her every word. *Wow. This feels good.* She'd never thought of a life on stage before now, but maybe she should have a go at the next production put on by the Kilbane Players.

"Out with it," Jeanie barked.

Or maybe not. "If the method is rare, then that says something defining about our killer." She began to pace in what little space she had. "Why not come up from behind and strangle him?" She headed for the shelves. Picked up a can of beans. "Or knock him over the head?"

"With a can of beans?" Macdara looked as if she'd just insulted his mother. It would be a waste of a good can of beans. Nothing like beans and toast for brekkie.

Jeanie pointed at the body. "Or . . . maybe it's not *murder.*"

Siobhán turned to Macdara. "Suppose he was murdered. How did it go down?"

Macdara sighed. "If he came in here to sleep it off, as Rory said, and he was passed out . . ." He glanced at the overturned chair. "Say in that chair. I suppose it wouldn't have been difficult at all to come up from behind, slip the rope around his neck, and pull." Macdara stared up at the rafter. "The rope would have been pre-tied, ready to go. Is there a ladder in here?"

"Rory Mack said so, but I don't see one, do you?"

"And the ladder from the back patio is yours?"

"Eoin brought it from home this morning." She looked at the rafter. "What are you thinking?"

Macdara sighed. "I don't see how the rope could be tied so tightly around that beam unless someone used a ladder."

"It's not possible to just toss it up there?"

"Of course. It's possible to toss it up there, but it's not possible to tie it off, unless yer man—or woman—had twenty-foot arms."

"Could someone have climbed on the shelves and reached it?"

The shelving unit on the side where Eamon had been found hanging was only a few feet from the rope.

Macdara examined the items. "The dust hasn't been disturbed. If someone climbed on these shelves, you'd think we would see a hand or shoe print, or at the very least items shoved over to the side. This hasn't been touched for ages."

"More proof that Rory Mack isn't a neat freak," Siobhán said.

"Doesn't Eddie Houlihan still do the cleaning here?"

Siobhán nodded. Eddie was an overweight twenty-six-year-old who kept to himself. Sweet kid, but possibly a bit delayed mentally. "What about him?"

"We'll have to speak with him."

"If there's no ladder, then there's no way Eamon Foley killed himself."

"Hold on, boss," Macdara said. "That's not true."

"You just said he needed a ladder to climb up and secure the rope. A dead man can't move a ladder. So where is it?"

"If the killer could have preplanned this, Eamon could have too," Macdara said. "Suicide victims often do. He used the ladder to secure the ropes early in the evening, then stashed the ladder."

"He didn't know the tournament was going to be moved to Sharkey's, so exactly when do you think he started planning this?"

"That's a good point," Macdara said.

"Someone else could have discovered the body. Took the ladder and the mop," Jeanie mused. "Decided not to report it."

Not reporting it, Siobhán could see. "Why would they take the mop and the ladder?"

"I'll focus on the body and leave that fun stuff to you," Jeanie said with a wink.

"It's plausible," Macdara said. "Good theory."

Siobhán knew Macdara was just trying to stay on Jeanie's good side, but they looked so proud of themselves she half-expected them to fist bump. Siobhán wasn't buying it. "Who would walk into a storage room, ignore a man hanging, and steal a ladder and a mop?"

Macdara crossed his arms. "It's still possible that Eamon is the one who secured this rope, then stashed the ladder."

"And the mop?"

"We have work to do, okay? Let's leave it at that."

"Murder is the only thing that makes sense."

"It's not the only thing," Macdara said. "I think suicide is the one that makes sense."

That seemed far-fetched, but Siobhán knew it was *possible*. But to her, it was even more likely that it was a murder. Made to look like a suicide. The killer assumed they would find him hanging, find the note, and then quickly close the case. *Game over.*

And yet . . . the killer was also taunting the guards. The strange note, the items in his pocket, the marked playing cards. *Can't beat the Dead Man's Hand . . .* if this was a murder, had it been premeditated, starting with the dealing of the Dead Man's Hand? Siobhán gasped. "Remember the blondie waitress who brought Eamon water?"

Macdara nodded. "The one accused of slipping Eamon a cold deck."

"That's the one."

"What about her?"

"Who was she?"

Macdara shook his head. "I thought she was with the poker crew. But then she disappeared."

"Exactly. Isn't that odd?"

"What's your theory?" Macdara watched her intently.

"Eamon said he was being set up."

"Okay."

"If this was murder, he was right. He *was* being set up." She nodded to the rope, then pointed at the suicide note. "For *this*."

"You're saying a killer made sure Eamon Foley got the Dead Man's Hand as some kind of sick warning of his imminent demise?"

"That's exactly what I'm saying."

"Are you serious?" Macdara almost sounded angry with her.

"Foreshadowing," Siobhán said. "We could be dealing with a sadistic killer."

"Diabolical," Jeanie whispered.

Concern was stamped on Macdara's face as he approached Siobhán. "Do you need a mug of tea? You look like you could use a mug of tea."

Siobhán knew he was teasing, but she didn't like him mollycoddling her during an investigation. She crossed her arms. "You asked for my theory. That's what I think so far."

Macdara nodded, reading her mood. "This waitress. What's her motive?"

"She might not have one. Someone told her to bring Eamon a bottle of water and slip him the deck of cards. Does it matter why? Money? Blackmail? Or she simply thought she was helping her hero. When we find her, you can ask her. The important bit is that whoever put her up to slipping him the cold deck had more menacing things on his or her mind than setting him up for cheating."

"Whether it's suicide or murder, we have the same conundrum," Macdara said.

Siobhán was right with him. "Exactly. Why not wait to kill him until *after* he wins a quarter of a million euro instead of *before*."

"How do you two do that?" Jeanie said. "Is this some kind of mind-reading trick?" She looked between them. "Usually, it's only husbands and wives who can finish each other's sentences." Heat crawled up Siobhán's neck. Now she wouldn't be able to look at Macdara for the rest of the morning. For the first time that day Jeanie laughed. "Could be one of the other players," she offered. "Competition is a killer."

"And we know who the competition is," Macdara said, picking up the evidence baggie with the playing cards.

The Queen of Hearts and the Shane of Spades . . . Clementine Hart and Shane Ross. And from what Eoin said, the three of them were brawling last night. Her brother was a straight shooter. If he thought they were brawling, she believed it.

Macdara closed his notebook and turned for the door. "We'll interview everyone who was here last night. If we're clear to move the body, I'll give Butler's a bell." Butler's Undertaker, Lounge, and Pub was the only funeral parlor in town and could double as a makeshift morgue.

Jeanie wasn't ready to move on, and was finally bonding with Siobhán. "It would be easier if you had to talk with everyone who *wasn't* here last night."

"Could he have been drugged?" Siobhán asked while she was still in Jeanie's good graces.

"I'll do a full toxicology. But it will take weeks, maybe a month to get the results."

"Rory Mack has already stated that Eamon was drunk," Siobhán said. "Supposedly not in any state to go back to the inn."

Jeanie knelt and gently moved the rope aside. His skin was red, the indentation of a V clearly visible. "These marks are consistent with death by hanging. But, of course, we'll do a full postmortem."

"We need to find out what deck those cards are from." Siobhán took out her notebook and began jotting down notes. Macdara cleared his throat.

"You know I'm a detective sergeant, don't you?"

Siobhán turned to see that Macdara was actually waiting for an answer. "Of course."

"Good. You wouldn't mind then if I take the lead on this?"

"Lead away," she said. She waited.

"Start with the storage room. If you can't find a secret entrance, I can't see making a case for murder."

Chapter 5

⚜

Once the body was removed, Siobhán headed back to the storage room. It would be a disaster if this case was closed as a suicide and a murderer got away. The thought of a killer running around during the Arts and Music Festival was horrifying. A game-playing, sadistic killer.

First things first. Suicide. She would go through it, step-by-step, see which way the evidence pointed. She took in the thick rope still hanging from the wooden beam and put aside the fact that someone would have needed a ladder to reach the beam and tie off the rope. Whether it was suicide or murder, the missing ladder was still a mystery they would need to solve. The rope was approximately twenty feet long. Eamon was at least six foot. If it was suicide, he had stood on the chair, adding another foot, and then kicked the chair out from underneath him. Would the measurement of the rope be slightly different if he had been sitting and strung up by someone else from behind? Math wasn't her forte but someone else could surely figure it out. If he was sitting down would the measurement of the rope be any different as opposed to standing? Unless the killer adjusted the rope *after* to mimic the measurements of a man standing on a chair and kicking it out from underneath him. Too far-fetched? Or were they dealing with someone that cunning?

And either way, how could they use rope distance as proof of which way it occurred? She doubted suicide victims were concerned with exact measurements . . . but maybe they would be able to tell from the fibers on the rope if it was used to pull Eamon up over the beam. Eamon Foley had been in good shape, but he was tall. It would have put some strain on a rope. Were there stray fibers on the floor?

Siobhán glanced at the pristine floor. Not now there weren't . . . *Is that why the floor had been mopped? Is that why the mop disappeared? Not only to hide footprints but rope fibers as well?*

She took out her notepad: *Check the fray of the rope. Check the beam for rope fibers. Check the mop for rope fires.*

Scratch that, she thought.

Find the mop. Check the mop for rope fibers.

"*Can't beat the Dead Man's Hand . . .*" *That's a taunt,* she knew it. *And the playing cards? The calling card of a killer?*

If Clementine Hart or Shane Ross was the killer, would either one of them be stupid enough to throw suspicion on themselves by placing those cards in Eamon's pocket?

What if that's *exactly* what they wanted her to think?

After all, they were dealing with cardsharps here. Someone was playing a very dangerous game.

Clementine Hart and Shane Ross stood to benefit
from Eamon's death. The top competition wiped out.
But, surely, they didn't think the poker tournament
would continue after this? At least not here, not now.
Maybe they didn't realize that? Or maybe someone
had a better motive to kill Eamon. Maybe the tournament had nothing to do with it? Still, it was hard to ignore a prize purse as large as this one. If this was murder,
it also appeared to be carefully planned. Where did the
rope come from? In order for it to be spontaneous, the
rope would have had to be lying around. At least that
fact would be quick to check. Hopefully, Rory Mack
would know if there had been a twenty-foot rope lying
about the storage room. *And if there had been, what an
eejit! Mixing alcohol with rope, a small room, and
wood-beam rafters was not a bright thing to do.*

*Brass knuckles. No money. No keys. No mobile phone.
A mopped room, with no mop. A missing ladder. Dead
Man's Hand. Dead bolt.*

Darn. Macdara was right. They had to figure out
how someone could have killed Eamon, locked the
door, and exited some other way with a mop and ladder in tow, not to mention keys, mobile, and billfold. It
was so crazy, it was almost comical. What if this was a
suicide? That still didn't explain it. Eamon could have
bolted the door—and as Jeanie tossed out there, mopped
the floors first as part of an obsessive suicide-contem-
plation ritual, but a dead man could not make ladders
and mops disappear. If Eamon had taken his own life,
it was planned in advance. He didn't strike Siobhán as
that type.

As far as the missing items from his pockets, those
were easier to explain. Knowing he was going to kill

himself, Eamon could have tossed them or given them away. Suicide victims often gave away their belongings before they died.

Or someone could have come across the body and rooted through his pockets without reporting his death. In that scenario the question of the exit and the dead bolt remained, not to mention you had to swallow the ludicrous thought that this bystander suddenly decided also to remove the ladder and mop.

Macdara was right. She really did need a mug of tea. Siobhán had not been prepared to go straight into a possible murder probe and quietly lamented her lack of caffeine.

Her mind returned to the suicide note. The page had been torn from a notebook. Where was the notebook? They'd found none, nor was there a biro with black ink lying around. Everything was missing!

Siobhán rewound and went back to the beginning: *A pregnant wife. Baby due any day now.* An image of Rose's hard eyes flashed in her mind. *Was the colorful pair having marriage problems?*

If so, could Eamon Foley have taken his life in this manner out of spite? Leaving her, knowing full well that just by waiting and winning he could have left her rich? Was this one last insult? Despite his winnings rumor had it that the Octopus was not good at hanging on to his money.

What in the world had happened here last night?

"Everything?" The skinny young guard looked as if she'd just slapped him across the face. "You want us to remove everything?"

"Everything," Siobhán said. "We need to check every inch."

"Where do you want us to put the items we remove?"

"Just outside the door."

"But isn't the entire pub a crime scene? If there was a crime, that is?" Two grim faces awaited her answer. Siobhán stepped out and examined the area just outside the door. Hundreds of people had been in here last night. The leaked urine had already been documented. She laid a plastic sheet on the floor. "This area is clear."

The guards did not move. The skinny one spoke again. "Let's say we find a great big hole in the wall. How did the killer put the shelves back, like?"

"First I want to know if there's a big hole," Siobhán said. "Then we'll deal with the shelves."

"I don't think it's possible that someone moved these shelves, escaped, and then *moved them back.*"

Siobhán resisted the old cliché—*we don't pay you to think*—even though it ran through her head. Besides, she was the newest guard on the force. Diplomacy was in order. "Our job is to examine this storage room. That's what we're going to do."

"Did the detective sergeant approve this?"

"Would I be doing this if the detective sergeant didn't approve it?" They stared at her, waiting. She sighed. "Yes. D.S. Flannery is the one giving you the order, I'm simply the messenger."

"Messenger," one said. "Is that what you call it?"

"They probably exchange a lot of messages," the other said under his breath.

"Excuse me?" *They know.* She and Dara had been fooling themselves. They all suspected the two of them were together, and she could only imagine what other guards were saying behind their backs. "Remove the shelves." Her voice didn't waver. She was grateful.

"We're on it."

With her gloves on, she began moving cans and rolls of paper towels out of the way so that she could get a look at the back wall.

It only took thirty minutes to confirm there was no passage or hole on the walls behind the shelves.

Siobhán looked down. "Now the floor."

They were incredulous. "The concrete floor?"

"Unless you see any other floor." She was losing her patience with these two.

They spread out, running their hands along the floor, searching. They found normal cracks, but no possible way of exiting through the floor. No hidden tunnels.

"That's it," the skinny guard said. "There's nothing here."

Siobhán's eyes landed on the window.

"You'd have to be a pigeon to squeeze through there," the guard quipped.

That left the ceiling. She looked up. The guards groaned as they followed her gaze.

"We have to make sure," she said.

"We're looking for Spider-Man, are we?" The guards laughed.

"Fetch the ladder from the patio, will you?"

"This is ridiculous," one of the guards said. "It was a suicide."

"The ladder," Siobhán said.

"You can see the ceiling is intact."

"It *looks* intact. But we have to get up on the roof and touch it, go over every inch and make sure nothing gives."

"You're joking me."

"I'm not."

"You don't mind if we double-check this with the detective sergeant, do you?"

Yes, she did mind. She minded very much. She minded so much, she used her mam's secret weapon. She smiled. "No bother at all."

Siobhán and Macdara stood just outside Sharkey's, staring out into a field as the scent of sugar and yeast filtered through the air. The guards had just informed them that there were no signs of any kind of disturbance on the roof. They photographed every inch. "We'll compare the handwriting on the note," Macdara said. "If it's Eamon's handwriting, and the postmortem doesn't hold any surprises, I don't see any other choice. I'm going to close this as a suicide."

Siobhán was running out of leverage. "If blood alcohol levels show he was blotto—which I'd guess he was—wouldn't you need some coordination to hang yourself?"

"Maybe it was just enough to allow him to do it."

Dutch courage. Where did that ridiculous saying come from? What did the Dutch do to deserve it? The Irish certainly drank and they didn't call it Irish courage.

Why did these questions haunt her at the worst times? Maybe it was a defense mechanism. "Where did he get the rope?"

"We'll have to ask Rory," Macdara said.

"You don't seriously think Eamon brought a twenty-foot rope with him and nobody noticed?"

Macdara flicked her a look. She was getting wound up. A second run might be in order. Or she could whittle something. It had been a while since she'd whittled. There was something calming about shaving little pieces of wood with a sharp knife. "The note. Maybe the brass knuckles. And the killer's calling cards."

"What calling cards?"

"The queen and the jack."

"I could make a case that the playing cards are *proof* that he took his own life."

"Do make it."

Macdara rose to her challenge. "He was furious with Clementine Hart and Shane Ross for accusing him of cheating. So why not take a dig at them—with both the note and the cards—before he goes out?"

"Why not *win* before he goes out?" She kept to herself her theory that he might have done it as a dig to his wife. She was trying to win the argument, not sabotage it.

"Maybe Nathan did announce his decision. Maybe Eamon learned he was out. Enraged, he takes his own life."

They were going in circles. "Right. Which suggests impulsivity rather than preplanning."

"Yes," Macdara said. "And?"

"What did he do with his money, sunglasses, mobile?"

"Someone could have robbed him after. Or he gave them away. Suicide victims often do that."

So we do think alike. "But you said it yourself. He would have needed time to tie the rope up to the rafters." Macdara sighed. In the distance Rory Mack leaned against his pickup truck. Siobhán nodded to him. "Do you mind if I speak with him?"

"You're doubting I was thorough?" It seemed a rhetorical question. He gestured to Rory. "Speak away, boss."

* * *

Macdara followed her as Siobhán stepped up to Rory. "What time did you leave Eamon here on his own?"

Rory scratched his chin. "Must have been almost four in the mornin'."

If he was correct, the time of death was narrow. She was no expert, but he looked as if he'd at least been dead for several hours, putting the time of death shortly after Rory Mack left. Or shortly after Rory Mack killed him. She needed to remember that every witness was a possible suspect until they were ruled out.

"What went on here last night?"

Rory glanced at Macdara, who nodded. Siobhán clenched her fist. Was it because she was female that they did this or because she was a new guard?

Rory shifted. "A few games, a bit of craic. You know yourself."

Siobhán had her biro poised over her notepad. "Who else was here by the time you left?"

"It was just me and the Octopus. I'm not running a hotel."

"But you let him spend the night?"

Rory nodded. "I thought it was for the best, given his missus is expecting and all. She probably needs her sleep."

"You're telling me you let him stay out of concern for Rose Foley?"

Rory threw his arms up. "He's a celebrity. He was langered. There was no harm in it."

"Did he *ask* if he could sleep here or did you *offer*?"

Rory took a minute to think about it. "He wanted more shots. I told him he had a big game in a few hours and he needed his sleep."

Macdara turned to Siobhán. "Wouldn't he be thinking along those lines himself if he planned on continuing the tournament?"

Macdara had a very good point. What professional poker player, even an Irishman who liked his pints, would do that to himself pregame? Maybe Nathan Doyle had announced his decision last night, and maybe it hadn't gone in Eamon's favor.

"I believe it was my idea," Rory said. "I thought he was just drunk. If I had any idea where his head was at, I wouldn't have left him on his own."

Siobhán made a note. *Bet the wife wasn't happy he stayed out all night.* "You mentioned taking naps in the storage room. Wouldn't you have a cot in there?"

"Aye."

"We didn't see it."

"I got rid of it. If you're a good enough detective, you'll figure it out for yourself and save me the embarrassment of tellin' you why."

"She is," Macdara said. "She will." He edged closer. "Is there any way in or out of that storage room other than the one door?"

"Not that I'm aware."

"Did you by chance mop the storage room last night?"

"Me?" Rory said, affronted. "No. Eddie does that."

"We're going to need to speak with him," Macdara said.

Rory nodded. "Suit yourselves."

"We'll need a list of everyone who was working here last night," Siobhán added.

Rory sighed. "No bother." It clearly was.

Siobhán shifted gears. "Did you have rope in the storage room?" Rory shook his head. "Did you see anyone in here last night with rope?"

Rory sighed. "We were jammers. It was wall-to-wall people in here most of the night. Everyone was having the craic! Music, dancing, drinking, playing cards. The Octopus was cleaning up. No. I didn't see any rope." He shook his head in disgust. "You're going to want to talk to Miss Queen of Hearts." Disdain dripped from his voice.

"Oh?" Siobhán said. "Why is that?"

"She was a raving lunatic. The minute it hit midnight she was after that official to disqualify Eamon. I tell ye. I'd be afraid of coming home to that one. No doubt she knows how to swing a frying pan."

Siobhán wished she were swinging a frying pan this very moment in the vicinity of Rory Mack's big head, but she kept her gob shut. It was better to let the witnesses talk even if they were offensive.

"You've stated that no decision was announced," Macdara said. "Is that still your story?"

"'Course it is. Yer man said everyone would reconvene at half ten in the mornin' for the verdict."

Someone didn't want to take the chance that Eamon would still be in the games. Siobhán thought of the playing cards still strewn on the tables. "You said Eamon was cleaning up in the games here last night."

Rory gave an appreciative nod. "That's putting it mildly. Boy-oh-boy, he was something else. Nobody could beat that man. I'm tellin' ye, he would have won this tournament."

"Who were last night's big losers?" Siobhán pressed. *And where is Eamon's big wad of cash?*

Rory slumped. "I don't understand why you're investigating. At the end of the day he's the one who done it. It's a right shame. 'Tis. But there's only one man to blame. No one could have predicted this."

"Your job is just to answer the questions," Siobhán said.

Rory's eyes shifted to the distance. "You're not going to ticket me over letting the lads have a few wee bets, are ye?"

Siobhán shook her head. "That's not our concern at the moment."

"Who were the big losers?" Macdara pressed.

"I'd say they're winners now," Rory mumbled.

Siobhán felt a chill go up her spine. "Excuse me?"

"A dead man isn't going to be collecting his winnings now, is he?"

No. He's not. . . .

"The big losers," Macdara said again. "Who are they?"

Rory did not want to talk out of school, but he had no choice. He gazed into the field. "You'll be wanting to have a chat with Henry Moore."

Macdara took out his notepad. "How much did he lose?"

Rory laughed. Shook his head. "Well, let me think, so. How much does that racehorse of his weigh?"

Chapter 6

"Henry Moore bet his prizewinning racehorse last night?" Macdara sounded outraged enough for the two of them. *Amanda Moore would be apoplectic.* It was her horse, and here was her da, betting him in a poker game.

"He did, yeah. Amanda looked fit to kill." Rory caught himself. "I didn't mean it like that." Siobhán imagined it wasn't far from the truth. A teenage girl and her horse? What on earth had Henry Moore been thinking?

He wasn't thinking. That was gambling for you. The addiction that drove some people insane. They were going to have to pay a visit to Henry Moore. If for nothing else than to save him from the wrath of his daughter. She wondered how long Gráinne and Eoin had stayed last night. She'd have to have a word with them too.

Rory stepped toward the pub. "I need the cure."

Normally, Siobhán disapproved of drinking as a hangover cure, but she wasn't here to lecture. It wouldn't be necessary anyway.

Macdara delivered the news. "You won't be getting inside your pub for a while. It's a crime scene."

"The entire pub?" Rory seemed more horrified by this than the news that a man had been found hanging.

"The entire pub," Macdara confirmed.

"What about the tournament?" Panic rose in Rory's voice. "Tell me we're still having the poker tournament?"

Siobhán and Macdara stood outside Room 100 at the Kilbane Inn. Margaret O'Shea, the innkeeper, leaned on her cane and watched them from outside the office. A frail woman in her seventies, she used to click around on a walker until someone gifted her the cane. She wasn't happy they were here, but their biggest offense was not letting her know *why* they were here. Gossip was her lifeblood, but Siobhán and Macdara had more important things on their minds at the moment.

It was, by far, the worst part of this job, the dreadful task of delivering shocking news to the loved ones. In this case it was doubly sad, with Rose expecting any day. Siobhán had their doctor on speed dial in case they needed it. Their gentle knocks turned into multiple bangs on the door before they saw the curtain twitch. "What do you want?" Rose Foley yelled from inside.

"It's Garda O'Sullivan and D.S. Flannery. Would you please open the door?"

"What time is it?"

"It's half nine."

"I'm sleeping."

"It's a police matter." The doorknob turned and the door opened. Rose stood, in a dressing gown that barely came to her knees, belly protruding, hair mussed, eyes red and angry. "May we come in?"

"Unless you're going to sit on me bed, there isn't room."

"We can stand," Siobhán said. "Is there a kettle in the room?"

"I have to make you tea too?"

"I was going to make you a cup."

"Don't bother. I have to pee every second of the day. I don't want any tea." Siobhán and Macdara stepped in. Besides the bed and a desk, there was little else to the room. Margaret didn't believe in decorating. A lone cross hung above the bed. "What did he do now?"

"Pardon?" Macdara said. Siobhán knew he'd heard her, but he was trying to draw her out.

"Is he in jail? Get in a fight?"

Siobhán swallowed. "Would you like to sit down?"

"No, I would not."

Macdara took off his cap. Siobhán took off hers. Rose took a step back, the first signs of alarm on her pretty face. "What is it?"

"We're sorry to have to tell you that we found your husband in Sharkey's Pub this morning."

Rose blew out air and rested her hand on her belly. "Passed out, is he?"

"I found him," Siobhán said. "He passed away, Mrs. Foley."

"He's what now?" She stared at them.

"He's no longer with us," Macdara attempted.

She crossed her arms over her chest. "I have no idea what you're trying to say."

It was a defensive mechanism, denial. The mind protecting the heart. "He's dead, Mrs. Foley." Siobhán had to give it straight.

Rose sank onto the bed, shaking her head. "That's not right. It can't be right."

"I'm so sorry."

"Oh, my God. What did he do? What did he do?" Her hands flew up to her mouth.

That is interesting.

Macdara caught it too. He stepped closer. "Had Eamon ever threatened to take his own life?"

"Threaten me?" She looked like a snake coiled, but ready to strike.

"No, no," Siobhán said. "Did he ever threaten to take his own life?"

"Never," Rose said. "He'd just as soon kill the rest of us."

Lovely. "I take it there were problems in your marriage?" Siobhán hoped her tone was gentle.

"How dare you," Rose said. "He was the love of me life."

"It was the way you said he'd just as soon kill the rest of us," Macdara said. "It sounded like maybe he didn't always treat you the way he should."

Rose stared at Macdara, blinking as if she were trying not to cry. This was a woman who only responded to men. Finally she bit her lip and nodded. "He could have done better."

Macdara placed his hand on her shoulder. "That's no disrespect to his memory, a fact is still a fact, and you can still love him, and him you."

"How did he . . . do it?" She gulped and closed her eyes as if bracing herself.

Siobhán winced, but vowed to give it straight. "I found him hanging in the storage room of Sharkey's Pub."

"Hanging?" Rose's eyes flew open. She shot to her feet. *"Hanging?"* She placed her hands over her eyes like a child playing hide-and-seek. "No, no, no." She dropped her hands, and abruptly wiped her tears. "Where is he?"

Siobhán had to step out of her way to avoid getting mowed down. "Pardon?"

Rose grabbed her handbag off the desk and strode to the door as if this was all a misunderstanding she was going to straighten out. She didn't seem to remember she was still in her dressing gown.

Macdara resumed his charm offensive. "He's at Butler's Undertaker, Lounge, and Pub."

Rose let out a laugh. "He'd like knowing that. Give him a pint while he's at it."

Siobhán felt a deep stab of pity watching her unravel.

"I'm afraid you won't be able to see him for a while," Macdara said. "The state pathologist has to do her work first."

Rose put her hand over her throat. "He was going to win the tournament. Heaps of money. Do you know what that kind of money means to a woman like me? Everyone here knows he was going to win!"

Siobhán nodded to Macdara. "Glass of water." He nodded and headed for the sink.

"No!" Rose shrieked. "I'll take that mug of tea." She dropped her handbag on the floor and stumbled back to the bed.

Siobhán sat next to her. She nodded to Macdara who flipped the switch on the tiny kettle situated near the telly. "I cannot imagine what you're feeling. But we are here for you. We are going to investigate thoroughly."

Rose shook her head. "It's not fair." She began to cry. "That money was for our baby."

The money, the money, the money. Was this just grief, or was Rose Foley really that greedy?

Once the mug of tea was ready, Macdara pulled out the desk chair and sat across from her. "We found a note."

"A note?"

Macdara nodded as he removed the evidence baggie with the note. "You can't take it out of the plastic evidence bag. But could you tell us if this is your husband's handwriting?" He held it up.

Rose's lips moved as she silently read. Her hand began to tremble. Siobhán gently removed the mug of tea as hot water began to splash out. "It is his writing. Why would he write that?"

Macdara exchanged a look with Siobhán. In his book this was strike number two for murder. If the pathologist didn't find something, the case would be closed as a suicide. "Are you sure?"

"I know my husband's penmanship!"

"Do you have any samples we can use to compare?" Macdara asked.

"Compare what?"

"To verify it's his handwriting."

"I just told you it was his handwriting. Are you calling me a liar?" She was getting too worked up. Siobhán made a point of looking at Rose's pregnant belly, then at Macdara.

He nodded and put the note away. "It's not that we don't believe you. It's our job to gather all the evidence we can."

"You need evidence that he killed himself?" Outrage poured out of her.

Macdara cleared his throat. It was his nervous little habit. Siobhán found it endearing. "In any death we have to consider foul play."

"*Foul play*," Rose repeated.

"Are you saying he might *not* have killed himself?" Rose asked.

"Correct," Siobhán said.

This time it was Macdara who threw her a look. He turned back to the widow. "We simply have to look into that possibility. Can you think of any reason why he would have taken his own life?"

"No. I can't. Not right now."

Siobhán gently touched Rose on the shoulder. "We will leave you to get dressed. You can come to Naomi's Bistro. We're closed for the festival, but you can sit by the fire and we'll make you breakfast."

"I'm not hungry."

"I understand. But you can eat a little something, can't you? For the little one?"

"Oh," Rose said, her hand landing back on her belly. "I forgot."

"It's settled then. In the meantime . . . is there anyone you'd like us to call?"

Rose shook her head. Siobhán and Macdara headed for the door.

"What will happen to the money?"

They stopped. Macdara took this one. "Pardon?"

"The winnings. I told you he was going to win and we all knew it. Can I still get my money?"

"I'm afraid it doesn't work that way," Macdara said.

Rose jammed a finger at Macdara. "Foul play is right! It's one of the players that did this. Show me that note again."

"We'll have time to go over everything later," Macdara said.

"You were trying to trick me! I don't know if it's his handwriting. Do you think he wrote me love letters every day?"

"You really mustn't worry about this right now," Siobhán said. "Let's all take a little break."

Rose jabbed her finger at them. "It's one of them players who did it. That pasty spades fella or the Queen of Hearts. Queen of *Black* Hearts."

Siobhán's radar went up. Was she referencing Clementine's skin color, or was Rose Foley the one who marked the playing cards? "By any chance, were you at Sharkey's last night?"

Rose pointed to her belly. "Are you joking me?"

"Is that a no?"

"I was here. I slept. All I do is sleep and pee."

"When you're ready, come to Naomi's Bistro," Siobhán said. Mother-to-be or not, grief-stricken or not, Siobhán needed a break from this woman. She could see how living with her might wear a man down to the bone.

Rose followed them to the door, still bellowing. "It's one of them players! You know it! I know it! Either you find out which one of 'em did it—or so help me, God, I will."

Chapter 7

Siobhán walked in the middle of the street, taking in her neighbors' tents, and trying not to take it personally that she received polite nods instead of the small talk that used to greet her. Local gossip, the weather, the latest items in the shops. Siobhán missed how easy she used to converse with her neighbors. The garda uniform was a repelling agent. Mike was setting up his fruit-and-veg stand; Annmarie and Bridie were stocking their tent with accessories and handmade gifts; Sheila had filled her space with hair products, while her husband, Pio, was propped up on a stool with a guitar. Chatter and music filled the air, along with the smells of hamburgers coming from the truck parked at the end of the street. Even Liam from the hardware store had a tent this year.

After the cold, gray winter, it seemed all citizens of Kilbane were out and about. They were finally ready for a lovely few days, but soon the news of what happened to Eamon Foley would ruin it all, spread through the village like a plague. It made Siobhán long for a tiny bit more of normalcy, so she headed off to see her siblings.

The tent for Naomi's Bistro was standing, looked solid, and the makeshift counter was set up. The menu would be limited: tea, coffee, scones, ham-and-cheese toasties, chicken salad, egg salad, and, of course, brown bread and lemon meringue pie. Her brood was all hanging around the tent. Her sisters, Ann and Gráinne, were writing the menu on the chalkboard sign; James and Eoin were breaking down boxes; James's girlfriend, Elise, was counting the money in the register. Ciarán was the only one not working. He was preoccupied with a deck of cards, and the minute Siobhán stepped up, he thrust them toward her. As usual, she resisted the urge to tame down his red hair or wipe the smear of dirt off his cheek. He was twelve-years-of-age, a fact she had trouble believing.

"Pick a card." Ciarán's face was a study of concentration as he held out the fanned cards, his little tongue sticking out of the corner of his mouth. He'd been obsessed with cards ever since he'd learned the poker tournament was coming to town. She was already dreading the moment he found out what happened to the Octopus.

"Not now, luv. I'm on duty."

Ciarán frowned. "But you're standing right here."

"Just popped in for a quick visit, luv."

"Then you can pick a card." Siobhán sighed and removed a card from the pile, and not the one he had sticking out like a sore thumb. His face crinkled in disappointment when she didn't pick it. She looked at the card. Five of clubs.

"It's *not* the king of diamonds," Ciarán said.

Siobhán laughed. "You're right, luv. It's not."

He beamed. She stuck the card back in and gave him a pat on the head. He swiped her hand away. "Did you know the Octopus drives a sports car?" Ciarán said. His eyes shone. "It's an orange Mustang."

"Orange is the new black," Siobhán said.

Ciarán frowned. "What does that mean?"

"Thank heavens you're back." Siobhán turned to her sister's voice. Gráinne stood in a short skirt and tight top, hands on hips, long dark hair fluffed, fingernails painted neon blue. She'd finally moved home for good, claiming New York wasn't all that. Siobhán was thrilled at first, but three months had gone by and Gráinne was spending most of it in front of full-length mirrors trying on outfits and painting her long nails rebellious colors. Siobhán's attempt to enroll her in a local college was so far in vain. Gráinne sighed. "Ciarán's driving us mental with the card tricks."

"You're already mental," Ciarán said.

"I won't argue with that." Gráinne mussed his hair.

Siobhán glanced at James and Eoin, huddled at the back of the tent. Eoin looked up, locked eyes, and then gave her a nod. It was clear what the nod meant. He hadn't said a word to anyone, not even James. Siobhán wished everything in life were as solid as Eoin O'Sullivan. She had a sudden longing for all the time she used to spend with her siblings. Times that were stretching further and further apart. She didn't know what was worse. The fact that she constantly felt guilty, or that they all seemed perfectly fine without her. Elise had moved on to organizing napkins, takeaway plates, and silverware.

"You look worried," Ciarán said.

The comment surprised Siobhán and she turned to her little brother. "Do I?"

He nodded. "That's a *tell.*"

"It is, is it?"

"Professional poker players don't let their faces show any emotion." Ciarán thrust his face forward and stilled everything but his blinking eyes.

"Unless they're trying to trick you." This was not going to be an easy bunch of suspects.

Ciarán frowned. He didn't like being tricked. The sound of hooves galloping arrested their attention. Amanda Moore raced by on Midnight. They were a blur of hair, shiny muscle, and speed.

"Deadly," Ciarán said. "She's *fast.*"

Amanda steered Midnight onto the footpath, nearly toppling into tents and folks on the street and kicking up dust behind her. "Move!"

Gráinne stuck her hands on her hips. "She's in a hurry."

She knows what her father did. Siobhán was already dialing Macdara. She maneuvered out of earshot as her siblings continued to converse.

"I want a horse," Ann said.

"Me too," Ciarán said.

"No way," Gráinne said. "You don't even pay attention to poor Trigger."

"We would if we could ride him," Ann said.

After warning Macdara about Amanda's flying through town on Midnight, and settling Rose into the bistro, Siobhán headed to the Kilbane Garda Station. She loved that she could walk to work. It helped her rev up in the mornings and decompress at night. Nathan Doyle had been summoned to the station and Macdara thought it best if they questioned him in one of the official interrogation rooms. Since there was no crime in riding your horse, even if she was speeding through a busy footpath and street, they had more pressing issues to deal with.

Siobhán was itching to talk to Henry Moore, give him a proper talking-to about betting a young girl's horse, but she wasn't in charge, as Macdara had taken to reminding her. Besides, Nathan Doyle could have critical information. She was anxious to hear what decision he had come to regarding Eamon and the games, and even more anxious to find out if he let the verdict slip to anyone last night.

They met him in the lobby. He carried a travel mug and looked as well rested as the other fools who had spent the evening at Sharkey's. He was gripping his beverage with both hands as if terrified someone was going to try and pluck it away from him. "Morning, Gardai."

"Morning," Macdara said. Siobhán nodded. Macdara instructed Nathan to follow them to IR1, Interrogation Room One. It was only large enough to seat four persons. The walls were the color of fresh cream. She didn't know if the theory was that a calming color would put suspects at ease, or those who liked to fidget would go mental staring at the blank walls. Macdara shut the door and everyone sat.

"I suppose you're eager to hear my decision." Nathan twirled his coffee mug.

"Have you heard any news this morning?" Macdara said.

His eyes flicked from Macdara to Siobhán. "Is there news?"

Siobhán cut in. "What did you decide?"

Nathan gazed intensely at Siobhán. "I know a lot of these folks have turned up to see the Octopus play. But I can't in good conscience let him continue." He stopped, waiting for a reaction.

Macdara leaned forward. "What did the video show?"

Nathan sighed. "If it was a cheat, they were good. The young blonde stood just out of the way of the camera."

"As if she knew it was there?" Siobhán asked.

"That was my read," Nathan said. "I learned nothing from the videos. In the end I had to resort to good old common sense."

Macdara pretended to write on his notepad. Siobhán knew he was pretending, for he was sketching a rabbit. "When did you come to this decision?"

"I was up all night. I knew last night what I was going to do. Hadn't changed me mind by this morning."

Siobhán tore her eyes away from Macdara's drawing. "Did you tell anyone?"

Nathan frowned. "No." He leaned forward. "Is this about Clementine Hart?"

Macdara stopped drawing and dropped his pencil. "Why do you say that?"

"She had nothing to do with my decision. I can handle the heat."

Siobhán retrieved Macdara's pencil and handed it to him. "What heat?"

"She practically attached herself to me last night. Barking that I needed to disqualify him. Threatened if I didn't, she would take it up the food chain." He sighed. "I was a last-minute replacement when the original coordinator dropped out. Doing a favor for a friend. It will be some craic, he said." He shook his head. "Some craic, alright. When you know better, you do better."

Macdara's face remained passive as he scratched out his rabbit. "Where were the two of you during this heated discussion?"

"Sharkey's."

"What time were you there?"

"I arrived at seven P.M."

"What time did you leave?" Siobhán asked.

"I left when it looked like Shane Ross and the Octopus were going to come to fisty-cuffs."

Macdara leaned in. "What are you on about?"

"Oh yes! They almost came to blows. Clementine's insistence that he be thrown out riled the Octopus up." He paused, then leaned forward as if he didn't trust the room was secure. "But I think our dark horse—"

"'Dark horse'?" Macdara cut in.

"Sorry. Shane Ross. That's me description of him. Shane Ross considers himself a knight in shining armor, I'd say. Before you knew it, he was standing between Clementine and Eamon, ready to do battle. That's when I left."

Is Shane Ross in love with Clementine Hart?

This time Macdara didn't draw a rabbit. He wrote: *Eamon/Shane . . . fight?* "What time was this?" Siobhán asked.

"I couldn't say."

"Try," Macdara said.

"I suppose it might have been nearing one in the mornin'."

"How sure are you?"

Nathan shifted, looked between them. "This isn't just about the tournament, is it?"

Macdara remained cool. "Why do you say that?"

"Something in the way you're questioning me."

Macdara folded his arms across his chest. "Eamon Foley is dead."

Nathan set his travel mug on the desk as if the news rendered him incapable of holding it. "What?"

Siobhán dipped back in. "I found him hanging in the storage room of Sharkey's early this morning."

"My God." He shook his head. "I never imagined." He clasped his hands and leaned forward. "Let me see. He was drunk when I left, and in a heated argument with Shane."

"Were they playing cards?"

"Of course. That's what everyone wanted them to do. They even let the town in on the games." He shook his head. "I heard rumors that several people in town lost way too much last night. I hate to say it, there will be a few heads relieved that he's gone."

"What heads?" Macdara asked. "What did they lose?"

"Is any of this helpful? Will it explain why he took his own life?"

"We didn't say that he did," Siobhán said.

"I thought you said he hanged himself?"

"I said I found him hanging. I did not say who did the hanging."

"We're exploring all avenues," Macdara said.

"Are you thinking it's murder? If that's the case, you're going to have a lot of suspects. That man with the racehorse?"

"Henry Moore?"

"Aye. He was stupid enough to bet him." He grabbed his travel mug, leaned back, and waited for their reaction to the news. When there was none forthcoming, he leaned in. "Looks like you already know about that little nugget."

"What else?" Macdara said.

Nathan snapped his fingers. "That's what flared up tensions between Shane and Eamon. He told him to declare the bet null and void. But Eamon refused. Said he won the horse fair and square."

"I thought you said it was Clementine who stirred up the tensions between them?"

"Pardon?"

Siobhán leaned in. "All that nagging?"

"Right, so. That came first. The argument over the bet came second."

"You said you left when they started arguing. The first time."

"Must have been the second." He looked around. "Do you not hang things on the wall on purpose, like?"

"Pardon?" Macdara said.

"This room. It could use a few things hanging on the wall." He pulled on his collar. "Is it hot in here? I feel hot." The man looked like a thermometer creeping up to the boiling point.

"We're just trying to get the facts straight," Siobhán said.

"Take a deep breath and see what you can remember." Macdara was playing the good cop.

"I definitely left after that business with the horse started. Clementine followed me out of the pub, all the way to my taxicab, stalking me almost—saying now I had to let Eamon go. I tell ye I should have canceled the entire tournament right then and there. None of them are stable." He sighed. "This is a fine mess, i'n it?"

"I would agree that's exactly what it is," Macdara said.

"I'm assuming the tournament is canceled now?"

"I'd say it is."

"I'm available to answer any questions, but I do hope I can return to Dublin as soon as possible. I have important business to attend to at home."

"What line of work would you be in?" Siobhán asked. She was genuinely curious. An accountant would be her guess. She could see him at a desk behind a mountain of papers tapping away at an adding machine, glasses slipping down his nose, curry sauce on his big belly.

"I'm a researcher."

Close enough. "What kind of research?"

He grinned. "I'm for hire. I have great credentials."

"Are you single?" It couldn't hurt to at least let Jeanie Brady know she tried.

Nathan Doyle raised an eyebrow. "If you ask me, I'd say yes. But I do know a Dublin woman who would have a fit if she heard me say that." He threw his head back and laughed, then studied Siobhán. "Why do you ask?"

"Just getting to know you." Siobhán smiled.

"Thank you," Macdara said, signaling the end of the meeting by standing.

"Don't talk to anyone about the case," Siobhán said. "And if you hear anything from anyone else, let us know right away."

Nathan lifted his travel mug and walked out the door.

Siobhán turned to Macdara as soon as Nathan Doyle left the room. "He's a bit odd, don't you think?"

Macdara nodded. "Reminds me of my math teacher in primary school."

She knew he looked like an accountant. "'Researcher'? What does that mean?"

"He didn't really say. Did he?"

"No. He did not." Siobhán folded her arms. "I think we should *research him* a bit more."

Chapter 8

Outside, the festival was in full swing. Children raced by, their faces painted in bright colors; Irish dancers tapped away on stage; folks passed by with their new treasures; Irish wolfhounds paraded by, their leashes held by proud owners; music spilled into the air. Siobhán stood by Macdara taking it all in. Siobhán wished it would last forever. "How long do you think we have until the rumor mill starts churning?"

Macdara sighed. "That's why I'm putting you back on festival duty."

Siobhán glanced at her list of suspects she was itching to question. "What about Henry Moore?"

"He's on the schedule. But I need you on festival duty."

"We also have to speak with Clementine Hart and Shane Ross."

"We have an entire garda force, boss. Please let me do me job."

He was right. She wanted her paws on every little bit of this investigation, namely because she feared someone higher up was going to jump to the wrong conclusion. However, on the food chain of life she was still prey, and prey had the best chance of survival if it didn't strut in front of the lion's den.

Festival duty wasn't so bad, was it? She should be happy. She tried smiling. She heard if you smiled, even when you weren't happy, you would soon fool yourself into thinking you were. *What's the saying Gráinne picked up in New York? "Fake it until you make it."* But minutes later all she had to show for it was growing resentment and a sore jaw.

Macdara tilted his head and gave her one of his looks. "What's that thing you're doing with your mouth?"

"It's called smiling. I hear people like when you do it."

Macdara laughed. "You could light up a room." He winked. "Or set it on fire."

She gave him a gentle shove. Then remembered the guards' comments this morning. "I think there are rumors going around about us. We'll have to be more careful."

"Don't mind them. They'd gossip either way."

They stood, taking in the merriment of the folks around them. There was something so jarring about all this celebrating, when a man who was very much alive last night was now lying in the basement of a morgue with a toe tag and a big question mark hovering over his death. "We're not canceling the festival then?"

"The town would revolt. Besides, if it was murder, and we cancel, all of our suspects go bye-bye."

"Got it." Siobhán glanced around. No one was watching them. She leaned in and kissed Macdara's cheek, then started to walk away. He grabbed her hand, swung her around, and brought her in for a real kiss. Her eyes flicked to the station just feet away.

"That was risky."

"Dinner. Soon. You and me. We'll go into Cork."

"Lovely." She felt a rush of pleasure as they pulled away.

"Be careful," he said.

"Always." She weaved away before he could see her fingers crossed behind her back.

Siobhán made her way through the crowds, past the Celtic tent, where children were performing an Irish Dance, then reluctantly past the chipper stand, where she would return later for a heavenly basket of curried chips. She'd nearly made it past Bridie and Annmarie's stand when they called her over. Lying to the public was one thing, lying to friends and family was torture.

She reached the stand and for a moment lost herself in all the gorgeous trinkets. Annmarie and Bridie made almost everything by hand. Scarves, hats, and jewelry. So much sparkle.

"We're so excited for the tournament," Bridie said, her eyes sparkling right along with the jewels. Her curly brown hair was pinned up by a pink rose she'd knitted. "Do you think you could do us a favor?"

"Depends," Siobhán said, hating that she had to pretend the tournament was still going to take place.

Annmarie held up a red scarf. She was a curvy woman with a lot of sass. Her hair was currently cut in a stylish bob with a streak of green. Siobhán smiled, recognizing Sheila's handiwork. Kilbane had its share of vibrant women. She wished she had more time to hang out with them as friends. "We made these for the players."

"I can't wait to see the Octopus," Bridie said. "I know they're just silly scarves, but—"

"They're not silly in the least. They're lovely," Siobhán said. "But I can't take them this moment."

"You're on duty, we understand," Bridie said. "Can you swing by later?" Later they would know about the Octopus. They would understand why she couldn't stay and chat. Siobhán nodded. "Thanks a million," Bridie sang. "I also have booties for his wife." She held up a pair. They were a gorgeous shade of green. "I don't know if it's a boy or girl, but he or she is Irish, so I went with green."

"They're lovely," Siobhán said. How quickly she'd forgotten about the baby. How could she be so short-sighted? Guards couldn't let their emotions cloud the investigation, but how could she not think about the fact that the baby would never meet his or her father? So many victims in a murder. Even ones who hadn't been born yet. Kind gestures would mean a lot. She smiled at Bridie. "I'll make sure she gets them." She took the booties. They were so tiny and soft. Like a newborn. Hopefully, it would bring a tiny bit of comfort to the widow.

"Hello?" Siobhán whirled around to find Tom Howell standing behind her, nervously twisting a gold chain around his neck. A tall man with slicked-back hair and a tan suit, he wore the expression of a frightened animal about to flee. He owned the only jewelry store in town, Celtic Gems.

"How ya, Tom?" Bridie called.

"Grand, grand. Yourself?" He ran his hand over his slicked hair and straightened his suit.

"Ah, 'tis lovely weather for the festival."

"'Tis, 'tis." He smiled at her, then turned back to Siobhán. "Would you mind stopping by me shop?"

"Is something wrong?"

He glanced behind him, then stepped forward and lowered his voice to a whisper. "I want you to look at some footprints."

"Footprints?"

Siobhán knew Bridie and Annmarie were listening intently, precisely because their heads were cast down like ostriches in the sand, but their big eyes and ears were tilted his way.

He stepped closer. "I know it sounds mental, but it looks to me as if someone was casing my store."

"Tell me more."

"Footprints. And not just in one spot. It's around the entire shop, like."

"Take some photos and I'll be over as soon as I can."

"Why can't you come with me now?"

"I'm on duty, but I'll let D.S. Flannery know."

He glanced down at the child's booties in her hand. "I see."

Siobhán tucked the booties in her pocket. "Someone will be over as soon as he or she can."

"Please. Hurry." With that, he turned and disappeared into the crowd.

"Footprints, is it?" Annmarie said. "How mysterious."

Bridie grinned. "Too bad. You should be able to enjoy the festival without worrying about such unpleasantness."

If they only knew . . . "Can't be helped." Siobhán smiled and said her good-byes and soon she was weaving her way back into the crowd as she took out her mobile and called Macdara. It went directly to voice mail. She relayed Tom's message and asked him to return her call. She would check in on the tent for Naomi's, and if she hadn't heard from Macdara by then, she'd use her lunch break to go over to Celtic Gems.

A line formed in front of the tent for Naomi's Bistro. Elise was tapping away at the register, Ann was handing out food and drink, and Gráinne was standing in a short skirt just outside the tent. She was posing, waiting for the Octopus to walk by. *If she only knew what he looks like now.* Siobhán shuddered at the thought and the image, and at herself for even thinking it. "Gráinne." Siobhán stood back as her sister finally sauntered over.

"How ya?"

"I sent Rose Foley over to the bistro. I thought you and James were going to sit with her."

Gráinne looked as if she'd bitten into something rotten. "Why would I do that?"

Siobhán turned, but couldn't see much through the window. The bistro was technically closed. Her heart gave a squeeze for the widow. Gráinne didn't know the woman's husband had just died, so she had to watch her reaction. But why did her sister have to be so stubborn? She was constantly doing whatever she wanted to do regardless of other people. Siobhán hated to think it, but oftentimes it felt like her sister was missing the empathy gene. "Is she still in there?"

"I left her out in the back garden. All she does is sit and stare. It's creepy. I can't imagine what he sees in her."

"You never know what someone is going through."

Gráinne narrowed her eyes. "What is she going through?"

"I just said you never know. Didn't I?"

Gráinne pointed a long red fingernail at her. When did she change the color? Didn't she have ambitions beyond the color of her nails? "What are you hiding?"

"I'm not hiding anything. I'm doing my job."

"Since when is that woman your job?"

"Garda! Garda!" Siobhán turned to see Henry Moore threading through the crowd. He was a big man, and not averse to shoving if he had to. She wanted to throttle him for betting his precious racehorse to the Octopus. Did the loss set him over the edge? Had he killed Eamon Foley?

"Yes?"

Worry creased his big face. "It's me Amanda. She's gone."

Ann popped up. "Gone?"

Siobhán placed her hand on Ann's shoulder and turned to Henry. "She flew by here a while ago on Midnight."

Henry Moore nodded. "I'm afraid she's run away."

"Why do you think that?"

"I found *this.*" He held up a note: *I hate you. Good-bye.*

A tear came into the big man's eye. Siobhán's heart squeezed. "She's a teenager. She didn't mean it."

Henry wiped his brow with the back of his hand. "It's my fault. It's all my fault."

"Go on." Siobhán was dying to see if he'd cop to it.

"I was at Sharkey's last night." Siobhán nodded. "I might have had a bit of a game with the players. Just for a bit of craic." He hesitated.

"Yes?"

"I didn't mean it. I had too much to drink. You know yourself."

"What happened?"

"It seems I bet our horse."

"*Your* horse?" Siobhán knew her tone was sharp, but she couldn't help it.

The comment landed. Henry Moore's face collapsed in shame. "Amanda's horse."

Gráinne gasped. "You bet your daughter's horse in a poker game?"

A rush of unexpected pride filled Siobhán. This time she was happy for Gráinne's take-no-prisoners approach.

Henry Moore stared at the ground. When he looked back up at Siobhán, there was desperation in his eyes. "Can you please, please tell Eamon Foley that I'll make it up to him? I can't let him have the horse. I have to find Amanda and tell her I'll fix it. Please. Help me fix it."

Is he being crafty? Trying to make himself look as if he doesn't know the Octopus is dead? "Any idea where she might have gone?"

"I can help look for her." Ann again. She tucked a strand of her cropped blond hair behind her ear and swallowed. She was the youngest O'Sullivan girl, just starting to grow out of her lanky phase, muscles filling out from playing sports. Amanda was one of her many friends. "I've gone riding with her. I could check our usual spots."

"I'll take you in my car," Henry said. He looked to Siobhán. "If it's alright with you?"

No, it wasn't alright. He was a suspect in a possible murder probe. Even if Macdara was leaning toward suicide, she was not. If there was the slightest chance Henry Moore did something even more naive or vile than betting his horse last night . . . she wasn't going to let her sister go off with him alone. "Write down where you would go riding," Siobhán said to Ann. "I'm sorry I need her here."

"No, you don't," Ann said. "I can help. Really."

"We've got the tent handled," Gráinne said with a wave of her hand.

"Thank you," Henry Moore said. "I'll feel better if we start looking."

"I said no." Everyone stared at Siobhán. "I'll let D.S. Flannery know. He'll send guards to help you look."

Ann wasn't happy with her. "You don't trust me?"

Siobhán shook her head. "Not now." She tried the smiling thing again. Everyone in her orbit frowned.

Ann stuck her bottom lip out. "James is the oldest. Maybe I should ask him."

Henry Moore held up his hands. "It's alright, luv. Whatever she thinks is best." He wiped his brow. "And you'll talk to Eamon Foley? See if he's willing to work something out?"

"Don't worry about that," Siobhán said. "I'll handle it."

Henry Moore threw a desperate look to Ann. "Can you please tell me where you think I should look?"

"I'll write down our places," Ann said. She threw a look to Siobhán. "If dat's okay with you?" Siobhán ignored the tone. She'd straighten out the misunderstanding later.

"Of course."

Ann made a list for Henry and he hurried away as Siobhán placed yet another call to Macdara. She left a second voice mail.

"How?" Gráinne said the minute she hung up. "How will you handle the Octopus?"

Ann crossed her arms. "Why won't you let me look for my friend?"

She sighed. "I'm privy to information I cannot share at this moment. Can the two of you just trust me for once?"

"I suppose," Gráinne said, not looking at all convinced.

"She's my friend," Ann said. "She would look for me."

"If you want to go . . . find James. Have him go with you."

"You don't like Henry Moore, is that it?" Gráinne pressed.

Siobhán desperately needed a cappuccino. And a basket of curried chips. And a new career. On an island somewhere. With loads and loads of books and chocolates and crisps.

"I'll go find James," Ann said.

"You're not to go anywhere alone or with anyone else," Siobhán called after her.

"I heard you the first time," Ann called back.

Gráinne met Siobhán's eyes. "They're growing up so fast," she said. "Will you stay here when they're all gone?"

Would I? All the placcs she could go. A big world out there. London. Paris. Even Galway or Dublin, or Kinsale. "*You* couldn't stay away."

"It's temporary," Gráinne said. "Believe me, I've got big plans."

"Do any of them involve university?"

"We can't afford it."

"We'll find a way."

Gráinne rolled her eyes. "Right now, I think you'd better concentrate on finding a missing girl and her horse."

Chapter 9

Siobhán mounted the official guard horse, grateful for her long legs, yet a little weary that the horse was going to get browned off, rear back, and send her tumbling to the ground. It had been ages since she'd ridden. Macdara mounted his with ease. These two belonged to the guards in a neighboring village. Both were chestnut mares with gorgeous black manes. Macdara thought the best way to find a girl who'd taken off on a horse was on a horse. Or two. Siobhán clutched Ann's map of Amanda's usual haunts. She glanced over at Macdara, sitting tall on his horse, messy hair blowing in the wind, blue eyes steady.

"Ready, boss?"

"Ready," she answered.

"Lead the way."

She pressed her foot gently into the side of the horse and they were off. These were well-trained workhorses, and within seconds Siobhán was no longer afraid of being ditched. She soon felt at one with the gorgeous animal and put everything out of her mind, except the wind through her hair and the feel of the stride. Once they were clear of the festival crowds and heading for the field behind the abbey, she took hers up to a gallop, confident Macdara could keep pace. They slowed as they passed the abbey, keeping an eye out for anyone camping out. Macdara had another team of guards searching the neighboring villages. If Siobhán were Amanda, she'd be out of Kilbane by now.

Once they were past their magnificent abbey, they maneuvered to the opening in the stone wall, which would allow them to ride the circumference of town. Siobhán wished they were out for a leisurely ride instead of looking for a runaway girl. It was a lovely spring day with the sun shining on the green fields, heather spilling out from the cracks in the wall, birds singing full-throated. As they galloped, Siobhán kept her eyes peeled for hoofprints in the ground. In the distance the steeple of Saint Mary's rose proudly in the air. They did a full loop, without any sign of Amanda or her horse. It wasn't until they were several streets away from Sarsfield Street, and nearing the back of Celtic Gems, that Siobhán remembered her visit from Tom. She reminded Macdara.

"We're here, might as well check it out," Macdara said. "I'll touch base with the other teams looking for Amanda. Let them know she's most likely hiding out at a friend's or in another village."

When they rode up to the front of the shop and dismounted, they found Tom Howell pacing in front like a madman. "Look," he said, pointing at the ground. "Footprints. Someone was pacing. A wild animal."

Macdara glanced at the camera above the door. "Did it trigger your alarm?"

Tom's head jerked up. "Exactly! It did not." He sounded as if this was proof of something nefarious. "I swear I set it. With all these strangers in town? I definitely set it."

He wasn't wrong about the footprints. It did appear as if a madman had been pacing back and forth alongside the building. A madman with massive feet.

Macdara was still interested in the security system. "What usually triggers the alarm?"

Tom stroked his chin. "Wind. Rain. Birds. People. It's a bit overreactive."

"And yet it did not react," Siobhán mused.

"Exactly!" he exclaimed. "You get it."

Siobhán used her mobile to snap photos of the footprints, then pulled a measuring tape out of her pocket, along with a pair of gloves

Macdara looked amused. "You carry all that in your pockets?"

"You have no idea," Siobhán said with a wink. Her pockets were as filled as her handbag.

"Size eleven," Siobhán said.

"That's my size," Tom said, staring at his feet as if they'd betrayed him.

"Common enough," Macdara said.

"Definitely a man," Siobhán said.

"If it's a woman, I'll let you bring her in," Macdara said with a wink.

"Very funny."

"I'll call this in. Get a cast of one of the prints. Let's try and find a clear one."

"A cast?" Tom said, sounding impressed. "Then what? Are we going to make every man in town step on it, see if the cast fits?"

"Yes," Siobhán said. "But we'd better do it before the clock strikes midnight and they all turn back into frogs."

"I think it's pumpkins," Macdara said.

She shrugged. "Are you sure these prints weren't here before?"

"I'm sure. I've been keeping the place pristine, hoping I could draw some of the festivalgoers this way. I was really hoping the poker players might spend some of their winnings here."

Tom stepped to the side to make a call. She waited until he was finished, then sidled up to him. "Have you had many heads in?"

He folded his arms. "No."

"Have you had *any* heads in?"

"You really like to rub salt in the old wound, don't you?"

As a businesswoman herself she knew how one's mood could rise and fall with customers, so she gave him a pass too. "Couldn't this just be kids messing?"

"Perhaps. When they start young and aren't punished, that's when they end up hardened criminals."

"Punishing children isn't a top priority for us this year, but we can take it up at the next department meeting," Macdara said with a wink.

Tom Howell did not seem in the mood for a laugh. "Does that mean you aren't going to investigate?"

"Take it easy." Macdara was using his jovial voice. "I'm only messin'. We will thoroughly investigate." He turned to Siobhán. "Write that down, will ya?" She bit her lip and nodded. He was in good form today. "In the meantime get your security company out to double-check your system. We have quite a bit we're chewing on at the moment."

"Eamon Foley's suicide?"

"How did you hear?" Word had traveled even faster than she expected.

He nodded his head to the farmhouse across the street. "Heard it from Greg Cunningham."

Greg Cunningham was an old man who kept racing pigeons. He kept mostly to himself. *How did he hear the news so quickly?* Siobhán wanted to know more. "Were you at Sharkey's last night, by the by?"

Tom stood up straight, almost toppling backward. "Pardon?"

"I heard it was some craic. I missed it. Were you there?"

"Heavens no. I'm too old and boring for that crowd."

And yet he suddenly wouldn't make eye contact. *Is he lying?* If so, it was a foolish thing to lie about, as the answer could be easily sourced. She followed his gaze to the property across the street. Greg Cunningham was standing by his fence, trimming bushes, keeping up a steady rhythm, impressive for his age. Siobhán nodded to Macdara. He followed her gaze to Greg and nodded. "See if he saw anything, I'll be here."

Greg Cunningham snipped faster as she approached, shrubbery falling to the ground like fairy dust. "How ya," he called without stopping.

"Afternoon," Siobhán said. "Grand fresh day, isn't it?"

"'Tis."

"Have you been outside long?"

"Aye."

He was a man of few words. As a normal person

going about her day, she appreciated that. As a guard she found it challenging. "How are the pigeons?" She glanced toward the coop. Their soft coos filled the air.

"They're flying it." He winked. "What's the story?"

"Have you seen anyone lurking outside Celtic Gems the past few days?"

Gary glanced up while snipping. "Was he robbed?"

"No, sir. But he suspects someone has been lurking around. There are footprints."

"Only person I've seen is Tom himself. Pacing out front. I t'ink he was expecting a big crowd."

Tom was pacing? Tom, with the size-eleven shoes? "Are you sure?"

"Aye."

Was Tom lying? Or was he losing mental capacity? Could he be unaware that he *was the one pacing in front of his store, leaving the footprints? Or is Greg lying?* Siobhán couldn't help but glance at the old man's feet. They were probably a size nine and she was being generous. There was probably no way to whip out her measuring tape and measure them without it being awkward. "Are you sure it was Tom? Could it have been someone else?"

"It could have been him *and* someone else. All I saw is him."

"How did you hear about Eamon Foley?"

He stopped snipping and regarded her. "That the poker player?"

"Yes. Tom says he heard the news from you. Where did you hear it?"

Greg shook his head. "It's a grisly way to go. Wife about to give birth too. How could a man be so selfish?"

It was more words at once than she'd ever heard Greg speak. He was stalling. "How did you hear?"

He held up his clippers. The blades glinted in the sun. "Say what you want about me pigeons. But they always come home."

"Mr. Cunningham, I need to know who told you." Greg Cunningham was close to being a total recluse. He didn't take up space in the pubs, and wouldn't be gossiping with the hill walkers in the morning. She'd only seen him in the bistro a few times over the years, and when he was in the shops, he shuffled through and kept his hat pulled down low. She was glad he had his pigeons, although it made her sad. If he had been born now, would he be diagnosed with a social anxiety disorder that they could treat?

Then again, diagnosing an Irishman, let alone getting him to follow treatment, was a challenging feat indeed. Freud's alleged quote about the Irish rose to mind: *"This is one race of people for whom psychoanalysis is no use whatsoever."* It made her want to give the famed psychiatrist a box to the head, but perhaps that just proved his argument.

Greg glanced at his pigeon coop. "What about Henry Moore's girl? Have they found her yet?"

Maybe it was time to reevaluate the label of recluse. He'd certainly been squeezing the grapes on the gossip vine lately. Siobhán glanced across the street and caught Macdara's eye. She waved him over.

Macdara jogged across. Siobhán met him just out of earshot of Greg. "Did he see something?"

"He saw Tom pacing in front of his own shop."

"You're joking me." Macdara turned as if to immediately confront Tom.

"But he's certainly hearing things," Siobhán said.

Macdara lifted an eyebrow. "Oh?"

"He knows about the Octopus. And Amanda Moore."

"Is that so?" Macdara frowned. "To whom would you be talking?"

Greg began to rake up his fallen shrubbery. "Just me pigeons."

"Your pigeons told you about the Octopus and the Moore lass?"

"Don't be ridiculous. Heard about the Moore lass from Henry Moore. He was out here looking for her."

"Why look here?" Siobhán asked.

"I suppose he's looking everywhere. And Amanda likes to come visit me pigeons now and then."

That was sweet. Made sense. Amanda was such an animal lover. A sixteen-year-old girl could not hang a grown man all by herself. *But what if she had help?* Her passion for her horse was epic. Hopefully, they would find her soon.

"And the Octopus?" Siobhán asked.

"That would be me pigeon," Greg said without a trace of sarcasm. Macdara and Siobhán exchanged a look.

"And where does your pigeon get his news?" Macdara said, barely holding his temper.

"Here and there," Greg said. "He picks it up in town."

Macdara glanced at the shears in Greg's hand. "Mr. Cunningham, these are serious questions."

"I'm just a man trimming me shrubs."

Siobhán eyed the bushes. "If you trim them any more, they're just going to be sticks." She imagined plucking one off and beating him with it. *Take that, Sigmund!* "Please answer the question. This is an official inquiry."

Greg sighed, put down his shears. He turned and started to walk toward his pigeon coop.

"Mr. Cunningham?" Siobhán called.
He didn't look back. "Follow me."

The pigeon coop was Triple D: dark, dank, and damp. Greg flicked on a light that buzzed and snapped. He shuffled to cubbyholes built into the wall. He stuck his hand into one and pulled out a fat gray pigeon.

"Aw," Siobhán said before she could help herself. The little thing was adorable. "Can I hold her?"

"'Course you can." Greg handed her the wee thing. It melted into a puddle of softness in her palm as it vibrated and cooed. *Bliss. Forget therapy dogs, they should use soft, fat pigeons. Every sad person should just sit and hold one until their heart eased.*

Macdara gave her another one of his looks. "Would you like to be alone with her?" She gave him a look of her own and reluctantly handed the pigeon back.

Greg removed a curled piece of paper from her tiny claws. "Layla brought this to me early this morning."

"Who's Layla?" Siobhán asked.

Greg gave her a dirty look and lifted his bird. "Me pigeon."

"Ah, right, so." Didn't quite fit the image she had of the famous Clapton song, but then again Greg on his knees for his pigeons didn't seem like such a stretch. She wondered how many hours she'd save in a day if she could stop innocuous thoughts from taking space in her head.

He handed Siobhán the note. It was typewritten: THE OCTOPUS HUNG HIMSELF IN FINNEGAN'S.

Finnegan's. The previous name of the pub. Rory Mack hated when folks still referred to it as Finnegan's. Whoever sent this note, one thing was for sure, he or she was a local. Siobhán handed it to Macdara. "Your pigeon brought you this note?"

"Layla," Macdara corrected.

She grimaced. "*Layla* brought you this note?"

Greg appeared to be growing tired of the humans. "I said so, didn't I?"

"Where did she get it?"

Greg kissed the pigeon's head and placed her back in the cubbyhole. She cooed. Siobhán tried not to melt. "Could be from anyone. All the locals know me pigeons. You wouldn't believe the t'ings people send." He walked over to another cubbyhole and pulled out a basket filled with tiny little notes.

"Wow," Siobhán said. "Are any of those recent?"

"Nothing from before the poker tournament came to town. But you can read through them if you like. Some of the messages aren't fit for delicate eyes."

Siobhán could only imagine. She hoped none of them were cruel. Tormenting a man through his own pigeons. Why did human beings pick on the vulnerable? It made her blood boil. "Why didn't you call the guards when you received this?"

"I didn't know what to t'ink." He gestured to the basket of notes. "There's one in there that says Elvis is alive and in Ireland." He nodded to Siobhán. "But I knew the rumor about the Octopus was true, once I saw this one's face. Lucky she's not one of the poker players."

Siobhán had a sudden urge to write her own note for Layla to pick up. "We'll be keeping this note."

"You will, so," Greg restated as if he was the one insisting.

Macdara stared at the pigeon as if he had a newfound respect for her. "Is there any way of knowing where Layla picked up this note? Do you have tracking on her?"

"I just track her by her coming and going. Most of my pigeons fly much longer distances. Layla only likes to fly about town. She's a bit soft in the head."

Siobhán leaned in and looked Layla in the eye. The old bird didn't blink or open her beak. Typical. Siobhán was happy when they stepped back outside into the fresh air.

Macdara gently took the note from her hand. "Have any of your other notes been typed?"

"No," Greg said.

"Can your pigeon type?" Siobhán wanted to lighten the mood.

"Aye, but she just pecks." The playful retort startled Siobhán, and then she laughed. Greg winked and turned back to Macdara. "I can tell you most of the lads' handwriting by now. Dis is the first typewritten note Layla has ever brought back."

"What time was this?"

"Half seven this mornin'."

Siobhán gasped. *Before* Siobhán discovered the Octopus hanging. Either the killer sent this note, or someone had discovered the body before she did. A third, remote possibility was that Eamon sent the note before hanging himself. But why? Was there an old typewriter in the pub? Why would he refer to it as Finnegan's? Eamon sending the note seemed the least likely scenario.

Beyond the "who" was the "why." Why did someone send the note? Was it simply a concerned citizen who didn't want to admit to finding the body? Why not place an anonymous call to the guards? The person had to know the Octopus would be discovered sooner than later. This seemed so bizarre. She turned to Macdara. "Do you think we can trace the typewriter?"

"I'm sure there's someone out there who could. But there're no letters missing, looks like your typical machine. The time it would take to go door-to-door asking if they have a typewriter, and would they mind typing out for us, 'The Octopus hung himself in Finnegan's,' is out of the realm of practicality."

"Right, so." It sounded like something a brilliant detective would do in a film.

"We might be calling you into the station to give an official statement," Macdara said.

Greg sighed, then nodded. "Will you be wanting me to bring Layla?"

"No," Macdara said. "But why don't you send her out again. See if she brings back another note."

"She was out all day yesterday. I won't let her go until tomorrow."

"Good man," Macdara said. "Give her a rest."

"Can you *send* a note with her?" Siobhán asked.

"I could. Can't promise the same person who sent that note will get it."

"Don't pigeons tend to fly to the same places?"

"Most do. I told you Layla's a bit soft in the head."

"Worth a try," Macdara said. He turned to Siobhán. "What did you have in mind?"

"Let's start with the basics," Siobhán said. She glanced at a small basket attached to the door to the coop. It was filled with pencils and pieces of paper cut into strips. "May I?"

"Knock yourself out," Greg said.

Siobhán took a piece of paper and scribbled one simple question: *Who are you?*

Chapter 10

By the time Siobhán returned to the street festival, word of Eamon Foley's death had spread. Folks huddled together chattering in high pitches, and the minute they spotted Siobhán, the seas parted as if she was contagious. When she neared the tent for Naomi's, she saw her siblings were surrounded by gawpers.

She felt a pinch on the back of her arm and turned to find Gráinne. Her instinct to scold was stifled by her sister's red eyes. "Why didn't you tell me?"

"It's work, luv." She put her hand on Gráinne's arm. Gráinne yanked it back. "You don't trust me."

"There are policies and procedures."

"Since when do you follow policies and procedures?"

"Since I became an official garda."

"I heard he hanged himself?" Gráinne had a boisterous voice. Heads turned.

"Let's go into the bistro. Where are the rest of ye?"

"Ann and James are out looking for Amanda." *Amanda.* She'd almost forgotten. There was too much going on. "Where are Ciarán and Eoin?"

A smile snuck across Gráinne's face. "They're at Eoin's tent."

Siobhán was going to have to get her hearing checked. "*Eoin's* tent?"

"C'm'ere to me." Gráinne grabbed her hand and began to pull her through the crowd. She heard snippets of conversations . . .

"Found him swinging from the rafters."

"Murder. Again. She's a magnet—"

They mean me.

"The Octopus."

Multiple women were crying. It seemed as if the smells of cigarette smoke, ale, grease, and sugar were stronger as well, as folks took to their vices to cope. With a glob of tourists to worry about, Siobhán prayed everyone would keep it together.

Who was she kidding? *Keep it together.* Whatever things were, they certainly were not being kept together. They had a man allegedly casing his own jewelry store, a teenage girl on the lam on a racehorse, and a soft-in-the-head pigeon bringing home notes from a killer. That was probably the very definition of *not* keeping things together. Not to mention the pregnant widow on a warpath. Was it too early in her career to retire?

"Here," Gráinne announced, pointing to a tent like a game show hostess. Eoin and Ciarán sat behind stacks of what appeared to be homemade comic books. On the front was a sketch of a girl, all in black and white, except for long red hair—Siobhán's color—although in Eoin's renderings the girl's head was literally on fire. She stared at the title: *Sister Slayer*.

Eoin grinned. "You're speechless. Deadly." He and Ciarán high-fived.

Siobhán picked up a comic and leafed through it. The redheaded girl was basically an Irish Wonder Woman. She turned the page to see the girl lifting a sheep over her head as if she were going to launch it like a projectile. He was selling them for five euro each. Despite the jarring content, Siobhán admitted, his drawings were superb.

"How long have you been doing this?" *Why have I never seen them?*

"Years. What do you think, so?"

"Years? You've kept these hidden for years?" Eoin winked. He wasn't blessed with traditional good looks, but he was full of confidence and charm. And a bit of swagger. "You're good."

"T'anks."

"Are they selling?"

He sighed, rotated his Yankees baseball cap. "It's early days yet."

"You should team up with Gordon's Comics." Chris Gordon's tent was propped up a ways down the street in front of his comic-book shop.

"He's an *indie* graphic novelist," Ciarán said. "Chris wanted a cut."

"A who now?" Gráinne demanded.

"Independent—indie—graphic novelist," Eoin said.

Siobhán stared at Eoin, wondering when they'd all started keeping secrets from her. She was proud and browned off at the same time. She wanted to cry, and pinch him really hard, and hug him all at the same time. She took a deep breath and smiled. *Sister Slayer*. "Good luck. These are brilliant."

Ciarán fixed her with a stare. "You can't just paw through them for free. Are you going to buy one?"

"Of course. I'll get my copy tonight. I have to get back to work."

"Why did he do it?" Eoin said. "The Octopus?"

Gráinne leaned in. "Siobhán thinks it's murder."

"What?" the boys said in stereo.

Siobhán couldn't believe it. "I never said that."

"You didn't have to. I can read your mind." She glanced at the comics. "I t'ink you picked the wrong sister."

"She's right then? You t'ink it's murder?" Eoin asked.

"It's an open investigation. That's all I'm saying. I want all of you to stick together. If you hear or see anything strange, let me know." Her eyes landed on the sketch of the redheaded girl holding the sheep above her head. "Anything else . . . strange."

"Someone murdered the Octopus?" Ciarán said, as if not a single utterance had pierced him.

Eoin let out a low whistle.

Siobhán nodded at Eoin. "I'm going to need to speak with you and Gráinne about anything you saw and heard that night. This evening. After supper."

Eoin and Gráinne exchanged a long look and then nodded. *Fantastic. More secrets.*

Ciarán lifted a deck of cards. "I was going to show him my trick." Trigger emerged from somewhere in the tent and jumped up on Ciarán's lap. Siobhán leaned in to scratch the mutt on the head. He licked her fingers. She was glad the dog was with them. Not much of a killer, but criminals didn't need to know that.

Siobhán could see the news of Eamon's death was affecting all of them. "It's a tragedy. We'll all say our prayers. Please. Stay alert."

"You think someone here is a killer?" Eoin said it matter-of-factly as his eyes roamed over the crowd.

"I do," Siobhán said. "I wish I didn't. But I do."

Siobhán didn't even get a chance to leave Eoin's tent. Rose Foley was making a beeline for her, belly leading the way. "Have you caught him?" she yelled. "Do you know who murdered my husband?"

People stopped, heads swiveled, exclamations rang out. "Murdered?" The crowd drew closer.

"Rose," Siobhán said. "Please." She gently placed her hand on Rose's shoulders. "Let's go somewhere private."

Rose yanked away. "Did you talk to Clementine Hart? Shane Ross? It was one of them that did it. They killed their competition!"

"I thought it was suicide?" a man yelled over the crowd.

"It was murder!" Rose yelled back. "My husband was murdered."

Accusing eyes landed on Siobhán as if she was personally responsible for their assumptions. "Calm down. Getting riled up is going to make it harder to investigate."

Rose, buoyed by the crowd, continued with her bullying. "Where is Clementine Hart? Where is Shane Ross? Take me to them right now."

"The guards are handling this. I promise you. In the meantime—"

"Forget it. I'm going to the garda station. If you won't answer my questions, I'll find someone who will." She glanced down at *Sister Slayer*, then back at Siobhán. Her look said it all.

Rose hurried off, faster than Siobhán had ever seen a woman with a belly that size move.

"Nightmare," Gráinne said. "She's going to go into forced labor."

"Like a slave?" Ciarán asked, scrunching his eyebrows.

"'Labor' as in *having a baby,* not as in the *workforce,*" Eoin said.

"But having a baby *is* work," Ciarán pointed out.

Siobhán ruffled his hair. There were moments she just couldn't resist.

"Did they find Amanda?" Eoin asked.

"No," Gráinne said. She gave Siobhán a pointed look. "Shouldn't you be doing something?"

"There are a lot of things I *should* be doing, a few I *could* be doing, and endless t'ings I *wish* I were doing."

They all stared at her. Eoin shook his head. "Maybe I did pick the wrong sister."

"Lesson learned." Siobhán grinned and walked away, while baskets of curried chips danced in her head.

By the time Siobhán made her way through the crowd to the garda station, the entrance was swarmed with reporters and folks wanting to get any drip of information they could. "Rose is getting everyone worked up," Macdara said when Siobhán made her way through.

"I'm well aware."

"Did you say something to her?"

"She ambushed me." She had to shout as people yelled out questions.

"Was the Octopus murdered?"

"Will the tournament be shut down?"

"Didn't he hang himself?"

Macdara sighed. "There's a fire lit now." He held open the door to the station. "And not the good kind."

"What's the 'good kind'?"

"A turf fire of course."

She could instantly feel and smell the burning peat. "What I'd give for a nice turf fire." If only they were cuddled up by one now, instead of wrestling with a hormonal widow. She took a moment to imagine it, then steeled herself and entered the garda station.

Nathan Doyle was leaning on the clerk's desk as if he owned it. Clementine Hart and Shane Ross were sitting in the waiting chairs on opposite ends, as if they wanted to be as far away from each other as possible. *Interesting.* You would think they would be huddled together gossiping about the news. Macdara hurried Siobhán past them and into the belly of the station, where guards sat at their desks in the open-concept room. Macdara had a large office, Siobhán shared a tiny one with other guards, and, otherwise, they worked out of the main communal space in the center. Lastly the station had a patio, a break room, and two interrogation rooms situated side by side. There was a window cut into the shared wall dividing the interrogation rooms, but a privacy shade kept subjects from being able to see into each other's rooms.

"We're going to interview Shane Ross in IR1, while Clementine Hart waits in IR2."

IR1 and IR2: Interrogation Room Number One and Interrogation Number Two. Siobhán liked knowing all the guard lingo. There was so much of it. Alphabet soup.

"Aye, aye, Captain," she said.

He narrowed his eyes. "It's too early for sarcasm."

"It's never too early for sarcasm."

"I think Shane will respond best to you, so I'm going to let you take the lead."

Excitement zipped through her. "No bother."

"Are you going to be good garda or bad garda?"

"Wait and see." He frowned. "I'm perfectly capable of switching it up. I'll start out good, and if warranted, I can bring down the hammer."

"Hammer away." Macdara entered the room and sat in the corner as if punishing himself.

Siobhán entered IR1 and pulled the black shade down between the rooms before ushering Shane Ross in. The rectangular table had four chairs. He seemed overwhelmed with the choices, so Siobhán finally pointed to a chair. He was pale and visibly shaking. Was it from the drink the night before, the shocking news this morning, or a combination?

Siobhán sat across from him, pulled out her notepad, and hit RECORD on the digital player in front of her.

Siobhán offered a friendly smile. "Let's start with where you were last night."

"We were all in Sharkey's last night."

"What time did you arrive, and what time did you leave?"

"I arrived at half seven. I left . . ." He scratched his chin. "Should I guess?"

"If you must."

"Half one?"

"Were there many around when you left?"

"It was still jammers. I assumed the rest were going to stay until sunup."

"Was it your intention all along to swindle the locals into playing poker?" Macdara's eyes flashed. She hadn't intended on saying it. He was settled in now, slouching in the chair as if this were a mere inconvenience. He sat up at the question.

"Eamon was the one who started playing poker with the locals." He traced his index finger on the table. "When yer man put his racehorse into the pot, I tried to stop it."

Siobhán reached into the cubbyhole underneath the table and then slid the clear evidence bag in front of Shane. Inside was the jack of spades with his mouth blacked out. Shane stared at it. She gave him a moment and then slid the evidence bag with the queen of hearts. He stared at the blackened heart and let out a low whistle. "Was it Eamon who done this?"

"Did you see him do anything like this?"

Shane shook his head. "He was a sick man, alright."

"It's quite possible that someone else did this," Siobhán said.

"Are you asking if it was me who done it?" He tapped the jack of spades. "You know that's what they call me. *Shane of Spades*. And Clementine, *Queen of Hearts*. So why would we do it?"

"Throw off suspicion," Siobhán said.

Shane crossed his arms and considered it. "If that's the case, it didn't work."

"Please answer the simple question. Was it you?"

"I've no memory of it."

Siobhán's ears perked up. "Are you saying you cannot accurately recall the evening?"

"You know yourself. Nobody can totally recall an evening like that."

"Did you black out?"

He grinned. "If I did, I don't remember."

The bluffer. She could not let him get to her. "I'm not referring to the playing cards. I'm referring to you. Were you so drunk that you blacked out?"

"You already asked me that."

"This time I want a straight answer."

"That's as straight as I can get. I was so drunk. If I blacked out, I don't remember." A smirk appeared on his face. He no longer looked boyish. Was his public persona just an act?

"I'm going to mark it as affirmative that you may have been the one to mess with these cards."

He sighed, slapped his hands on the table. "I didn't mess with the cards." He looked at his fingertips. "I'd have black marker all over me."

"You could have washed them by now."

He shrugged. "I suppose."

"Did you see anyone with a black marker, or scissors, or messing with playing cards in any way?"

"No." He slid the bags back to Siobhán. Then he raised an eyebrow and held up his finger. "Except for that kid."

The back of Siobhán's neck tingled. "What kid?"

"The little redheaded one." He stopped and stared at Siobhán, then cocked his head. "Is he yours?"

"Pardon?"

Shane tilted his head, and from the gleam in the poker player's eye, Siobhán knew the blow he was about to deliver seconds before it left his cruel lips. "Ciarán O'Sullivan, is it?"

Chapter 11

Ciarán? Was he really talking about *her* Ciarán?

Macdara moved from his corner seat and took the chair next to Siobhán.

"Pick a card." Ciarán had been obsessed with the tournament and the Octopus long before they'd landed in town. She shouldn't be shocked. And yet she was. He was just goading her. She wasn't going to take the bait. If Ciarán had been at Sharkey's that evening, Gráinne or Eoin would have mentioned it. Right? Right? Siobhán chose her next words carefully. "I'm sure you saw my brother Ciarán at the festival."

"At a tent selling graphic comics." Macdara leaned forward with a grin. *"Sister Slayer."* He saw it? Siobhán didn't dare make eye contact with him. "I bought ten copies m'self."

What was he doing to her? *Distracting me so I can't*

overreact. It worked. She was distracted. Her cheeks were so inflamed, they could start a turf fire.

"I didn't see him at the festival," Shane said. "I saw him at Sharkey's. Wondered to m'self, who would let such a young lad loose in the middle of that craic? I'm no role model, but even I wouldn't have let any of my young ones be around dat crowd." He pinned his eyes on Siobhán. She stared back and mentally started naming everything in the room. *Table. Chair. Biro. Notepad. Recorder. Curtains. Fist. Fist. Fist.* "I suppose he has no one to look after him. Is that right?" *Stab, stab, stab.* Macdara's leg touched Siobhán's under the table. *Steady, steady, steady.* "He leeched around until an older lad pulled him out by his ear."

"Moving on," Macdara said.

But Shane wasn't ready to move on. "'Pick a card, pick a card, pick a card.'" A smile crept across his face.

Siobhán lurched to her feet and leaned across the table. "Shut. Your. Gob."

Shane crossed his arms and smiled. "Something wrong?"

Macdara gently tugged her back to her seat. He leaned over and whispered, "Need a break, boss? Cup of tea?"

"No." She took a deep breath.

"I have a few questions," Macdara said. He began talking. Siobhán couldn't listen, her temperature was skyrocketing.

Ciarán! Children were often seen in pubs in Ireland. With their families for a bite, or music, or a special occasion. But not Sharkey's. How did she not know Ciarán was out all night? She mentally retraced her every movement that evening. She'd tucked him into bed around half eight. A bit early for him, but he was so worn-out from the festival.

Correction . . . he *pretended* to be so worn-out from the festival. *He played me.* She had taken a book to bed, and was asleep soon after, dead to the world. And while she slept, he snuck out and went to Sharkey's. The very thought, imagining him making his way to the pub all by himself . . . down dark streets . . .

Ciarán was just a baby. Maybe not in his eyes. Twelve years of age was still a baby. Which one of her brothers had hauled him out by his ear? Eoin? James? Why had they kept it from her? She was the de facto mother, whether any of them liked it or not. She tugged the collar of her uniform away from her neck. She felt like punching a hole through the wall with her fist. Even the thought of whittling did nothing to calm her down. She'd whittle something pointy and sharp. Macdara's voice came back into focus.

"Did you see him with a black marker?"

"No."

"How did Henry Moore react when he lost the horse?"

Shane shifted in his seat, as if his arse wasn't used to such hard surfaces. "Who?"

"The man who lost his racehorse," Siobhán said. Shane took a moment to clock the anger in her voice.

"How do you t'ink? Said if Eamon laid a single hand on his horse, he'd see him dead."

Macdara leaned forward. Siobhán momentarily forgot all about Ciarán. "He said what?"

"His exact words. 'I'll see him dead before you get a hand on that horse.' "

Siobhán slipped in. "That can't be right."

Shane frowned. "'Tis. Exactly."

"No. Not *exactly.* So try again. In *his* words."

"What do you mean?" Shane was on defensive again. *Good.*

"If Henry Moore had said that to Eamon, he would have said, 'I'll see *you* dead before you get your hands on me horse.' "

"That's what I said."

"No. You said, 'I'll see *him* dead . . .' "

"Semantics." Shane waved his hand and blew air from his lips.

Semantics, or is Shane making this up as he goes?

"What did Eamon say in return?" Macdara asked.

Shane rubbed his head, leaned back in his chair, and crossed his arms. "He said, 'As you wish.' "

"Like from the movie *Princess Bride*?" Siobhán said.

Shane folded his arms across his chest. "Never seen it."

"You should," Macdara said. "Excellent film."

"He's seen it," Siobhán said. "Everyone's seen it."

"I haven't seen it."

"Try again," Macdara said.

Shane slouched. "I might have seen half of it."

He stopped speaking, but Siobhán could tell there was something else. "Go on," she said. "Out with it." She was the bad garda now and back in charge of the interview.

Shane grinned. "You caught me. Brilliant film." He bobbed his head. "Revenge always makes for a great story, don't you t'ink?"

"What would you know about revenge?" Siobhán kept a smile on her face.

Shane shook his head. "Me? Nothing." He opened his arms. "I'm a man of peace."

Siobhán leaned forward. "Someone else?"

"It's just a rumor."

"We like rumors, don't we?" She turned to Macdara.

He nodded. "I will admit it. I do like a good rumor."

Siobhán smiled at the bluffing eejit across from her and imagined the day he left Kilbane for good. "Rumor away."

Shane sighed. "All that yelling Rose is doing about her husband being murdered?"

"What about it?"

"It's all an act. A little drama for the crowds."

"That's not a rumor," Siobhán said.

Shane glanced at Macdara.

"She's right. Not a rumor. Will you be needing a dictionary?"

Shane shook his head. "The *rumor* is that Eamon wasn't the father of dat baby."

"Who might be spreading that rumor?" Macdara asked.

Shane glanced at the black curtain separating the interview rooms and jerked his thumb toward it.

"We're going to need a verbal answer," Siobhán said.

"Clementine Hart." He threw up his hands. "That's all I know. Am I free? I'd like to go home."

Macdara shook his head. "You were planning on staying for the tournament over the rest of the weekend. I'd appreciate it you'd stay."

"Is that an order?"

"Do I need to make it one?"

Shane stood. "This is ridiculous. The man hanged himself."

"His widow doesn't think so."

"And I told *you,* that widow is playing you."

"Based on a rumor you heard from Clementine Hart?"

"Eamon Foley said his little swimmers were no good." Shane waited for his message to land. "He'd been to a doctor and everything. Why don't you see if you can get your hands on his medical records? Crowing like Rose's pregnancy was some kind of gift from God. How did he phrase it?" He stared at Siobhán. "You're big at phrasing."

She forced a smile. "I am."

"'A miracle baby.'" Shane scoffed. "Dat's what he said. The only miracle was that he was dumb enough to believe it could be his baby." He shook his head and drummed his fingers on the table. "It was a gift, alright, but not the heavenly sort. She was knocking boots with someone else, and my guess is he finally figured that out for himself. That's why he killed himself. Mystery solved, Detectives. You're welcome."

Siobhán wrote a single word on her notepad: *Sterile?* Was there any truth to this? Would they be able to get his medical records? Shane was still talking out of his mouth.

"Rose Foley is a miserable shrew and he wanted out of that marriage. If he *wasn't* sterile, who knows how many snot-nosed brats he'd have running around? You know that's why they really call him the Octopus."

Macdara kept an impassive face. "Do tell."

"He needed eight hands for all the colleens he bedded."

"You're saying he was having an affair?"

"That's a soft word. Too soft for the likes of him." His head swiveled to Siobhán again. "He likes them young too, that really riled up the missus. There was a black-haired beauty last night hanging all over him. What was her name?" He snapped his fingers. "Gráinne O'Sullivan." He whistled. "Nice one, that."

Macdara screeched his chair back as Siobhán whittled an imaginary spear and stabbed him with it. "Stay the weekend. That's an order." Siobhán knew it wasn't enforceable, but it was worth a shot.

Shane gave a curt nod. He stood, then whirled around and jabbed his finger at the pair of them. "Don't be telling anyone you heard that rumor from me. If there is a murderer running around, I don't need to give the killer a reason to come after me."

Siobhán and Macdara huddled outside the interrogation room. Concern was stamped on Macdara's face. "How ya doing, boss?"

Siobhán collapsed against the wall. "I blew it. I let him push all my buttons."

"That's not my read."

"It's not?"

"The only reason he turned up the volume was because you were making *him* nervous. If you ask me, that was all the acts of a desperate man determined to hide the truth from us."

"It didn't feel like that."

"That's why I'm telling you. You did good."

"I'm going to kill Ciarán."

"Go easy on the lad."

"If you say, 'Lads will be lads,' I'm going to clop you over the head."

"What if I say, 'You best watch that redheaded temper'?"

"I'd clock you for that too."

"What lad *wouldn't* sneak out to see the famous Octopus?"

Maybe that's what was really bothering her. What mother wouldn't realize that? She wasn't his mother. She didn't have the instinct. No matter how hard she tried, she'd never replace the real thing. She'd let Ciarán down. The person she was most angry at was herself. Her mam would have had an ear out for a creak in the step. Or she would have been waiting at the bottom of the steps in her blue robe and knowing look. She would have sensed it the way some folks could feel the rain in their bones. "I keep seeing him around all of that drinking, and gambling, and smoking—and as it turned out, death."

"He wouldn't have had all that in his head."

"I keep having to try and figure out what my parents would have done. It's not fair."

"No. It's not." He stared at his shoes. "You want me to have a word with him?"

"No." Macdara was a good influence, but he wasn't blood. He wasn't their father. They'd keep this in-house. "Why didn't you have more guards posted at Sharkey's?"

"We had plenty. Most in plainclothes. All say the same thing. It was a circus. You know yourself."

Siobhán nodded. "Any news on Amanda?"

"I'm going to check in with my guards now on that. I suppose you're going straight to Ciarán?"

Siobhán shook her head. "I'd better wait until I have me temper a bit under control. Besides, I thought we were meeting with Clementine Hart next?"

"We were supposed to." Macdara held up his mobile. "I got a text." He turned his screen to her. "She left the station."

"What?" *These players! Maddening.* "Why would she do that?"

Macdara shrugged. "Said she'd be at the festival."

Why would she do a runner? "I'm on it."

"When you find her, schedule a new appointment—

make sure she's motivated to stick to this one—and text me the details."

"Is anyone watching the widow?"

"I've got guards on all our suspects."

"Good thinking."

"Why, Ms. O'Sullivan, is that a compliment I hear?"

"Make it last. I won't be giving them out like candy."

Macdara laughed. He looked as if he wanted to lean in for a kiss, but as usual resisted. "Good luck."

"Can I have the evidence bags?" Macdara took the playing cards in plastic bags and handed them to her. She expected a fuss, so she looked at him with surprise.

"They're just props. The original ones are in the evidence locker." He gave her a wink that made her feel like she was floating.

Siobhán smiled to herself as she left the station with the playing cards in their plastic bags. Macdara Flannery always did like a good prop.

Chapter 12

It wasn't hard to spot Clementine Hart, not only because her gorgeous dark skin was in contrast with the pale Irish folks surrounding her, but because she had a regal presence, making the Queen of Hearts an apt nickname indeed. As Siobhán approached, she spotted Ciarán at the head of the fan pack, holding out his deck of cards. She had to force her mind elsewhere. She was going to have her word with him, and whichever brother dragged him out by his ear, but right now she needed to focus on Clementine Hart.

But as soon as she had taken a step inside the circle with Clementine, she was bumped from behind. She whirled around to see Ann, her blond hair tousled, cheeks shiny red, standing before her breathless.

"I found her!"

For a moment Siobhán was lost. "Who?"

"Amanda."

"Where was she?"

Ann's face clouded over. "I can't be giving away our hiding places."

Siobhán sighed. Another thing she'd have to deal with later. "Where is she now?"

"With the guards. They're bringing her home now."

"Good girl." Siobhán wrapped her sister in a hug.

Ann pulled away. "Can I go see her?"

"I think the family will need some time."

"She asked me to come over."

"I thought you had camogie practice?" Ann was a star at the stick-and-ball game.

"No practice during the festival."

Siobhán wished there was. At least one of her brood would be preoccupied with something healthy. "You can invite her to the bistro tomorrow. Let the family have their time." Ann's shoulders sank with disappointment. Siobhán drew her in again. "It's only a day. Where's James?"

"I dunno. He took off again." Ann leaned in, her voice low. "I think he and Elise had a row."

James was keeping a low profile. Siobhán had assumed it was because of his addictions. But maybe there was more going on. They were all silently falling apart, and Siobhán had no idea how to put them back together. That's it. She was going to have to schedule a family supper. Not tonight. But sometime soon. "Why don't you go off and enjoy the festival then?"

"With a murderer running loose?" Ann jutted out her hip.

"If you stay close to the locals, you'll be fine." Siobhán did not want her siblings, or any of the folks in town, to stop living their lives. They would catch this killer. Her eyes flicked back to Clementine. She was still engaged with her fan club, but she threw a nervous glance at Siobhán, studying, it seemed, her shiny garda cap.

"Amanda is going to be my best friend," Ann crooned. "Muscles in her arms like a lad. From carrying heavy buckets of water to and from the barn." Her eyes practically glowed. "I bet she can fight like a lad too."

Ann sounded infatuated. She was coming into an age where she would be finding herself. Some roads were harder than others, but Siobhán would make sure she always felt loved and supported. Or maybe Amanda would turn out to be a best friend. You could never have enough love, no matter what. Siobhán gently grabbed the back of Ciarán's jumper, whirled him around, and nudged him toward Ann. "Why don't the two of you spend some time together?"

"I'm spending time with Clementine," Ciarán said. Clementine sported the expression of a kidnapped victim.

"Clementine and I have plans," Siobhán said, mostly for Clementine's benefit. "Why don't the two of ye help Eoin sell his comics, alright?"

"Graphic novels," Ann corrected.

"Graphic novels, so," Siobhán said.

"Can we get curried chips?" Ciarán's eyes shone with excitement. How could he look so sweet and innocent, yet be keeping secrets from her at the same time?

She glanced at Clementine. The same thing could be said of murder suspects.

Siobhán wished she could have curried chips. Wander the festival without a single thought of cardsharps. "Go on then. Bring Eoin a basket too." She dug in her pocket, handed Ann the euro, and gently shoved them off.

She turned to Clementine with a smile and spoke

loudly so the rest of the hangers-on would hear. "Ready for our lunch date?"

"Lunch date or interrogation?" Clementine shot back, flashing a wide smile.

"I'm a multitasker," Siobhán said. "No reason it can't be both."

Siobhán found she needed the comfort and quiet of the bistro, so she brought Clementine in and they sat at a table in the back dining room with a view of the garden. Spring was springing all over the place. There were bluebells, with their little purple heads bowed down; patches of broom, which were so sunny and bright; pansies and violets, along with pink and red roses, to name a few. Her mam could have named all of them. Their herb section was looking fabulous, thanks to Eoin, and every so often he would pick them and hang them upside down in their kitchen like Mam would do. Siobhán liked plucking mint and dropping it into hot water, or even just inhaling it.

Siobhán also liked watching the bees, butterflies, and dragonflies zipping around. Nice work if you could get it. At the end of the day the little things mattered most. The tiny little miracles every human being deserved. Another reason it so incensed her when a life was cut short. She couldn't bring Eamon Foley back, but she could find his killer. She made herself and Clementine a mug of tea and grabbed some brown bread cooling in the kitchen.

"This is amazing," Clementine said after her first several bites.

"It's me special talent," Siobhán said.

"Can I have the recipe?"

"No."

Clementine raised an eyebrow, then laughed. She jabbed a finger at Siobhán. "I like you."

"Thank you." Siobhán liked her too. But she didn't say it. She was on duty. Besides, Clementine could be a killer.

"I didn't stay long at Sharkey's," Clementine volunteered.

"You didn't stay long in our interrogation room either," Siobhán quipped.

"I have a hard time sitting still. It's not like I'm hiding anything." She opened her arms and grinned. "All here."

"Why didn't you stay long at Sharkey's?"

"I wanted to be rested for the tournament and the men were behaving like absolute animals."

Siobhán tried to shove the image of Ciarán among all those animals out of her mind. "What time would you say you left?"

"Half eleven."

"Are you sure?" That sounded way too early. Shane claimed he left at half one.

"I wanted to be in bed by midnight."

Siobhán found herself lost for a minute in Clementine's English accent. She demurred for a moment about the immaturity of men, bonding with the woman she wished were her friend. She pulled out the playing cards and laid them on the table between them.

"Interesting." Clementine reached for the bags and then stopped. "Can I touch them?"

"They're safe in the plastic, you can, sure."

Clementine picked up the playing cards and studied them closely. "Seems like something the wife would do, doesn't it?"

Shane was right. Clementine was gunning for the

widow, throwing her under the tractor at the first opportunity. "Why would she do that?"

Clementine didn't hesitate. "We were the competition."

"Whoever did this wanted to send some kind of message. What message would the widow be sending?"

Clementine shook her head. "That's your territory. I have no idea."

"Was Rose Foley at Sharkey's that evening?"

Clementine nodded. "She was storming in as I went out."

Siobhán didn't need clarification. Every single time she'd seen Rose, the woman seemed to be on a warpath. Rose Foley had lied straight to their faces. Insisted that she had gone to bed. "Nathan Doyle mentioned you spoke with him that evening."

Clementine crossed her arms against her chest. "He's an odd one, don't you think?"

Siobhán agreed, but kept her gob shut. "He said you were pressuring him to announce his decision."

"What decision?"

Clementine knew very well what decision. She was stalling. *Why?* "About whether or not Eamon Foley was to be banned from the tournament?"

Clementine made a steeple with her hands. "*Pressuring* him? Is that what he said?"

"Yes."

"What a weakling."

"Pardon?"

She tapped her long red nails on the table. "He says 'pressure,' I say 'persistent.' If I had been caught cheating, do you think he would have taken the evening to think about it?"

"I would hope so," Siobhán said. "He needed to review the tapes."

"Why couldn't he do that right away?"

"Namely because of the crowd. It would have been irresponsible not to control when and how the decision was rendered." Clementine rolled her eyes, but didn't argue. "Why were you so persistent? Why couldn't you wait for his decision in the morning?"

"Once it's after midnight, it's the morning." Clementine smiled.

"You said you left at half eleven."

Clementine's smile faded. "I'm still on London time."

"London time is the same as Cork time."

"Is it?" She smiled. "You have to be persistent to make it in this field as a female. Isn't it the same for you? As a female guard?"

"What time did you really leave Sharkey's?"

"I don't know. I wasn't paying attention to either London or Cork time." Her smile was long and easy.

"Why did you lie?"

"I thought you wanted an exact time. I'm a people pleaser." She held out her hands. "Cuff me if you must."

"Are you making light of lying to a guard during an active investigation?" Siobhán hated having to take this tone with a woman she imagined would be a best friend. In an alternate universe where no one was ever murdered.

Clementine's eyes narrowed. She wasn't used to being challenged. "It wasn't a lie. It was a bluff." She shrugged. "Hazard of the trade."

"If you bluff to a garda, that's a lie." This wasn't a tea party, even if they were drinking tea.

Clementine sat up as if she'd just been scolded for

poor posture. "I apologize. I don't know why I lied. I wasn't paying any attention to time whatsoever. I just wanted that nerdy bloke to make his decision!" She took a deep breath. "He's the one who followed *me* out of the pub."

"Who followed you out of the pub?"

"'Doddering Doyle.' That's what I call him."

"Nathan Doyle followed you out of Sharkey's?"

"Yes."

"What did he want?"

"I believe he thought he was flirting. Can you imagine? That pasty, middle-aged bloke?"

"Did he make a move on you?"

Clementine's expression turned angry. "Something is off about that man."

Siobhán's ears perked up. She had the same instinct. "In what way?"

"How did he get the position of coordinator? He doesn't even know the game of poker."

"What have you based that on? Have the two of you played a game?"

"He asked me if I could recommend a *book*. Imagine? Useless."

Siobhán scribbled on her pad, wondering if she could figure out a smooth way to ask for the name of that book. "Ciarán is mad to learn about poker. Would you mind giving me a suggestion as well?"

Clementine laughed. "I never read a book on the game in my life. I learned by doing. Rolling up my sleeves. Sitting down at the table with all those useless beasts. That's how you learn."

Siobhán picked up the cards again. "I need you to answer directly. Did you do this?" She jiggled the bag.

Clementine stared at them. "What if I did?"

"You're saying you did?"

"No. I'm saying, what if I did? What do those scribbles have to do with anything?"

Siobhán glanced at the cards. *Or a taunt. A message* . . . Plus, they were found on the body. She could not divulge any of this. "It's a simple question."

"Hazards of your job, I suppose. Everything looks sinister." Clementine looked at the cards again. "If it's a threat, does it mean someone intends on cutting my heart out?" She leaned forward. "Should I be looking over my shoulder?"

"I think it would be wise for everyone to be aware of their surroundings until this matter is closed."

Clementine blinked. "I want to go back to London."

"We're asking that everyone remain for the next few days. You planned to be here anyway."

"What if I don't remain?"

"I have no idea. It wouldn't look good, I can tell you that."

"Fine. I'll stay. But I'm leaving when the weekend is done, and that is that." She yawned. "Are we finished here?" She looked at her watch. "It's time for my catnap."

"Just a few more questions." Siobhán doodled in her notebook. "Did you argue with Eamon Foley that evening?"

Clementine tapped her lip with her fingernail. "I wouldn't say 'argue.' "

"What would you say?"

"I might have called him a few names. After he insisted he was going to take that poor man's horse. I might have told him he was going to be kicked out of the tournament."

"I'd prefer you not talk about what you *might* have done and instead focus on what you did do."

"Eamon was enraged that evening. He'd been caught cheating and was going to be thrown out of the tournament. And rumor has it that baby wasn't his. That would be a lucky break for the child. He had plenty of reasons to do what he did that night."

"Where did you hear the rumor about the baby?"

"Shane might have said something."

"He said he heard it from you."

"There you go then."

"Do you think this is a game?"

"Everything is a game, Garda. Life is a game."

"I'm not playing."

Clementine offered her palms to the sky. "The game continues regardless."

"You're not helping yourself."

"What evidence was at the scene that makes you think it was murder?"

"I can't discuss that."

"Are my fingerprints at the scene? My DNA? Strands of my hair?"

Siobhán was losing control yet again. Clementine was simply better at this than she was. She'd make a great garda herself. "Did anyone see you after you left Sharkey's?"

Clementine traced the edge of the table with her finger. "If I'd known how fragile Eamon Foley truly was, I wouldn't have badgered him." She leaned in. "I wanted to beat him fair and square."

"Then why press for him to be thrown out of the tournament?" Clementine arched an eyebrow and remained silent. Siobhán felt she'd won a small victory. She had her there.

"If someone in that pub did it, it seems they would have had to be sober."

"Why do you say that?"

"Eamon was a scrapper. Fought as good as he played. It would have taken great coordination and strength to hang a man like the Octopus."

"Go on." Siobhán wanted to keep her talking. Let her think she was in control.

"I didn't see any sober people. Except Doddering Doyle."

Clementine was really shining a spotlight on him. *Deflection?* "What did he say to you when he followed you out of the pub?"

She sighed. "He wanted to know what I planned on doing if he *didn't* kick the Octopus out of the tournament."

Why was she just hearing about this now? And didn't Nathan say he made his mind up early on, even if he kept the decision to himself? If so, why would he ask Clementine that? They needed to question this group while they were in the same room with each other, to weed through the lies. Siobhán wished there were a foolproof lie-detector test other than plying them with too many pints of Guinness. Maybe Declan should get all their suspects blotto and see what he could learn. "Go on."

"I quoted the famous 'hell hath no fury' line." She grinned. "He was shaking in his boots." She leaned in. "I bet he marched right in and announced the Octopus was out."

"No. He didn't."

"He should have." She shook her head. "I felt a bit sorry for the bloke."

"Why is that?"

"Imagine the pressure. If he threw Eamon out of the tournament, he'd have an angry mob against him. If he let him stay, he'd have me and Shane against him. A terrible spot for a weakling." Clementine certainly looked proud of herself. She picked up the jack of hearts. "My guess is that Eamon killed himself. But if he didn't . . . there's one person I can think of who might have done this." She made the card move, as though dancing.

"Shane Ross?"

"With the Octopus gone, he moves up to a second-place ranking."

"And you move up to number one," Siobhán said lightly.

"Doesn't matter. I was still number *two*. Shane didn't stand a chance with the two of us in the tournament. But he's arrogant enough to think he can beat *me*."

"But Shane had to know that if the Octopus was found dead, the tournament would be canceled."

"Not canceled. *Postponed*." *True. Is Shane that desperate for the winnings? Could he be in financial trouble?* "Shane was really livid about the horse too. I didn't know the bloke was an animal lover. He looked like he wanted to tear Eamon apart with his bare hands."

"Did you see any rope lying around the pub that evening?" Clementine shook her head. "Did Eamon talk about having problems with Rose?"

"He wasn't friendly with the other players. We all keep our distance. Otherwise it's too hard to have a poker face. However . . . you could see it. I could feel him tense up every time she entered the room." Clementine rose and stretched. "Feels like we've been sitting for ages."

It had only been twenty minutes, but Siobhán was finished with her for now. She needed to think it all through. After Clementine's exit, Siobhán stepped out into the back garden. Clementine had thrown suspicion on a multitude of others. Rose. Eamon. Nathan. Shane. Sleight of hand? Was that all, or did she have other cards she was holding back? There was a final option: Clementine Hart was a cunning and cold-blooded killer.

Chapter 13

Jeanie Brady wanted to meet Siobhán and Macdara at Sharkey's to go over her preliminary findings. She also wanted to have another look at the storage room where Eamon was found hanging. The three of them stood in the middle of the space and tilted their heads back to take in the rafters.

Jeanie hummed for a minute and then stopped. She began counting off on her fingers. "His widow admitted the handwriting on the note appeared to be that of her husband. The markings on his neck and face are consistent with hanging. The chair was knocked over. The publican, presumably the last to see the deceased, confirmed that the Octopus asked if he could sleep in the storage room, and the door was bolted from the inside." She stopped. Then looked at Macdara and Siobhán as if waiting for them to argue with her.

Siobhán stared at the rafters. "Did we learn anything from the knots?"

Macdara shook his head. "Well tied. The person knew what they were doing. But a common tying method." He sighed. "It's a strong case for suicide."

Siobhán eyed the window again. "What about Layla?"

"Layla?" Jeanie said.

"Sorry," Siobhán said. "She's a pigeon." Siobhán walked over to the window and looked up. "It was closed when I came upon the body. But what if it had been open?"

"It's only a venting window. Not big enough for a person to get through."

"But it is big enough for a pigeon," Siobhán said.

Macdara nodded. "Interesting."

Jeanie tilted her head. "I'm lost."

"A local man owns racing pigeons. Saturday morning before I discovered the body, he received a note informing him that the Octopus was hanging in Finnegan's."

"Finnegan's?" Jeanie said.

"It was the original name of this pub."

"Well, isn't that odd," Jeanie said.

Macdara looked uneasy. "All we know from that pigeon is that someone else discovered Eamon's body before you did. It doesn't prove murder."

"There has to be a reason. Everyone was supposed to meet here by half ten. Why send the note with the pigeon at all?"

"Concerned citizen. Too afraid to call the cops. Comes into the storage room, sees the body hanging . . . doesn't want to be associated with it—then, in flies a pigeon."

"That means there's a typewriter in this pub somewhere."

"We'll look. If not, it won't be our only missing item." He sighed. "But I'm afraid it still isn't a case for murder."

"There is one more thing," Jeanie said. She looked at them as if she relished delivering the news.

Macdara stepped forward. "What is that?"

"Eamon Foley was wearing a bulletproof vest."

Siobhán gasped. She turned to Macdara. "Rose hinted that he was in some kind of trouble in Dublin." Macdara opened his mouth, then shut it. "We should at least check that out, right?"

"How?"

"You were a detective sergeant there. You must know people in Dublin."

"I've already reached out."

"And?"

"I haven't received the report yet. But if he was in some kind of trouble, that just makes me lean toward suicide."

"What suicidal man would wear a bulletproof vest?" Surely, this had to be a game changer.

"He was afraid of someone," Jeanie said. "Doubt it was the pigeon."

Macdara frowned. "We need to figure out where the vest came from."

"Bulletproof vest, brass knuckles . . . as if he had his own little army," Siobhán mused.

Macdara nodded. "Who knows what he was up to in Dublin?"

"Drugs?"

"As I mentioned, the toxicology report will take ages," Jeanie said. "But we didn't find any on him. However . . ." She smiled again. She liked waiting for reactions.

"Yes?" Siobhán said.

"You weren't far off from Eamon having his own little army. The vest is garda issue."

Macdara jumped on it. "He was wearing a police vest?"

Jeanie leaned down and lifted an object out of her bag. There in a plastic bag was a bulletproof vest. *AGS* could be seen in the upper-right corner. *An Garda Síochána.* This investigation had just taken a bizarre turn.

Siobhán and Macdara stared. "Where in the world did he get that?"

Macdara took the plastic bag with the vest. "I don't like anything about this."

"Exactly," Siobhán said. "Someone is messing with us, and we've already established it's not the pigeon, and it's certainly not a dead man."

"Eamon Foley could have set all of this up—staged his death to confound us," Macdara said. "A true player until the end."

Siobhán turned to Jeanie, who was unnaturally quiet, and for once there was no sign of pistachios. "Is there anything else in your findings that would lean toward murder?"

"Multiple contusions on his arms," Jeanie said. "It could indicate he was manhandled, or came to during the incident and there was a scuffle."

"Anything else?"

"There is some wear on the rope that would suggest it was pulled over the beam. But in and of itself, it's not conclusive. Who's to say the rope wasn't already worn in certain places?"

"Which way are you leaning?" Siobhán was curious to hear Jeanie's instincts.

Jeanie threw her arms up. "I'm befuddled."

Macdara strode over to the door, shut it, and slid the bolt, then pointed to it. "You tell me how the killer got out."

Siobhán sighed. "If I have to explain the door, then you have to explain the bruises."

"I was thinking herself," Macdara said.

The wife. He had a point there. It was easy enough to imagine Rose digging her claws into her husband. *Literally.* But unless the Octopus suspected his wife was packing heat, Rose was not the one he feared.

"Even with the vest, and the brass knuckles, and the bruises," Jeanie said, "D.S. Flannery is correct. I simply cannot rule it a murder unless you figure out how the killer got out and then bolted the door again." She looked thoughtful. "How talented is this pigeon? If she can open and slide bolts, I'd say it's 'fowl play.' Get it? *F-o-w-l.*" She threw her head back and laughed.

Siobhán wasn't in the mood for a laugh. She stared at the bolt. "It's murder. I know it."

He sighed. "Our suspects will be leaving on Monday. At best, you have twenty-four hours to prove it."

Jeanie saluted. "I will keep my report open until the two of you can complete your investigation." She strode out, humming once again.

Siobhán and Macdara exited the storage room, but stayed in the pub. Siobhán began to pace. She stopped underneath the far corner where a camera was mounted to the ceiling. She pointed. "Have you checked the camera?"

She watched as Detective Sergeant Flannery's face reddened. "I requested the footage. Haven't heard back." He pulled out his mobile and dialed. "Rory, where is that footage from your security cameras? Drop whatever you're doing. We're here now."

* * *

They sat at the bar stools while they waited for
Rory. It was an odd sensation, a pub emptied of its patrons. Missing a trad band in the corner, lads lined up
for the pool table, pints of ale sliding across the
counter. Banter, and gossip, and the gentle unwinding
of a day. A pub without its patrons was like a swimming pool drained of water. If only those beer taps
could talk.

Rory Mack entered, already rambling his apologies,
toting a laptop. "Sorry. Sorry. I forgot about the cameras. Guess it was the shock."

He strode over to the corner of the room where a
camera was situated, and stared up as if it were a leak.
"I don't see the little red light." He set his laptop on the
counter and let out a curse a few clicks later.

"What?" Siobhán hovered over his shoulder. White
fuzz danced on the screen.

"The camera has been shut off." He ran through the
history. An image of a jam-packed pub popped on the
screen. "Here's from Friday day." They watched a few
seconds of faces, raised pints. She couldn't make out
the particulars. Then the screen turned to fuzz. Rory
cursed again and leaned in. "Half five," he said. "It
blew at half five, Friday evening."

*The security cameras went on the blink. Just like the
cameras at Celtic Gems . . . coincidence?* Siobhán didn't
like coincidences.

"Did it blow?" Macdara said. "Or did someone tam-
per with it?"

Rory considered the question. "Only two ways to
shut it off. Manually or through this website. I certainly would have seen someone climbing a ladder in
the corner of me own pub, like."

"Speaking of ladders," Siobhán said. "We've been

through every inch of this pub and we haven't found
yours."

Macdara rubbed his chin and turned to Rory. "When
did you last see the ladder?"

Rory looked up. "I used it Friday day. I hung dat."
He pointed to a banner hanging from the ceiling: *Welcome to the Players!* Siobhán had been in and out of
the pub numerous times and hadn't even looked up.
She would have to do better. "When I finished, I put it
back in the storage room."

"Where?"

"Leaned it against the back wall. Near the window."

She turned to Rory. "Did anyone have access to
your laptop?"

"It sits behind the pub when I'm working. The place
was jammers. Someone could have messed with it. But
it's password protected."

Siobhán knew that was hardly a barrier. "Do you
have the password written anywhere?"

"Of course not."

She nodded. "As long as it's not something simple,
like Sharkey's. . . ."

Rory beamed and shook his head.

"Or Finnegan's," Macdara added.

Rory's face reddened. He opened and shut his mouth
several times. Then he shook his fist. "You can't trust
anyone!"

"Do any of your employees still refer to this place
as Finnegan's?"

Rory frowned. "Most everyone does. You'd t'ink a
neon shark would have done the trick, but no. Finnegan's,
Finnegan's, Finnegan's."

So it could have been any local yoke.

"Do you have a typewriter in the pub?"

Rory pointed. "That one?"

Siobhán and Macdara stared. There by the cash register on the back of the bar was a typewriter. The antique kind that Siobhán loved.

"At least one item is still here," Macdara said. "We're going to need that list of all your employees."

"Especially those scheduled to work Saturday morning," Siobhán said.

"Is that all?" Rory said, sounding like it was a giant bother.

"We're taking your laptop as evidence," Macdara said. "When you get it back, change your password."

Rory cursed again. Siobhán was starting to wonder if he knew any other words. Maybe she'd get him a dictionary for his grand reopening. As Rory was leaving, Siobhán asked him again about the rope. "I told ye. I didn't have rope lying around me pub. Someone else brought it in." He let the door slam behind him.

Siobhán didn't hesitate. "Now are you starting to see that something sinister took place?"

Macdara nodded. "The coincidences are piling up." He started to pace. "On one hand, what man who is about to kill himself is going to be concerned with a camera?"

"Correct. Only a *murderer* would be concerned with the cameras."

Macdara stopped. Looked at the banner. "What man would bring a twenty-foot rope to a poker game?"

Siobhán didn't hesitate. "Only one kind of man."

"And what kind is that?"

"The kind who has a plan to get away with murder."

Chapter 14

Macdara continued his pacing while Siobhán propped herself on a bar stool. They had been in Sharkey's for a while as they went over and over the case. "How on earth would the killer know the Octopus would end up sleeping it off in the storage room?"

"Perhaps he or she made sure the Octopus would be in no state to go home. Either that or the killer acted on an opportunity."

Macdara stopped pacing and tilted his head. "Go on."

Siobhán hopped off her stool and used the pub as her stage as she tried to work through it. "The killer saw the state the Octopus was drinking himself into, then he came across the rope. Say at the beginning of the evening. The wheels start turning."

"Wait," Macdara said. "You're the one who said

that if this was murder, it all started with the Dead Man's Hand."

Siobhán sighed. "Yes. I did say that." *Why was his memory so sharp?*

"This is either premeditated or impulsive. But you can't have it both ways."

"I know. Doesn't stop me from *wanting* it both ways."

"Let's get some fresh air," Macdara said. "I need to see sky."

Siobhán couldn't agree more. Outside, they found Rory Mack waiting for them by his truck.

He waved them over. "You're going to want to see this." He peered into the back.

They walked over and followed suit. Under a scrunched-up tarp lay a ladder. Rory put his hands up like they were going to arrest him. "I didn't do this. I swear. I put it back in the storage room."

Macdara gave Siobhán a look before turning back to Rory. "This is the first you've noticed it?"

Rory pointed to the tarp. "I've had this down on the bed for days. It was only now I noticed there was something underneath it."

"So it's possible it's been in here since you used it Friday day."

"I definitely put the ladder back in the storage room. Someone else must have hidden it in my truck."

Macdara sighed. "Why would they do that?"

Siobhán scanned the bed. "Nothing else was in the truck?"

"No."

"When is the last time you used the back of the truck?"

"I hauled tent poles for Liam. That was early Friday

morning. No ladder. Then I used the ladder Friday afternoon. Put it back in the storage room."

"When I first asked you about a ladder, you said it should be on the back patio," Siobhán said.

Rory's face reddened. "I know. That's where it was *before* Friday. I had just woken up when you asked me. My apologies. I swear to ye. I used the ladder Friday afternoon to hang the welcome banner for the players and then put it in the storage room. I knew the place would be jammers and I didn't want eejits on the patio playing around with it, or tripping over it and suing me."

"Have you touched the ladder?" Macdara asked.

Rory shook his head. "I was waiting for you."

"We'll be taking it as evidence," Macdara said.

"You might as well," Rory said with a sigh. "You've taken everything else."

The slouched lad at the tent for Liam's hardware store saw Siobhán's approach and straightened up like he'd been on a deserted island and she was the first human he'd seen in years.

Siobhán gave him a smile and a nod. "How ya. I'm looking for Liam."

He kicked the street with the tip of his shoe and sighed loudly. "He's back at the shop."

"T'ank you."

"Do you need any hand tools?" He waved his hand over shiny hammers and screwdrivers.

"Not at the moment."

He grabbed the rubber circle in front of him. "O-rings?" He stood a ruler up. "Anything to measure?"

"Just here to see Liam, luv."

"Tent poles?" He gestured to a heap of them lying in the corner of the tent.

"Everyone's tents are all set up, luv."

"You aren't going to buy anything?"

"Have you sold any rope?"

No rope was visible anywhere on his table. He glanced at the items like they had betrayed him. "That's what you want? The one thing I don't have?"

Get used to it, lad. "I don't want it. I want to know if you sold any."

"No." He leaned in. "Is this about the Octopus?"

"Did he come to your tent?"

His face caved in disappointment. "No." He threw up his arms. "No one comes to this tent! We shouldn't even have a tent. Me boss is a—"

"Watch it," Siobhán said. "I know Liam very well and he's employing you, so you'll be wanting to think very carefully about what comes out of your mouth next."

He clamped his lips shut. "Yes, ma'am."

"Garda."

"Yes, Garda."

"At least you get to watch people go by. That's one of my favorite things to do."

He squinted. "It is?"

"It's better than telly." He frowned, as though it was impossible to imagine such a thing. "In fact, you can be my special lookout."

"What am I looking for?"

"If you see anything suspicious."

"Like what?"

"Anything that doesn't fit. Arguments. Thievery. That sort of thing." He stood straighter, his eyes scanning the streets. "Good lad."

Siobhán headed for Liam's hardware shop, entered,

and found Liam behind the counter going through receipts. "How ya," he said without looking up.

"Grand, grand. You?"

"Ah, 'tis a grand fresh day."

"'Tis. Perfect weather for the festival."

"Aye." His reading glasses slipped down his long nose. He pushed them up and finally glanced up. "Can I help you find something?"

"I wanted to speak with you."

"Go on."

"I'd like to see what kind of rope you sell."

He put down his receipts. "Thinking of using an old lasso on your suspects, are you?"

Siobhán gave a nod. "Couldn't hurt, could it?" He laughed as he came around the corner, then headed down the aisles. "How's the missus?"

"Grand," he said, turning into aisle three. "Still has an ache in her hip when it rains, don't you know."

"Sorry to hear. Tell her to come in for a mug of tea when this festival is behind us."

"Will do." At the end he gestured to shelves. There was all kind of rope. Clothesline, jumping rope. She did not see the rope used to hang Eamon. That was the real deal—thick, the color of straw. She had a picture on her mobile from the one in the evidence room. She brought it up and showed him.

"Do you sell this kind?"

"Aye." He scanned the shelves, bending over to search the bottom. "There should be some left. I don't see it."

"Left?"

"Special order. I had some left over this time and it was on this bottom shelf."

"Special order for whom?"

Liam paled. "Rope is a common item."

"But you just said 'special order.' "

"It was the wrong turn of phrase."

Siobhán didn't think it was. Liam had blurted something out and he was trying to take it back. "Do your receipts list which items were sold when?"

He sighed. "It would take a long time to dig through them."

"I'm going to have to ask you to do that."

"'Course you are." He didn't sound happy about it.

"It would help things along if you tell me who it was that the special order was for."

He sighed. "Henry Moore."

Siobhán perked up. "When did he order it?"

"Don't be jumping to any conclusions, Garda. It's a *standing* special order. He uses it to train the horses."

An image of Henry Moore and Amanda walking by with Midnight leapt to mind. This was before the hanging. Amanda was leading the horse with rope. She'd forgotten all about it.

"When was the last time Henry Moore purchased it?"

Liam scratched his chin. "Last month, I'd say."

"Can you find the receipt?"

"Does this have something to do with the lad hanging himself? Did Eamon Foley use this rope?"

"I can't say."

"*Can't* or *won't?*" He turned and headed back to the register. "I'm sure lads can get rope a lot of places. Charlottesville. Online. Limerick. Cork. I'm not the only game in town."

"Did anyone come in recently—since Thursday, say—to buy anything from the shop?"

Liam went behind his counter and pulled out a book. He opened it. It was a financial ledger. Every line was handwritten. Old-school accounting. She liked Liam.

He ran his finger down the page. "Nobody purchased any rope in the past week."

He was parsing his words again. Nobody bought any rope. Did anybody buy anything? "Have any of the poker players been into the shop?"

Liam set his jaw. "One."

The hairs on the back of Siobhán's neck prickled. She had been expecting him to say no. "Which player?"

"The third one."

"The third one?"

"Aye. Yer man calls him the dark horse. Said his money was on him. I suppose we'll never know now, will we?"

"Shane Ross, is it?"

"Aye. Dat's the one."

"When did he come in?"

"Friday afternoon."

Before everyone descended on Sharkey's. "What did he buy?" Liam stared at her for a moment, only blinking. She edged closer. "Liam?"

"It's going to be bad for my reputation if folks can't come in and purchase items without me blabbing to the guards."

"Shane Ross isn't going to be a regular customer, and I'm conducting an official investigation, so spill."

He folded his arms across his chest. "He bought two items."

"Go on."

Liam had perfected the stare of the put-upon man and he was sporting it now. "He bought a black marker and a pair of gloves."

Chapter 15

❧❧

Gloves and a black marker. A dark horse was right. Had Shane been the one to mark the playing cards? And what about the gloves? It was spring. Why did a visiting poker player need gloves in the spring? They were going to have to get him back in that interrogation room. Liam thought he was done, but Siobhán had more questions. "What kind of gloves?"

"Workman gloves."

That was odd indeed. "Did he say why he wanted them?"

"I don't pry into the lives of my customers," he said. "Unlike some people."

"And I don't sell hammers," she said. "Unlike some people."

He blinked rapidly. "Fair enough."

"I'm going to need a photocopy of that page from

your ledger. And do you mind showing me the kind of gloves he purchased?"

Liam sighed. "Are you going to tell him I told you? That's bad for business."

"This is an official investigation. I can only promise I won't hire a little plane flying a banner announcing your cooperation."

Liam frowned, and then gazed out the store window like a wild animal trapped in a cage. "I used to play the trumpet in a traveling band. Did you know dat?"

"Must have been some craic."

"Compared to this, I'd say it was."

At a loss as how to respond to that, Siobhán was saved by the *ding* of her mobile. She glanced at the text. It was from Macdara. **Drop what you're doing and meet me at the inn.**

Liam never looked so happy as when he watched her go. She sighed and wondered if she'd ever get used to that side effect of her new job.

Once again Margaret O'Shea took her time making her way up to Eamon Foley's room, where Siobhán and Macdara waited. With each step she pounded her cane.

The suspense was killing Siobhán. "Why are we here?" Macdara nodded to Margaret. "She just gave me a bell. Turns out Rose and Eamon Foley asked for separate rooms."

"Trouble in paradise?"

"Apparently, Rose asked Margaret to let her into Eamon's room this morning."

Interesting. "Did she now?"

"Aye. Margaret called me instead."

"Good woman." Margaret was a pill, but in this case it worked in their favor.

"Would you be wanting me to open his room or her room?" Margaret shouted down the corridor.

"His room," Macdara said. "It would be illegal to go into her room without a warrant."

"It's me inn, I don't need the gardai to be telling me what to do. There could be all sorts of shenanigans that require me to go into a room, don't you know." Margaret finished her trek and then took her time unlocking the door.

"Did they say why they wanted separate rooms?"

"I asked, alright. Given they were married and she was with child." Margaret's eyes shone with mischief. *Given that Margaret is like a vampire and gossip is her lifeblood.* "What did they say?"

"They said he was going to be staying out until all hours of the evening with those card games of his and she needed her *beauty* sleep." Margaret rolled her eyes. "If you ask me, there's something in here the widow doesn't want you to see."

Siobhán's ears perked up. "Why do you think that?"

"She was hissing and spitting when I wouldn't let her in."

Siobhán sighed. "That's her normal state."

Margaret flung the door open and began pounding the pavement back to her office. "You'll be wanting to return the key to me office when you're finished."

Siobhán put her hand on Macdara's arm. He turned. "What?"

"Remember what Rory told us?"

Macdara frowned. "Which time?"

"He said he let Eamon spend the night because Eamon claimed he didn't want to disturb Rose."

"Good memory. Maybe Eamon just said that because he was too langered to go home."

"Or maybe Rory Mack is lying."

"Write it down. We'll circle back to it."

They stepped inside. The furnishings were always sparse in the inn, a single cross hung above the bed, a small rendering of the Virgin Mary hung above the door, and the Bible and phone rested on the end table. The bed was tidy. "We'll have to ask when it was cleaned. We know he didn't sleep here Saturday night, so my guess is whatever time he left the room on Friday was the last time he had been here."

Siobhán nodded and scanned the room as they both donned gloves and booties. A bag was tossed on a chair, clothes and a carton of cigarettes tumbling out of it. Near the sink a cup was filled with a toothbrush and a small tube of toothpaste.

"Bare bones," Macdara said, going through the clothes in the sack.

Siobhán approached the nightstand. She had been in Margaret's rooms before. The Bible was always tucked inside the drawer. Was Eamon a man of faith? She slid the drawer to the nightstand open. She registered a flash of black metal. A firearm sat squarely in the drawer. From purely an aesthetic point of view, there was something beautiful about its compact but deadly curves. She wouldn't touch it, not even with her gloves. "Dara," she said. "We've got a firearm."

Rose Foley agreed to answer their questions, but only if they went for a walk. "I cannot sit still," she said. "Not until my husband's killer is found." They took the road hugging the medieval walls surrounding the town. Rose kept a good clip. For a few minutes Siobhán allowed herself to drink in the rolling green fields and feel the soft warm breeze on her cheeks. It was hard to compute such violence when you looked out at the Irish fields. How had man made such a mess of things when the earth was so bountiful? Rose's harsh voice cut through Siobhán's moment of gratitude. "I heard the girl has been found. I want my horse. Are you going to get him for me?"

Macdara gently steered her in a new direction. "We have other matters to discuss."

Siobhán kept her lecture in her head. *That was not a sanctioned poker game. Understand? It was illegal. You don't have a legal right to the horse.* It was true that poker games went on all the time and the men usually honored their bets, even if they lost a truck, or livestock, or in extreme cases the family farm. It was also true the guards normally stayed out of it. But this was anything but normal. If the widow was innocent, Siobhán felt for her, but that didn't mean she was going to take a racehorse away from a sixteen-year-old girl. Not if Siobhán could help it. They stopped as they neared Saint Mary's Church, ancient graves visible in the distance. The widow leaned against the wall, gazing out at the churchyard. Siobhán gave her a moment of peace and then broke it.

"What had your husband so spooked?"

"When you're as good as he was, everyone wants a piece of ya."

"This goes beyond that," Siobhán said. "And earlier you said he had some trouble in Dublin. We need to know exactly what kind of trouble." Had someone followed the Octopus here from Dublin? Maybe it had nothing to do with their poker players. It would be easy enough for someone to slip into the festival crowds.

Rose stared off into the distance. When she spoke, her voice was quiet for the first time. "Somebody was asking him to do something he didn't want to do."

"Something he didn't want to do?" Siobhán echoed.

Rose nodded. "That's all he would say." She turned her back on the cemetery. "He said one more thing."

Siobhán leaned in. "Yes?"

"He told me to stay away from Shane Ross."

Siobhán felt the back of her neck prickle. "Did he say why?"

"He said he'd learned something about him." Rose pushed off again. "Something dark."

Something dark . . . "What does that mean, 'something dark'?" Given the way Eamon Foley appeared to live *his* life, Siobhán was leery of discovering what he considered dark.

Macdara had no such qualms. "What was it?"

"He didn't say," Rose said, picking up her pace. "That's how I knew it was bad."

"You didn't press him for details?"

Rose stopped, turned, and leaned against the stone wall. Siobhán was grateful for the rest, and ashamed she was having trouble keeping up with the pregnant widow. Rose tucked strands of her hair behind her ear, battling as the breeze whipped strands around her cheeks. "You didn't know my husband. He had a hardness to him. You'd be sorry if you pressed too much."

"Was he violent?" Siobhán asked. "Toward you?"

Rose flinched. "We had our fights. Sometimes he would throw things and I would duck. Sometimes I threw things back."

Siobhán dropped the last piece of news. "Did you know your husband owned a firearm?"

Rose stared at Siobhán. "What are you talking about?"

"We found a firearm in *his* hotel room," Macdara said. Some facts had to be kept hidden during an investigation. Others they were forced to use to get suspects to talk. In this case his message was meant to hit on two fronts. The gun, and the fact that they had separate rooms.

A look of worry crossed Rose's face. "I hope you're not trying to make something of our room arrangement. I don't sleep well at night anymore." She rubbed her belly. "Eamon knew he'd be drinking, and gambling, and staying out late. That's the only reason why we had separate rooms. My husband is gone. Do you intend to take away my dignity too? Spread nasty rumors?"

"No." Siobhán was telling the truth. "We're only interested in finding out the truth."

"Then find out what my husband had on Shane Ross." Her eyes landed on them. "What if Shane found out that Eamon knew his deepest, darkest secret? He could be my husband's killer."

"What about the firearm?" Macdara asked.

Rose shook her head. "Someone must have planted it. I've never seen my husband with a gun. Never ever."

"Margaret said you were anxious to get inside his room. Why was that?"

"I wanted to wear one of his shirts. I miss his smell."

It was plausible, but Rose certainly didn't seem like the sentimental type. As far as the six stages of grieving were concerned, she seemed deeply entrenched in the anger phase.

Macdara jumped in. "If he was afraid of Shane, isn't it possible the gun was his and he didn't tell you?"

Maybe that explains the bulletproof vest and brass knuckles. Protection. Fear. Is Rose telling the truth? Is Eamon Foley terrified of Shane Ross? What kind of secret could Shane be hiding, to scare a man like the Octopus?

Siobhán recalled how he strolled into O'Rourke's that Friday evening, looking as if he didn't have a care in the world. He was wearing those mirrored sunglasses. She was obsessing on those. *What happened to them?*

Rose shrugged. "I don't see why it matters. He didn't shoot anyone and no one shot him. Why are you chasing your tails over a gun found in a nightstand?" Her pretty cheeks flushed red. "What?" she barked.

Siobhán stared at her long enough to make her squirm. "How did you know we found the gun in his nightstand?"

Chapter 16

The bells at Saint Mary's tolled. Rose Foley seemed lost in their chimes. Siobhán stepped forward and repeated her question. "How did you know we found the firearm in your husband's nightstand?"

Rose set her mouth in a thin line. "I guessed."

"No," Siobhán said. "I don't think you did."

She scoffed. "Where else would he keep it? Under his pillow?"

"We're going to need you to come to the station," Macdara said. "Make a formal statement."

Rose blinked. "And if I refuse?"

"You're welcome to call a solicitor, but refusal is not an option."

"Are you accusing me of something?"

"We can if you like," Siobhán said cheerfully. Macdara gave her a look.

"The sooner you make your official statement, the

sooner we can eliminate you," Macdara said in a sooth-
ing tone. Siobhán would have preferred he delivered it
with a pinch to the back of her arm but to each his own.

"I'm about to give birth. You think I'm strong enough
to do . . . whatever you think I did?"

"It's just a formality," Siobhán said. *You could have
had help.* "We must get an official statement."

"I wasn't anywhere near that pub Saturday night."

"Funny," Siobhán said. "We have witnesses who
swear you were."

"Liars!"

"The pub also had cameras," Siobhán said. She didn't
bother to add that they'd been disabled.

Rose winced and bent over.

"Are you alright?" Macdara said.

"Stress is not good for the baby. If you stress me
out, I'm going to go into early labor."

"We'll have a doctor on the ready," Siobhán said.
Rose, it turned out, was just as sneaky as her husband.
Siobhán wasn't buying the act for a second. Was Dara?

"As Garda O'Sullivan mentioned, there were security cameras in Sharkey's. We'll be able to see if you
were there. Best you tell us yourself."

"I was in and out," Rose said, straightening up. She
began to walk. Siobhán and Macdara were forced to
follow. Siobhán kept at her.

"Why did you lie?"

"Because I know what you people think of me. A
traveler. Right? A tinker? A gypsy? A no-good, lying,
dirty, cheating eejit."

"We think nothing of the sort," Siobhán said. "You're
not helping yourself or your husband by lying."

"Come to the station," Macdara said. "We'll order
you some supper."

"I don't need your pity supper."

"It's not pity. You need to keep up your energy," Siobhán said.

"I'll accompany you to the station if, and only if, we go and collect my horse after."

Siobhán didn't hesitate. "I'm afraid that's not possible. The horse is a piece of evidence in an ongoing investigation." Macdara hid his surprise laughter with a cough. Rose stopped and whirled around, her pretty forehead wrinkled. Siobhán dug in her pockets and brought out the green booties. "I've been meaning to give you these. A gift from two of our local crafts ladies, Bridie and Annmarie."

Rose stared at them. "I'll still be wanting me horse." She snatched them up anyway and held them in her trembling hands.

"Come on," Macdara said, offering the widow his arm. "Wait until you try our curried chips." By the time they took Rose to the station, and booked the gun into evidence, Siobhán finally remembered the receipt from the hardware store. She presented it to Macdara.

"Black marker and workman gloves," Macdara mused. "We're dealing with a colorful crew here."

"Indeed."

"Are you thinking Shane Ross is the one who marked the cards?"

"He must have had some reason for buying that marker. And if he was up to something nefarious and the Octopus found out . . ." Siobhán glanced at Rose, who was still holding the baby slippers in her hands. Siobhán felt a twist of pity for the widow. "Do you think it was a coincidence she guessed the gun was in the nightstand?"

"No," Macdara said. "And she wanted in that room for a reason."

"She wanted to get the gun before we did."

Macdara nodded. "That would be my guess. But she's right about one thing. The gun was never used. So what is the significance?"

"It definitely confirms Eamon's state of mind."

"She could be telling us the truth about Shane Ross. I'm going to see if we have anything on him in the system." Macdara sighed. "Looks like several of our suspects are going to have to come in for round two."

Siobhán nodded. "And here we thought the games were canceled."

Siobhán was on her way out of the station when she heard her name being shouted across the floor. She turned to find Susan, their newest desk clerk, standing before her, shoving her thick eyeglasses up the bridge of her nose with her index finger.

"How ya," Siobhán said, waiting.

Susan wasn't one for pleasantries. "Have you seen my bingo flyers?"

"Your what now?"

Susan turned and pointed to the counter. "I spent ages making them. For the bingo fund-raiser. They were sitting right there!"

"I'm sorry. I haven't seen them."

"A thief right in the station!"

Siobhán shrugged. "I'm sure you can print more."

"It's a sin to waste paper," Susan said. "I love trees."

"Maybe they're being passed around and your job is done."

Susan frowned. Siobhán gave her a nod and a smile and took off before she was enlisted to help her look.

* * *

Out in the fresh air, walking down Sarsfield Street, Siobhán began to plot. It would be helpful if they could gather all their suspects in one place. A wake for Eamon Foley would be the perfect opportunity. If it were set for Monday evening, most of them would do the decent thing and stick around. As it stood, they had all planned to leave Monday morning. This would be pushing the limits, but not too far. Any man or woman who didn't do the decent thing and stay for the wake would rise to the top of their suspect list.

Ideally, they would hold the wake at a proper place, like Butler's. But it was a proven fact that criminals liked to return to the scene of their crime. And this criminal was clever, but he or she was also arrogant. They liked playing games. Sharkey's would be the perfect place. Would the others be horrified if she suggested it? The reopening would also keep Rory Mack calm. Father Kearney could be there to bless the space and give a short mass. The storage room would be kept closed, with flowers and a cross outside the door.

The widow was key. If Siobhán could get Rose Foley on board, no other person would dare throw up an objection. A fund-raiser for the baby in Eamon's memory should do the trick. It was also the right thing to do, a little kindness she could extend in his memory. She would work on her pitch to Rose. She just hoped she didn't have to throw in a horse.

She would get Rory Mack to fix the cameras in Sharkey's, maybe add a few more. They would be able to watch the tapes after the wake. One never knew what could be stirred up by forcing people to interact. Lastly the widow could benefit from a bit of comfort during this terrible time. That is, unless, of course, they were dealing with a black widow.

* * *

Siobhán entered the bistro, eager to change out of her uniform, start a fire, and prop herself near it with a big mug of tea and brown bread with butter. Just a bit of comfort. Some alone time would do her good. But when she entered the front dining room, there stood Ann and Amanda Moore, the tearstained pair of them melting into each other like inconsolable candlesticks.

"What's the story?" Siobhán called out, dreading the answer.

Ann looked up, her face red. "I know she's a widow. And a mammy-to-be. I should be kind. But she's done it again!"

"Rose Foley?" Siobhán had come home partly to forget about that woman. The universe could be cruel.

Ann nodded. "She showed up at the farm with some terrible man, insisting she take the horse. Where's she going to keep it? In the inn?"

"What terrible man?"

Amanda's face was red with fury. "Some terrible old man with a belly."

That did not narrow things down. But it sounded like Nathan Doyle. Why was that poker official always around the widow? And why had Macdara let Rose leave? "I just left Rose Foley at the garda station. I made it clear the horse was evidence in an ongoing investigation."

"She didn't listen, did she?" Ann said.

"Okay, okay. Amanda?" Siobhán went over and touched her arm. "Does she have the horse now?"

Amanda finally pulled her head up. "My da wouldn't let her take it. She said she's coming back. With a pack of wolves!"

"What?"

Amanda huffed as if that should have been crystal

clear. "Fans of Eamon. She said she's coming back with a pack of scrappers."

Not a chance. "We're not going to let her take your horse. You must promise not to run away again. I'm reporting this to the guards now."

Amanda's face was scrunched in rage. "I hate her. She'll never get Midnight. Never!"

There was that word "hate" again, the same one she'd used in the note to her father: *I hate you.* Their mam had never let any of the O'Sullivans use the word "hate."

"You might not like something, and that's alright to admit, but 'hate' is a heavy word and it will only darken your heart." Naomi O'Sullivan had been such a wise woman. They didn't appreciate it then, but Siobhán sure did now. But Amanda wasn't her daughter, and she was already fit to be tied, so Siobhán kept the words of wisdom to herself. She took out her mobile, called Macdara, and told him about the widow's latest escapades.

She could feel his sigh through the phone. "You're joking me?"

"Why did you let her leave the station?"

"She said she wasn't feeling well."

"And you believed her?"

"What would you have me do?"

The girls were hanging on to every word. "Any idea why Nathan Doyle was with her yet again?"

"Aye," Macdara said. "He was at the station. Offered to take her home."

"Interesting," Siobhán said.

"You've got the wrong end of the stick."

"How do you know what end of the stick I have?"

"I know that tone. He was doing me a favor."

"A favor? Marching up to Henry Moore's farm,

where we forbid her to go, to try and drag a racehorse away from a young girl? Where is she going to keep it? At the inn?" Siobhán glanced at Amanda, who seemed proud her line was being used and gave her a thumbs-up.

Macdara sighed. "Believe me, I'll speak with him. Are they at the farm now?"

"Henry Moore ran her off. She said she's coming back with reinforcements."

"A pack of *wolves,*" Ann said.

"Scrappers," Amanda clarified.

Siobhán repeated the comments. Macdara laughed. "That sounds a bit dramatic."

Siobhán lowered her voice and stepped farther away from the girls. "Teenage girls."

Macdara laughed. "Tell Amanda we won't let her take the horse." Siobhán clicked off and turned back to Amanda and Ann. "D.S. Flannery will handle it."

Amanda did not look relieved. "I'm afraid of what my da is going to do. If she does come back, she'll be sorry. He doesn't like to be cornered."

The comment struck Siobhán and she was forced to turn it over. Had Eamon tried to corner Henry? Witnesses stated he had pleaded with Eamon to let him win his horse back. Eamon had refused. Did Henry lash out in a fit of rage? He was the one who kept the rope on special order. Siobhán handed the phone to Amanda. "Dial your number. I'll speak with your father."

Ann was staring at Siobhán's cappuccino machine. "Can I make us one?"

Amanda handed her the phone. "It's ringing."

Siobhán addressed Ann with a nod to the cappuccino machine. "It's late in the day. You might not be able to sleep. I'll put the kettle on instead." Henry Moore's voicemail kicked in and she left him a message. "Mr. Moore we are aware of Rose's recent visit. The guards are going to handle it. They are on their way to your property now. Do not—I repeat—*do not* take matters into your own hands. Amanda is here with Ann. We'll mind her until things calm down." She said good-bye and hung up. Amanda was hovering close to the cappuccino machine.

"I don't mind if it keeps me up. I intend to stay awake and guard Midnight with my life."

She was so earnest. It broke Siobhán's heart. "You're going to hurt my feelings."

Amanda scrunched up her face. "Why?"

"Because I'm a guard. It's my job, along with the rest of the team, to protect ye, and I'm telling you, that's what all of us are working day and night to do. You can sleep without a worry. Understand?"

"You weren't there the first time she came for me horse."

"I didn't say we were mind readers. But now we know. And we're on it." Amanda nodded without an ounce of enthusiasm. "How about some cocoa with marshmallows?"

This was greeted with a bit more excitement. So much for putting her feet up. Siobhán smiled and told the girls to sit. It felt nice to do a little mothering. As the kettle boiled and she spooned hot chocolate into mugs for the girls, her mind drifted back to the case.

Where is Rose now? What youthful indiscretion will Amanda get into next? And why isn't Henry Moore answering his mobile?

Chapter 17

The young ones were in bed. James had finally called. He'd gone into Limerick. Said it was too tempting to drink in the festival atmosphere. Siobhán suspected it also had something to do with his recent rows with Elise, but she didn't ask. She needed Elise's help with the tent at the festival. Besides, the girl was growing on her. She hoped they'd work it out. "Do whatever you need to do," Siobhán said. "We miss you, but we're all fine."

"I'm coming home tomorrow," he said.

"We'll have a family supper then." She hadn't realized how much she counted on those family times until they'd missed a few. It would do them all good. She'd have to invite Elise as well, it would be rude not to. Siobhán was about to turn in for the night when there came a light knock on the door. She smiled to herself as she went to answer it. It was Macdara's knock. Six in total, the last four at a good clip. She opened it, and he stepped in and kissed her. They had so few of these stolen moments that she treasured them. It didn't last long. When they pulled away, his face soon showed his anxiety.

"What's the story?"

"Shane Ross is scheduled back in for questioning, but I can't get ahold of Rose Foley."

Siobhán groaned. "Do you think she went back to Henry's farm?"

Macdara leaned against the doorway. "No. I have guards posted there, and against my advice he's keeping vigil."

Siobhán sighed. "Like father, like daughter. What did Nathan say about the incident?"

"He said she pretended she needed to go for a long walk. It wasn't until she was marching up the drive to the farm that he realized he'd been played. He did his best to calm her down. He said Henry Moore flew into a murderous rage."

"'Murderous rage'? That's a quote?"

"'Tis."

"My word." She saw the wheels turning in Macdara's head. "Do you think Henry Moore murdered Eamon?"

"I don't *want* to think that."

"But?"

"What wouldn't a father do to protect his daughter? Multiple witnesses say he was on a mission to get Eamon to change his mind about the horse."

Siobhán nodded. "It's a strong motive. Then there's a matter of the rope." She couldn't imagine Amanda's life if her father had murdered a man because of her horse. Pain on top of pain, so twisted it would be impossible to remember how it all started. There was a point in any plotting of a crime where it wasn't too late, where common sense could prevail, and lives could be saved. If Henry Moore was guilty, that point had already been crossed. "You checked the inn for Rose?"

Macdara nodded. "She's cleared out. Her room is empty."

"Fantastic." She grimaced, then led him inside the dining room, where she held up a finger before entering the kitchen to put on the kettle. When she came out, Macdara was making a fire. She felt instantly warmer, knowing it meant he was going to stay for a spell. She returned with mugs of tea and brown bread.

"I don't know how you make the time," Macdara said, relishing the treat. "But I'm so glad you do."

"It calms me," Siobhán said. "Making it. My daily break." She always made it right after going for her morning run. She loved the routine. Run, shower, and then she made brown bread before getting dressed for work. Lately she'd had to triple the batches for the festival. Elise, who was on a mission to figure out Siobhán's secret ingredients, was miffed that Siobhán would rather triple her work than let her make it. Maybe she was being foolish. But it felt like the last private connection she had with her mam. They used to make it together, and now Siobhán was continuing. Some mornings she imagined her mam next to her as she made it, chattering away about the plans for the day.

She would have let her siblings in on it, but none of them showed any interest in doing anything other than eating it. That suited Siobhán; when you were from a big family, you had to share everything. This was one little thing she had all to herself. That, and the handsome, messy-haired man by the fire. Macdara leaned back in his chair and stared at the dancing flames.

"Can we just sit here for a moment and pretend the rest of the world doesn't exist?"

His smile still made her stomach flutter. She hoped that would never go away. "I doubt it," she said, taking his hand in hers. "But we can surely try."

The next morning Siobhán walked into the garda station to find Nathan Doyle in the middle of an intense conversation with Macdara. Her curiosity piqued, she ambled over. "Any word on Rose?"

"No," Nathan said. "She took off after the farm. I have no idea where she went."

"Thank you for coming in," Macdara said.

Nathan nodded. "Anytime." He turned to leave.

That was odd. Why was he leaving so quickly? Siobhán called after him. "How did you get interested in poker?"

"I like a good competition," he said with a wink.

"Do you play yourself?"

"Not like the pros."

"Do you play at all?"

Nathan tilted his head. "Are you challenging me to a game?"

She felt a touch on her elbow. Macdara. He gave a nod to Nathan. "Thank you for coming in."

"Not a bother." Nathan turned to leave.

Siobhán wondered why Macdara was letting him go so easy. "I have a few more questions."

Macdara gave her a look and almost seemed to throw an apologetic glance at Nathan. Nathan waited by the door. Macdara leaned into her ear. "What are you doing?"

"Questioning a suspect."

"We have bigger suspects to deal with. Shane? The gloves?"

She glanced at Nathan, who was watching them with great interest. She smiled and held up a finger before turning back to Macdara. "He said he was a researcher. Did you ever research that?"

"As a matter of fact, I did. We can discuss it later."

"If you'll stop fussing with me, I can ask him right now."

"We have a missing, pregnant widow on our hands."

"Exactly."

"What are you trying to say?"

"He could have her somewhere."

"What? Like held captive?"

"Why not?"

Macdara shook his head. "You're on the wrong path. Let me take the lead."

"Just find out exactly where he works. If he is who he says he is, case closed."

"I'll handle it."

"What is going on with you?"

"What do you mean?"

"I don't know. You're acting squirrelly."

"Right now, I want to find Rose Foley."

He didn't deny it. Why didn't he push back? Darn it. He was hiding something. Siobhán wanted to repeat that finding out who Nathan Doyle was could help them find Rose Foley, but she knew that obstinate look on Macdara's face.

Macdara gestured to Nathan. "Thank you for your time. That's all for now."

"You sure?" Nathan pointed at Siobhán with a grin. "She looks like she wanted to ask me something."

"We're all good," Macdara said. "Talk to you later."

Nathan winked and disappeared out the door. Siobhán whirled on Macdara. "We should follow him." She headed for the door. Macdara put his arm out as a barrier.

"I need you at the festival." Normally, Siobhán wouldn't even be working on a Sunday, she requested it as family time, but this weekend it was all guards on deck. Technically, if she was assigned to the festival, she could spend a bit of time at Naomi's tent enjoying her family. But murder shook all that up. It was nearly impossible for her to focus on anything other than finding the killer.

"Since when?"

"Keep an eye out for Rose Foley."

"What are you going to do?" She'd crossed another line. He folded his arms across his chest. He was keeping something from her.

"There are times when you simply must do as I ask. And trust. Trust that I know what I'm doing."

She sighed. "Fine. I'll go. But I don't like it. There's something about that man."

Macdara turned away. "I'll try to find you for lunch." He gently shoved her out the door.

Unlike the sun they'd enjoyed the past several days, the Irish skies were swollen with black clouds, a warning of the lashing that was expected in the afternoon. Siobhán had predicted that after the games had been canceled, a large number of tourists would have gone home. If anything, it seemed like even more people were squeezed into their small village. They gathered in clumps on the streets to gossip about the murder, and as Siobhán suspected, waited to catch sight of the

widow or one of the players. Despite the weather and
the possibility that a killer was among them, the atmosphere was strangely jovial. Musicians serenaded
folks from street corners. Siobhán had always regret-
ted that no one in her family had ever taken up musical
instruments, for she so enjoyed listening to live music,
and was always jealous of those families who would
jump up from the dining-room table to grab their vio-
lins, guitars, banjos, bodhráns, squeezeboxes, tin whis-
tles, and spoons. Music could go a long way to calm
people down. Today she was grateful for the musicians. Coupled with the smells of curried chips and
sweets, it was easy to pretend nothing was amiss. *Take
that, stormy skies.*

Unless, of course, it was your job to remember that
something was very much amiss, and Siobhán kept her
eyes peeled as she walked up and down the streets. The
killer could be mingling freely with the locals, plotting
his or her next move. She walked up and down the
street for nearly an hour, relieved that on the surface
everything seemed normal.

Just as she was wondering if Macdara was going to
have a spot of lunch with her, there he was, just up the
street standing off to the side. She was about to approach, when she saw he wasn't alone. Nathan Doyle
stood with him. She stopped in her tracks. *Odd. Definitely odd.* Hours ago, it seemed, Macdara didn't want
Siobhán talking to Nathan. Now they were huddled together. Was this why he distracted her with festival
duty? What was going on? Whatever they were talking
about, it looked intense. Exactly how they looked
when she walked in on them this morning at the station. There was no doubt she was being left out of
something. But what? Before she could decide on a

course of action, they were moving, heading away from the festival, their pace brisk.

Follow them. She couldn't help it. Macdara was hiding something from her, and she knew it in her bones.

He was also the detective sergeant and the one in charge. He'd told her to stay at the festival. He was already breaking one of his cardinal rules by dating her. If Siobhán started ignoring his commands at work, it wasn't a leap to believe it would put a crack in their romance. She should stay exactly where he wanted her, walking the streets of the festival, looking out for their suspects.

Only none of their suspects were here. And she couldn't shake the feeling that he was simply trying to keep her busy. That was insulting. Besides, wasn't it *almost* her lunch break? And was she really to blame for going on a little stroll? And if she happened to stroll in the same direction as Macdara and Nathan Doyle, could he really prove it was deliberate? Kilbane was a very small village. There were only so many directions one could stroll. She edged out of the crowd so she could pick up the pace. She'd missed her morning jogging routine lately, nothing wrong with using her almost-lunchtime to do a little jogging. They took a left at the end of the street. What was in that direction? Celtic Gems, for one. Had Tom summoned Macdara? Why was he allowing Nathan Doyle to tag along? Had they found Rose?

They turned right and disappeared down the street. Now she could break into a run, hugging the side of the road in case they looked back and she needed to duck and cover. They took the left at the end of the road and seconds later she followed.

*   *   *

Celtic Gems sat ahead, just on the left. It was a tiny white farmhouse zoned for business. The shop took up the front room. When she was younger, she used to imagine what it would be like living amongst all those jewels. Imagining that she lived there. In these dreams she pictured herself sneaking into the shop at night and trying on every piece. Feeling like royalty, she'd cover her fingers and wrists with rings and bracelets; her neck gleaming with emeralds, diamonds, and rubies. She laughed at it now, especially since she rarely wore jewelry. It wasn't practical when she was running the bistro, and even less so now that she was a guard.

There was no sign of Macdara or Nathan. They must have popped into the shop. She stopped to catch her breath. If they came out and spotted her, she'd better have a good excuse. She hardly had a reason for being here.

Unless . . .

She could say that she'd promised Tom she'd check in on his well-being. Ask him if he'd spotted any more footprints outside the shop. Macdara would see right through her. Her best bet was that he wouldn't see her. But a grown garda inching her way toward the jewelry shop in broad daylight was not the most professional look. If Macdara caught her, she would need a plausible lie on the ready, and a darn good one at that.

She stood just outside the shop. Through the front window she could see three men inside. She edged closer. Their backs were to her. Macdara, Nathan, and Tom Howell were hunched over the counter. Tom Howell opened the glass case and removed a tray of diamond rings. He set them on the counter. Macdara seemed to be the focus of this encounter, Tom was pointing out various rings, Macdara picking them up and examining them.

Siobhán stared, her stomach a new recruit for the circus. This could not be happening. *Is this what it looked like? Is Detective Sergeant Macdara Anthony Flannery thinking of proposing?*

Chapter 18

All sleuthing vanished from Siobhán's head as she hurried away before they caught a glimpse of her stunned face. They had never talked about marriage. She'd thought about it, of course, for it was near impossible to be in love and in a relationship and not at least think about it. She assumed they steered clear of the subject because of the obvious. Siobhán had her hands full with her siblings, and the bistro, and now her new job. They were already treading lightly, highly aware of the complications of dating and working together. Now in the middle of a murder probe, Macdara was looking at diamond rings.

With one of their suspects . . .

It didn't add up. The next time she saw Macdara, he would mention it, wouldn't he? There would be a logical explanation: *"By the way I took Nathan Doyle to Celtic Gems with me to look at diamond rings because . . .*

"It's such a manly thing to do. . . .

"Lads will be lads. . . .

"We were going to go golfing, but the skies looked like they were about to open up, so we decided to look at sparkly things instead. . . ."

Ludicrous.

There was no plausible explanation.

Part of her wanted to march back immediately and demand answers. But she didn't. When it came to her job, Macdara was her superior and a darn good detective sergeant. If he was keeping a part of the investigation under wraps, he had his reasons, and eventually he would tell her what was going on. Patience was needed. Mandatory, one might say. She could do that. She would just put it out of her mind.

Is he going to propose?

She would say yes, wouldn't she? Wouldn't she?

Did she want to marry Macdara? Someday. Probably. Of course. Someday. Maybe. Definitely. Didn't she? Wasn't she just supposed to know? Feel it? It wasn't that she didn't love Macdara. She'd never felt this way for any man in her life. She knew all his irritating bits—she could list them in her sleep—and yet she could still see herself growing old with him. But there was another part of her, a part that didn't want her life wrapped up in a neat little wedding bow. It felt like a door closing on future possibilities. Would he want to start having children? She was too new of a guard. It was hard enough proving yourself as a female guard. Would he move into the bistro? That was the only solution. His flat was around the corner from the garda station. Not bad for a bachelor, a clean one-bedroom apartment with a small garden out back, but she could hardly move in with him.

Was he expecting her to move in with him? Would they find a new place together? "Together" meant her entire brood, even James? She wouldn't be able to call a place home if James wasn't welcome. And from the looks of it, he was gearing to break up with Elise. James may very well end up being a lifelong bachelor. Part of her had always wondered the same about Macdara Anthony Flannery.

What would her siblings think? They adored Macdara, but did they want to live with him? Daily she felt as if she was letting her siblings down. She was the only mother figure left in their lives. Why weren't men the ones that got pregnant?

It took less than three blocks to throw Siobhán into a tizzy. She didn't even know what she was making for the family supper she'd arranged this evening. Some mother or wife she'd make!

He was not going to propose. She was mental. Definitely not going to propose. This had something to do with the case and nothing to do with her.

Why not? He wanted to marry her someday, didn't he? Didn't he?

She headed to Mike's fruit-and-veg shop. Then she'd pop to the butcher. She would lose herself in prepping for supper. Chicken curry. James's favorite. There, that was one problem solved. If only the other ones could be rectified so easily.

"What's the matter with you?" The question came from James, sitting at the front of the table, eyes lasering into Siobhán.

"Is something wrong with the chicken curry?" From the way they were all diving into it, she'd dare him to utter a complaint.

"Nothing wrong with ours," James said, eyeing her plate. "What's wrong with *yours*?"

She looked down to find her plate hadn't been touched. She'd taken a bite. Hadn't she?

What diamond did he choose? Will I like it? Did he choose a modest one, or one that could light up a dark path in the dead of night?

"She's thinking about the case," Ciarán said. "That's why she's such a good garda."

The Mysterious Case of Macdara Flannery and the Diamond. "You caught me." Siobhán took a bite. It was good curry. She wished Macdara was there to taste it. She wouldn't be expected to cook his supper every night, would she? What was wrong with his two hands? Not that she wouldn't enjoy cooking for him . . . most of the time. Some of the time. Well, enough of the time. They could always go out for curried chips. They would need a bigger table if they were married. As it was, they had to squeeze Elise in. She supposed they could push more tables together. Tables were the least of her worries. What was their biggest worry? Why not get married? She was too modern of a woman to think they had to be married to be in a fulfilling relationship, but it was the next logical step. Wasn't it?

She pushed her plate away. Outside, thunder cracked and rain began to lash at the windows. Siobhán was grateful to be inside with her brood. Tents flapped in the wind. In the end it was the weather and not a man's death that brought an early end to the Arts and Music Festival. Lightning cracked and all heads swiveled to the window.

"Deadly," Eoin said with a grin. The O'Sullivans always did love a good storm.

"Are you thinking about the case?" James asked.

"I could hardly discuss it if I was."

"You're joking me," Gráinne said. "We could wire your jaw shut and you'd still be talking out of the side of your mouth."

Siobhán ignored the comment. "Wouldn't be professional."

"It's never stopped you before." Gráinne stabbed at her food and smirked.

"Is there any chance it's a straight-up suicide?" James asked. Goodness. They really believed she was brooding about the case. Maybe she should have been an actress. Or a poker player.

"It's so difficult for loved ones to accept," Elise said. "Yet, people take their own lives all the time."

"This is not the conversation I wanted to have at the table," Siobhán said, glancing at Ciarán and Ann. Imagine, if she forced her siblings to live with two guards. They couldn't have all their dinner talks revolve around death and crime. Would Macdara want to talk about work at home? Where would he sit? If there was only one plate of leftovers, would James and Macdara fight over it?

Her scalp started to itch. There had to be another explanation. "Do you know of any men who like looking at diamond rings," she asked casually. "For the craic?"

"For the *craic*?" James put down his fork. "No."

Eoin scrunched up his face. "Are you jokin' me?"

"Yes!" Ciarán said. "I'll have a look."

"Ciarán has a secret girlfriend," Ann taunted.

"Ew," Ciarán said. "I do not."

"Ciarán's getting married."

"I am not."

"Settle," Siobhán said. Ann stuck her tongue out at Ciarán and then grinned. He scowled.

"Why on earth are you asking that?" Elise said. She leaned forward. "Is *that* what's going on?"

"No," Siobhán said as she felt her cheeks flare.

"Is what what's going on?" Ann said. Her head swung from Elise to Siobhán.

"What are you two on about?" James said.

Siobhán threw a desperate look to Eoin. "How are the comic books selling?"

"Graphic novels," Ciarán corrected.

"Fair to middling," Eoin said. "Kilbane may not be ready for *Sister Slayer.* But they'll catch on."

"No, no, no," Elise said, wagging her finger. "You're changing the subject. Why did you ask about men looking at diamond rings?" She slid a look to James. He turned red on the spot and refused to look at Elise.

"I said no," he said softly.

A pained look flashed across Elise's face. It was obvious *they* had been discussing marriage. Is that what was sending James running for the hills? Elise looked like the type of woman who would run after him, even if she had to drag him back. *Poor James.*

"Sometimes things pop out of my mouth for no reason," Siobhán said.

"Not true," James said.

"It's true for me," Ciarán said. "Most of the time."

Ann reached over and ruffled Ciarán's red hair. Ciarán shoved her hand away. This was supposed to be family supper. And here she was fixated on Macdara and those diamonds. Those shiny, shiny diamonds.

"Are you and Macdara thinking about marriage?" Elise, again. She was like an unyielding searchlight.

"No," Siobhán said. "I mean. Thinking about it. I am. I don't know. It's nothing."

"If you're not going to eat that," James said, gesturing to her plate with his fork, "can I have it?"

"I'd better eat it or I'll pass out," Siobhán said. She hadn't been eating much at all since she'd found Eamon Foley hanging from the ceiling like a sack.

"Oh, my God. Are you pregnant?" Elise yelled it out.

Forks clattered to their plates. "No," Siobhán yelled back, feeling heat crawl up her neck. "No, no, no."

"Touchy," Elise said.

"How was your time away?" Siobhán said to James. *Save me.*

"I'm grand," James said. He didn't want to talk any more than Siobhán did. This family supper was not turning out the way she'd planned.

"I wish we were more musical," Siobhán said. All her problems might go away if someone would just stand up and play the violin.

"You are acting peculiar," Ann said.

"Why? Because it would be nice if one of you could play the violin, or squeezebox, or spoons, or guitar, or bodhran, or tin whistle right now? What's so peculiar about that?"

A hand landed on her shoulder. Elise. "I'll clear the plates and put on the kettle." She beamed at the table. James slouched in his seat. "Who wants dessert?"

It wasn't until they'd finished the lemon meringue pie made by Elise, and cleared the table, that Siobhán announced they needed to have a family meeting. James took the opportunity to escort Elise to the door.

She could hear them arguing as her siblings sat watching her with guarded expressions. James returned and landed in his seat with a big sigh.

"Thank you," he said.

"For what?" Siobhán was genuinely curious.

"Calling this 'family meeting.'" He used air quotes. "I've tried breaking up with her. She pretends nothing happened."

"That's not why I called the family meeting."

"Who's in trouble?" Gráinne said, looking around. "Eoin?"

Eoin slumped in his chair. "What did I do?"

"Ciarán," Siobhán said. He sat up, his cheeks already turning red, just like hers often did.

"T'anks be to God," Gráinne said. "Can the rest of us go?"

"No." She took her time. *Let them feel the stress.* "Imagine how shocked I was to hear that Ciarán was at Sharkey's on Friday night." She made sure to make eye contact with each and every one of them. "And imagine what a fool I felt like when I realized that every single one of you knew about it and are therefore complicit in lying by omission."

"That's a thing?" Ciarán asked, mouth hanging open.

Siobhán pointed at him with her index finger. "You better believe that's a thing."

"Comments like those are the reason we rue the day you became a guard," Gráinne said.

"Would any of you like to deny it?"

Heads remained bowed. She was guessing about them all keeping it a secret, but now that it had been confirmed, she felt her temper tap-dancing. *Focus.*

"I'm sorry," Ciarán said. "I wanted to see the Octopus."

"We minded him," Gráinne said.

"We brought him home before midnight."

Siobhán looked at James. He sighed. "Eoin mentioned it. I told him you probably already knew, and if you didn't . . ."

"If I didn't?"

He looked away. "If you didn't . . . there was no harm done."

Siobhán looked at Ann. It was her turn to confess. They were all going to confess. "I heard them sneak out. I didn't want to go. I didn't tell you because you're always so worried about everything anyway."

"I don't expect much from you," Siobhán said, already hating herself for sounding like an echo of their mam. "But I do expect honesty. If you wanted to go so bad, Ciarán, you should have come to me."

"Would you have let me go?"

Siobhán bit her lip, lamenting the timing. She could hardly lecture them about honesty and then tell a white lie. Could she? "Probably not. And it turns out, I was right."

"I wish I would have been there too," Ann said. "Amanda was there."

This was news. "How do you know that?"

"She told me."

She looked to Gráinne, Eoin, and Ciarán.

"I saw her," Ciarán said. "She wouldn't pick a card."

"Where did you see her?"

"Sharkey's."

"I understood that part, luv. Where in Sharkey's?"

"She was on the back patio. I saw her *smoking*."

Siobhán put her head in her hands, then looked at Ann. Ann threw her arms up. "I've never seen her smoke, I swear to ya, and I would never, ever smoke. I'm an *athlete*."

"Are you going to punish me?" Ciarán's voice trembled. She hated this.

"You'll have extra chores," Siobhán said. "You saw Amanda smoking on the patio. Did you go out onto the patio?"

Ciarán shook his head. "I waited for her to come back in. I was ready with the cards. She pushed them away. Called me a loser."

This must have been after she found out about the horse. That might explain the rebellious behavior. "Then what?"

"She went up to the lad doing the cleaning."

Siobhán sat up straight. "Cleaning?"

"Mopping."

"In the middle of all of those people?"

"They spilled a lot."

I bet they did. She did not want to picture it. "What was his name?"

"He's talking about Eddie Houlihan," Eoin piped up.

"Mikey's boy," James confirmed.

Eoin nodded. "He's worked there for ages. Back when it was Finnegan's."

Eddie Houlihan was on their list of people to speak with. There had been so little time. The lad was very overweight and painfully shy.

"He started at Finnegan's when he was sixteen," James said.

"Why did Amanda go up to him?"

Ciarán shrugged. "I think to sneak her a drink."

"Did he?"

"I didn't pay attention. I just wanted to practice my card trick."

"Extra chores for you. For all of you. No one is ever allowed to lie to me—either to my face or by omission again. Are we clear?"

Heads nodded all around.

Ciarán held up his hand. "But I can still sell Eoin's graphic novels?"

"Are you ever going to sneak out of the house again?"

"I don't think so."

"You don't *think* so?"

Ciarán crossed his arms. "You told me not to lie."

"And?" Siobhán demanded.

"And I can't predict the future." He threw his arms up in frustration.

"Lots of extra chores," Siobhán said. He put his head in his hands. "Now that we've sorted that out, is there anything else any of you saw or heard that evening that was unusual?"

"I swear to you, we didn't stay long," Eoin said. "There was music, and gambling, and drinking—the usual craic."

Siobhán brought the playing cards out of her pocket. "Ciarán, did you do this?"

He cocked his head. "Those black marks?"

"Yes."

He squinted. "Why would I do that?"

"You tell me. You were seen with playing cards."

"What do those cards have to do with the case?" Gráinne cut in.

"I can't tell you."

Gráinne rolled her eyes. "Looks like honesty is a one-way street."

"It's my job."

"I agree," James said. "From now on, complete honesty from all of us."

"Are you going to be honest with Elise?" Gráinne said. She couldn't help but push people's buttons.

"I've tried. There's something wrong with her ears. They filter out everything she doesn't want to hear."

"That's not part of this discussion," Siobhán chimed in.

"We did hear one strange thing," Eoin said. He and Gráinne exchanged a look.

"Go on."

"The widow," Gráinne said. "We heard her crying and yelling at someone."

"It was on our way out," Eoin said. "They were outside. She was saying over and over again, 'You can't, you can't, you can't.'"

Siobhán sat up straight. "Who was she with?"

Gráinne shook her head. "Whoever it was, he or she was standing against the building. She was in front. We couldn't see."

"It wasn't her husband though," Eoin said.

Siobhán leaned forward. "Are you sure?"

Eoin nodded. "He was inside playing cards." He took his phone out of his pocket. "I had just snapped a picture." He turned it to her. There was Eamon Foley at a table, focused on his hand. The rest of the players were locals.

"Anyone else you can eliminate? Was Shane playing cards? Clementine?"

Gráinne shrugged. "I wasn't paying attention, we were trying to get Ciarán home."

"I wasn't paying attention either." Eoin studied his phone. "Do you think this is the last picture ever taken of him?"

Alive, Siobhán added in her head. *The last picture taken of him alive.* "I don't know. He was probably photographed a lot that evening." In fact . . . "Please e-mail that photograph to me." Most mobile phones had time stamps. Should they put out a request for folks to send in their images from that evening? See if they could figure out the person Rose Foley was pleading with?

"We thought about telling you," Gráinne said. "But it seemed like a private conversation."

"Privacy takes a backseat when you're conducting an investigation."

"We thought it was suicide," Eoin said. "But you don't think it is, do you?"

"She's not going to tell us," Gráinne said. Then added softly, "Because she's good at her job."

"Did you hear her say anything else?"

They shook their heads. "She was crying, but sounded mean too." This from Ciarán.

"Did this person say anything back? Was it a male or female voice?"

"We didn't hear a peep from the other person," Gráinne said.

"You can't, you can't, you can't . . ." Had she been speaking with Nathan Doyle? Had he dropped a hint *to her* that he was going to throw Eamon out of the tournament? Or was she simply assuming he might and pleading with him not to kick Eamon out of the games?

"He would have won. The money was supposed to be for our baby." Rose had said something like that when they first interviewed her. Did Eamon Foley have an insurance policy?

If Rose was worried he wasn't going to be able to

play, did she switch the plan to death to get an insurance payout?

It wouldn't matter. Siobhán didn't know of a single policy that would pay out if the death was ruled a suicide.

But that's not entirely what mattered. What mattered more was: *Did Rose Foley know that? And would she be strong enough, in her condition, to pull the rope?*

Chapter 19

The next morning Siobhán changed her usual jogging route, opting to run close to Celtic Gems. Not that getting close to the shop was going to answer any of her lingering questions about what Macdara and Nathan had been doing there, but nonetheless she found herself running past it. As she neared, she spotted Shane Ross leaning against the building, smoking a cigarette. She stopped, wishing she wasn't breathing so heavily, as it appeared to amuse him.

"Hey," she said when she could finally speak. He nodded. She approached, glancing at the darkened windows of the shop.

"I'm waiting for it to open," he said.

"Having a morning gem emergency?" She smiled, hoping he would see that she saw his lie for what it was. Absolutely ridiculous. Wait for a coffee shop or breakfast shop to open, absolutely. A doctor, no problem. A mechanic, understandable. A *jewelry* store? She was tired of being messed with.

He shrugged. "As soon as I've finished me shopping, I'd like to go home."

"*Home?* You're staying for the wake, aren't you?"

He shrugged. "I suppose. But I'm bringing me suitcase. The minute it's over, I'm out of here."

"What shopping do you plan on doing here?"

He grinned, then tossed his cigarette to the ground. "I was going to propose to me girlfriend."

"Was?"

"That was the plan. I said if I won the tournament, I'd ask her to marry me. Now that's it canceled . . ." He stared into space. "I was just going to look at the rings."

What on earth is in the air around here? Suddenly all the men in Kilbane want to look at diamond rings? Well, three of them. Still. That's three more than normal.

He approached with a shy smile on his face. "I just had a brilliant idea."

"Oh?"

"Will you come back with me when they're open?"

"Why?"

"I need a woman's opinion."

"Then my opinion is you don't need my opinion."

"C'm'ere to me. Don't be like that."

"I don't know your girlfriend." She didn't even know he had a girlfriend. "Why didn't she come with you?"

"I get too nervous with her around. Need to maintain my poker face."

"I see."

"Please. It will hardly take any of your time. Just let me know what ring you would choose."

She still didn't believe him, but it wouldn't hurt to keep him talking. It was challenging enough not to grill him about the purchase he made at the hardware store, but Macdara made it clear that he wanted to take the lead. But that didn't include helping a man pick out a diamond ring, did it? She was all about the love. "I can meet you here at half nine."

"Wonderful." His smile was that of a man who had a secret. She glanced at his shoes. They looked big. Size eleven? If he was telling the truth, and was considering proposing to his girlfriend, maybe he'd been the one pacing the store. More angst than menace in that case. She'd shake him like a tree later, see what fell out.

"See you then," she said, and headed off to finish her run.

Tom Howell placed the tray of sparkly little diamonds on the counter. They were so beautiful. Siobhán had spent little time looking at jewelry. Her mam had only owned a few pieces, her diamond engagement ring being one of the finest Siobhán had ever seen, namely because it was passed down by her grandmother, and she loved the history it held within. She always thought she'd wear it when she married, although she had yet to discuss that with Gráinne or Ann. For now, her mother's ring was in a box on top of Siobhán's dresser. Looking at these, all so shiny and new, Siobhán had to admit there was excitement when she thought about being given one just for her. As she glanced at the variety of styles and sizes, she wondered which one Macdara would choose.

"You look frozen," Shane teased. "Which is your favorite?"

"Tell me a bit about your girlfriend," Siobhán said. "Is she a dainty jewelry wearer, or do you think she would prefer the bling?"

"Most prefer the bling, alright," Tom Howell said with a wink.

"First you need to stick to your budget," Siobhán said.

"Forget all that." Shane waved his hand. "I want you to tell me which ring you like. If money were no object."

"I might have very different tastes than your girlfriend." *I certainly hope so.*

"Indulge me."

She sighed, and looked at the rings. There was one obvious stunner and she tried not to stare at it. Tried not to imagine it on her finger. Should she pretend she liked the smaller ones? Her eyes gravitated back to the stunner. The diamond was set up a little higher than the others, a decent-sized beauty also dotted with emeralds forming a Celtic cross around the diamond. It was nearly impossible not to fall in love with it. It probably cost more than an entire year of her garda salary.

Tom Howell pointed to the object of her affection. "I see you can't take your eyes off this one." He winked. "The lady has expensive taste."

Shane Ross laughed. "It's gorgeous. Just like the lady."

"They're all beautiful," Siobhán said. "I'd be happy with any of them."

"Sure you would," Shane said, rolling his eyes.

"If I were in love, I'd be just as happy to wear a copper wire 'round me finger." That was true. She didn't need diamonds to love Dara. A stiff drink now and then did the trick.

Shane arched an eyebrow. "Are you saying you're not in love?"

There went her face, another little flash fire. *Does he know something, or is he just fishing at night?* She turned her attention to Tom. "Have you had many in during the festival?"

"No. The action has all been at the tent." He gave her a look, no doubt trying to remind her of the trouble he'd had, including the footprints. She had hoped he would mention Nathan and Macdara's visit. But he was keeping their secret. Men certainly stuck together.

"Shane has been waiting for you to open. He's probably been to the store multiple times. It's a very nerve-racking event, thinking of proposing."

"Indeed," Shane said.

"What size shoe do you wear?"

Tom was suddenly alert and following Siobhán's trail.

"Eleven," Shane said. "Why?"

"Eleven," Tom said. "And have you been pacing outside me shop?"

Shane laughed. "You caught me."

"Finally," Siobhán said. "A case solved!" She turned to him. "You weren't planning on robbing Tom, were you?"

"Robbing *him*? At these prices I t'ink he'll be robbing me."

Tom threw his head back and laughed. He placed his hand on his heart. "I'm so relieved."

Shane nodded to the diamonds. "I need to think on it. What time do you close?"

"I'll be closing this afternoon to go to the wake."

Shane rapped on the case with his knuckles. "Right. I have some thinking to do."

"I'd be happy to offer a small discount. I'm a big fan."

"Mighty appreciated."

Siobhán accompanied Shane outside. She really hoped Tom would have opened up about Macdara and Nathan's visit. She was going mad with wonder. Maybe Shane could help. She turned to him. "How well do you know Nathan Doyle?" Sometimes it was best to take a direct approach.

Shane raised an eyebrow. "I'd never met him until this trip. He's an odd one. Likes to delegate."

"What do you mean, 'delegate'?"

Shane shrugged. "He isn't cut out for the job. Even asked me and Clementine to help. Fetch this or that for Rose Foley. And he wouldn't win a hand of poker against a child."

"How did he get the job?"

"That's above my pay grade." He took out a cigarette and lit up as they walked. "If you want to know who I don't trust . . . it's Clementine."

"The Queen of Hearts?"

"If you ask me, they should be calling her 'the Queen of Black Hearts.'" He flinched. "I didn't mean because of her race. I meant her disposition."

Black hearts. Just like someone had blacked out her heart in the playing cards. The very marker Shane purchased from Liam's shop.

"What about Clementine's disposition?" Siobhán liked Clementine Hart. Shane, on the other hand, was a dark horse. Just like Nathan Doyle said.

"Do you know she carries around the queen of hearts, always on her?"

"Really?"

"The cards you showed me? Jack of spades with the mouth blacked out, queen of hearts with her heart blacked out?"

"Yes?"

"I think it was Clementine herself who done it."

With your marker? Why don't you fess up to buying it? "Because she carries the queen of hearts with her?"

"Playing cards weren't the only thing. That night she was also carrying around a black marker."

Siobhán could not believe he just said that. With no mention that he was the one who purchased the marker. He lied so easily, it was frightening. "You never mentioned that earlier."

He tapped his head. "It only came to me."

"Would Clementine have had any reason to harm Eamon?"

"She was convinced she was number two."

"She was ranked number two," Siobhán corrected. Shane Ross was seething with jealousy.

"If she did it—and I'm not saying she did—but if she did, it was the competition she was trying to kill."

Just like she suspects of you. A cardinal rule of lying was to stick as closely as possible to the truth. Was this his confession? "Even if you're right, and she was trying to kill the competition, wouldn't she have waited until Nathan rendered his decision? See if Eamon was still in the tournament?"

"I'll leave the detecting to you. Cards is my game. I'm just telling you, I saw her with a black marker. And playing cards."

"Have you been into our local hardware store? Liam's?" Macdara was going to kill her. But "strike while the iron is hot" was an expression for a reason, and the iron was currently scalding.

Shane frowned. "Where did that come from?"

"We're trying to trace a few items and Liam mentioned he saw you in the shop."

"I figure I might as well help out the locals while I'm here."

"Did you purchase anything?"

"I have a feeling you already know."

"Why don't you tell me?"

"I bought a pair of gloves."

"And?"

His eyes narrowed as he stared her down. "A black marker."

"What for?"

"The old woman at the inn."

"Margaret wanted a black marker?"

He shook his head. "She asked if I'd help her carry in some firewood. I didn't want to get splinters. Makes it hard to play cards."

Margaret did have a wood-burning fireplace in the lobby and she was known to send anyone who was willing out to fetch a pile. But wouldn't she have gloves folks could borrow? It would be necessary to speak with Margaret again. "And the marker?"

"Ask the delegator."

"Nathan Doyle?"

"That's the one."

"He asked you to buy him a black marker?"

"He did."

"Did you ask why?"

"I figured it was for one of the charts. But, no, I didn't ask."

"Why are you laying this all at Clementine's feet then?"

"I bought the marker. Gave it to Doyle. Then Clementine is the one I saw clutching it all night."

She didn't know if she believed him or not. He was so smooth. From now on, her default was going to be to assume everything that came out of his gob was a lie. Especially when he appeared cool and collected. Maybe that was his *tell*. His calm, calm exterior meant he was bluffing. "What kind of interactions did you have with Eamon Foley?"

"He was a bit gruff. But friendlier in some ways than I'd anticipated."

"How do you mean?"

"He was asking me a lot of questions."

"What kind of questions?"

"It was like he was writing a book on me."

This was new information. She thought of Rose's statement. How Eamon had found out something about Shane Ross. How he warned Rose to stay away from him. How did Rose put it? *His deepest, darkest secret.* But if Eamon had been afraid of Shane Ross, would he have been grilling him? Shane certainly wasn't acting as if he knew Eamon had been afraid of him.

"What kinds of questions was he asking you?"

"What does that matter? I know what he was doing."

"What?"

"Trying to crawl inside me head, intimidate me. Know the enemy. I didn't fall for it. Didn't tell him a t'ing." Shane pointed his finger at her. "Have you spoken to Eamon's doctors yet?"

Siobhán didn't answer. He probably knew they couldn't get their hands on medical records that quick.

Or he didn't care. "Checked on his little swimmers?" he continued goading.

"Show some respect. A man is dead."

Shane glowered. "He took his own life. I've no re-spect for that."

"You might want to keep that to yourself at the memorial." Siobhán was relieved when they finally parted ways. Killer or not, there was indeed something dark about Shane Ross.

Chapter 20

Siobhán was on her way to the garda station when her mobile rang and Macdara's name and handsome face flashed across the screen. She answered.

"Where are you?"

"On my way in."

"I need you to meet me at the Kilbane Inn. Rose Foley's room." Siobhán turned around and hurried over. Macdara was waiting for her outside of Rose's room.

"I thought you said she'd cleared out."

"That's what I heard." He ushered her in and pointed. Rose Foley's handbag sat in the center of the bed. "That's not a good sign, is it?" Macdara said. "A woman leaving her handbag."

"No," Siobhán said. "Especially after she's checked out." Siobhán removed a pair of gloves she always had tucked into the inside pocket of her uniform, put them on, and opened the handbag. Inside was just a coin purse and lipstick. "She may have another handbag. I don't see her wallet or keys. . . ." *Just like the Octopus.* She stopped. "This feels staged."

Macdara edged forward. "How do you mean?"

"Like she wanted us to find this here. She wants us to worry." Something was nagging her. *Keys. Keys.* She thought of Ciarán crowing about Eamon's orange Mustang. "How did the two of them get here?"

"I assumed they drove."

"Ciarán said Eamon drove an orange Mustang."

"That's right."

"So where is it now?"

Macdara stared at her. "I don't know." Macdara snapped his fingers. "I heard talk of how paranoid he was to park it around here. I think he made Nathan Doyle find him a secret parking spot."

Siobhán jotted down a note. "I'll ask him about it."

"No worries. I'll do it." Macdara retreated to the corner with his cell phone, then turned back to her. "I left Nathan a message. In the meantime the guards are on it. They'll give me a bell when they suss out the car. I can't believe we overlooked that." Siobhán tried not to gloat. She was happy she was the first to think of it, but she should have worked it out earlier. They left the room and headed out. As they passed Margaret's office, Siobhán thought about speaking to her about the firewood, but a CLOSED sign hung on the door. Besides, Macdara appeared to be in a hurry. "Where to now?"

"While we're waiting for word on the car, I thought we'd stop into Henry Moore's farm."

"Do you think Rose is there?"

"She keeps circling the place."

Like a vulture. "Have you called the hospital? Maybe she went into early labor."

"I checked. She's not in hospital."

"I had a talk with Ciarán. He says he saw Amanda Moore at Sharkey's Friday night. He also saw her talking to Eddie Houlihan. Have we questioned him yet?"

"No. We'd better put them both on the follow-up list."

"I also ran into Shane on my morning jog."

"Ran into where?"

"Just in town." *At Celtic Gems. You know, your favorite place to hang with the bros. . . .* "We got to chatting and he said he bought the gloves to move firewood for Margaret and that Nathan Doyle asked him to buy the marker for one of their charts."

"That sounds plausible."

"He was casting a lot of suspicion on Clementine Hart."

"How so?"

"He said he saw her with the marker Friday night. He also said she always carries around the queen of hearts in her pocket."

Macdara gave her a sideways glance. "Someone's been busy."

"Any response from Eamon's doctor?"

Macdara sighed. "We don't have the official death certificate yet. I'm afraid that's going to take time."

Siobhán nodded. It was one of the things she found most frustrating about investigating. The red tape. The waiting. This rumor could either be a lie and would take them on a wild-goose chase, wasting time and money, or it could be the crux of the entire case. If Eamon Foley wasn't the father, and he found out . . . well, it changed everything. That kind of news was devastating. Had it triggered him to take his own life?

They headed away from the inn. "Let's head to the

station," Macdara said. "We'll take one of the guard vehicles to Henry's farm."

"Good idea." The official vehicle would bring an added layer of professionalism to the visit. Henry Moore was on the verge of going rogue and needed to be reminded that this was *their* investigation. "Can we stop at the bistro on the way?" It was going to be a long day, and Siobhán was dying for a cappuccino and a ham-and-cheese toastie, not to mention checking in on her brood. The festival was over, but they would be taking down the tent and putting everything away, so she at least wanted to offer her moral support.

"Good idea, I wouldn't mind a cappuccino of courage before we confront Henry Moore."

"Music to my ears," Siobhán said.

James and Elise were standing in front of Naomi's Bistro, and anyone could see they were in a row. Siobhán pretended not to listen as she headed inside.

"I can't believe you," Elise said. "You said you loved me."

Oh, boy. The breakup saga continued. *After all the work Elise did for us this weekend? Terrible timing, James.* If she didn't have so much on her plate, she'd sit him down and give him an earful. *Why are men so awkward when it comes to emotional matters?* Siobhán was going to have to give her a good paycheck. *Poor lass.* James never did like commitment. All his loves were little time bombs ticking away to the detonation date.

"Trouble in paradise?" Dara whispered as they entered.

"Trouble the moment he realizes it's *not* paradise," Siobhán replied. She headed to her beloved cappuccino machine, and as it whirred, she looked out the window, watching Elise cry.

"You're staring," Macdara said.

"He's going to end up alone."

"He has all of you."

"Some days that doesn't seem like much of a consolation prize."

"I thought you didn't like her."

"She grew on me."

"The devil you know," Macdara said with a chuckle.

"Indeed."

"Maybe they'll work through it."

"You never know." She and Macdara exchanged a look, as everything they'd managed to get through these past few years passed between them in a matter of seconds.

Siobhán made their drinks and then found Gráinne in her bedroom, chatting on her mobile and surrounded by at least five bottles of nail polish. Buoyed with caffeine, Siobhán left a grumpy Gráinne in charge of taking down the tent.

Wrestling with a finicky tent pole, Gráinne was still at it when Siobhán and Macdara headed off Macdara's grin said it all.

"The O-ring is caught," he whispered to Siobhán. It had latched onto the edge of the table. Gráinne wrestled with it like it was a mortal enemy, dragging the table across the street instead of releasing it.

Siobhán hated to admit that Gráinne struggling was amusing to watch. "Should we help her?" she whispered to Macdara.

"Give her a few more seconds," Macdara said, clearly enjoying it as well. Eoin ruined their fun by ambling over and sorting it out in seconds. "I loosened it for you," Gráinne said.

"It's not a jar of pickles," Eoin shot back good-naturedly as Siobhán and Macdara headed to the station.

Henry Moore's farm was a gorgeous sprawling place with a solid white barn and a stone farmhouse. Amanda was in the field brushing Midnight. He was a magnificent creature. Henry Moore stepped up as soon as Macdara and Siobhán emerged from the car.

He held his hands up as if they were here to arrest him. "I haven't seen or heard from dat woman since I threw her off me farm."

A sheepdog ambled up and sniffed Siobhán's shoes. She scratched its head and it backed off, affronted. It had taken Trigger a while to like her as well. Was she some kind of dog repellent? It rubbed against Macdara's legs, and when he patted it on the head, the shaggy thing practically purred.

Macdara cleared his throat. "We'd like to hear from you exactly what happened when she was here."

"And Amanda," Siobhán added. "We need to hear from her as well."

Henry Moore jabbed a shovel into the ground. "Leave her out of this."

"You wouldn't want to keep talking to Garda O'Sullivan in that tone," Macdara said. "And we will need to speak to your daughter."

Henry's eyes slid to the left; then he put his fingers in his mouth and whistled. Amanda turned and headed their way. "How about Midnight? Will you be wanting his statement as well, like?"

If only the horse could talk. "We'll wait for Doctor Dolittle on that front," Macdara said with a smile. "Now how about you start from the beginning?"

"There isn't much to tell. That woman stormed up here with yer man and a rope."

Siobhán had to interrupt. "She had a rope?"

"Said she wasn't leaving me property without *her* horse. Can you believe dat?"

Yes. Siobhán could believe it. Did he not remember being the drunken eejit that bet the horse in a poker game with the Octopus? "A rope?" she said again.

Macdara took a step forward. "Did she leave the rope?"

"No. She took it with her."

"I understand you have a standing order for rope with the hardware shop?" Siobhán hoped her tone was light.

Henry Moore stabbed the ground with his shovel. "Is there a problem?"

"Did you bring rope with you to Sharkey's that Friday night?"

Henry Moore squinted. "Of course not. Why would I do that?"

"You'd better not be here to take my horse," Amanda said as she approached. Her cheeks were flushed, her nostrils flared. She stared at Siobhán. "You promised."

"No one is here to take your horse."

"I hope you're listening," Macdara added. "Because if we have to send guards out again looking for you and your horse in the middle of a busy investigation, we're going to be mighty sore about it."

Amanda regarded Macdara as if deciding whether to punch him or ask him to dance. "Yes, sir." *Dance it is.*

"Did Nathan Doyle say or do anything while they were here?" Siobhán asked.

Amanda scrunched her eyebrows. "Nathan Doyle?"

"The big fella who was with her."

Macdara shifted beside her. Anytime she mentioned

Nathan Doyle lately, Macdara was like a jumpy rabbit. Definitely something up with him and that man. She was going to get it out of him today.

"He only spoke with her. Whispering to her, like," Amanda said.

"Seemed the fella was trying to calm her down," Henry Moore said. "I have no quarrel with him."

"He should stay off our property," Amanda said. "Everyone should stay off our property!"

Siobhán wasn't going to indulge Amanda. She turned back to Henry. "Can you tell us if the rope looked old or brand-new?"

Henry Moore shaded his eyes from the sun. "Why are ye on about the rope?" He dropped his hand and leaned in. "Do you think it has something to do with the rope the man used to hang himself?"

"You sound confident it was a suicide," Siobhán said.

"I t'ink it was. I don't know any man who would go to the trouble. There's much easier ways to kill someone." He slid a look to his daughter, obviously trying to clean up his descriptions. Amanda Moore didn't look the least offended.

"I think it's a brilliant idea," Amanda said. "If you want to get away with murder, that is. Although poisoning would be good too." The adults all stared at her. She didn't seem to notice.

Henry Moore stood still, but his face registered surprise and then concern. "Do you see what these tragedies are doing to our young ones? All the shows on telly about solving crimes? It's a disgrace, I tell ye. A disgrace."

"It's life, Da. Same as you always said. Life on a farm means getting close to both life and death." She faced Macdara and Siobhán. "I've seen things born, and I've seen things die. It doesn't scare me."

Siobhán made a mental note that she didn't want Ann spending too much time with this girl. "How long were Rose Foley and Nathan Doyle here?"

"No more than ten minutes. He had to drag her off, screaming and threatening."

"Any chance she said where she was going next?"

"Why don't you ask yer man? He's the one who was with her."

"You never answered my question about the rope."

"It looked brand-new, I'd say."

"Was it the exact rope you buy from Liam?"

"I didn't pay much attention." He was on high alert now. "You're saying the rope I buy is the exact rope used to hang the Octopus?"

Siobhán did not respond. Henry Moore whistled. "It's common enough. And Liam doesn't just sell to me, don't you know."

Macdara leaned in and whispered to Siobhán. "How many times have we questioned him and this is the first time he says that Rose brought rope with her?"

Siobhán nodded. "What are you thinking?"

He glanced over at Amanda. "We need to question the stonewalling father and teenage psycho separately."

Siobhán stepped up to Henry. "We'd love a mug of tea."

He leaned on his shovel and sighed. "You best come in then."

Chapter 21

The farmhouse was plain but tidy. Henry put the kettle on, placed biscuits on the table, and tended to their tea. Macdara kicked off the pleasantries. "Where's the missus?"

"On a bus trip to Waterford with the ladies."

"Ah, lovely," Siobhán said. She loved Waterford. Her mam always collected Waterford Crystal. For a second she lost herself in the pleasant memory. Soon all the reluctance seemed to go out of Henry Moore and he began to talk.

"It was a foolish thing, betting the racehorse. But I had a pair of aces and a pair of fives. It seemed like Lady Luck was shining on me." Henry Moore clenched his fist. "Turns out she wasn't a lady a't'all."

"Blaming Lady Luck," Macdara said with a wink. "That's a first."

"What went down after you lost the racehorse?" Siobhán said. "I'd like to know every little detail."

"That's a woman for you. Making you relive every second of the worst day of your life." Henry looked to Macdara, hoping for a shared laugh.

"That's a *guard* for you," Macdara corrected. "I'd like every detail m'self. If you're going to disparage her for it, you'd better toss me under the same tractor."

"Apologies." Henry bowed his head. "Sensitive, are ye?"

Macdara placed his hand over his heart. "I am indeed."

Siobhán was torn between gratitude that he'd come to her defense and fury that she didn't rise to it herself. She felt sorry for Amanda. She worked that farm as good as any lad, maybe better. Siobhán had a suspicion that no matter what Amanda did, it would be lacking in her father's eyes. It must be a frustrating way to grow up. No wonder Amanda was so attached to her horse. Animals loved a person unconditionally. The purest form of love, untainted by ego. She made a mental note to bring a little treat home for Trigger.

"Take us back to Friday night," Siobhán said. "And your interactions with the Octopus."

"I might have lost me temper," Henry said at last. "He was mocking me. Dancing around like an eejit crowing how he now owned a racehorse." Henry shook his head. "He wouldn't know the first thing about dat horse. Not the first thing."

Yet, you bet the horse anyway . . . Now that Siobhán knew the wife was out of town, Henry Moore's foolishness made a bit more sense. Had she been here to stop it, he might not be a murder suspect right now. Along with her firecracker of a daughter.

"Dancing around. What else?"

"I tried to get him to play me again." Henry Moore rubbed his face as if trying to wash the memory out of his skin. "I had that sinking feeling in my gut. I needed to make it right." He looked up as if pleading with them. "I just wanted to make it right. But Eamon said he was done playing. Asked for another jar. He was already wobbling. Started bucking around and cracking a whip like he was on me horse."

Your daughter's horse . . .

Siobhán stirred sugar into her tea. "Amanda was there, wasn't she?"

"I swear, I didn't even know she was there." He shifted uncomfortably. "And don't go lecturing me. The wife is the one that disciplines her. I'm useless. That night everyone was there. You know yourself."

He's talking about Ciarán. Her fists clenched. She reached out for a biscuit. Then two.

"Go on," Macdara said.

"Eamon danced around in the middle of the pub. Bucked like he was on a horse." He winced. "Pretended to whip a horse." He dropped his head. "That's when Amanda lost it. I heard her scream. I knew that scream was me Amanda, even before I turned and saw her in the corner with her friends. They were all dressed like grown women on the prowl. I blame the guards for not putting a solid boot down on the evening. Why did you let it get so out of control?"

Macdara didn't rise to the bait. "You heard Amanda scream and then what?"

"She got Eamon's attention."

He was stalling. "Got his attention how?" Siobhán prodded.

Henry Moore could barely lift his head. "You sure someone hasn't told you this already?"

Macdara sighed. He was getting impatient as well. She slid the tin of biscuits closer to him. "We need to hear it from you."

Henry sighed and pushed away from the table. "She jumped on his back."

"What?" This was news, and Siobhán could see it all so clearly. Why had all their witnesses left this out of the story? Siobhán had a feeling the place was so packed and chaotic that everyone there had a different experience.

"Then what?" Macdara urged.

"She was pulling his hair, and he was whipping around, trying to buck her off him. I was pleading with her to get off. But she was crazed. It's all me fault. I didn't know she was there. I had a pair of aces and a pair of fives! A group of lads started to circle him. That's when Shane Ross and the black woman cut in—"

Siobhán interrupted. "Do you mean Clementine Hart?"

"If that's her name, I do."

"Yes," Siobhán said through clenched teeth. "That's her name."

"I figured you'd know who I meant." He waved his hand as if Siobhán was being ridiculous. She clenched her fists. She wasn't here to fix people; the more they let their true selves shine, the more she'd learn. But still. She wanted to swipe the biscuit tin from the table and spend a few minutes knocking him over the head. *God, that would feel so good.*

"Then what?" Macdara questioned.

"I managed to pull Amanda off his back. Shane and Clementine each grabbed one of Eamon's arms and dragged him outside. Shane came back in and assured us all—every last one of us—that they wouldn't be taking our money, or my horse, or anything else that was bet."

Shane Ross playing the white knight or plotting Eamon's demise? Yet another little tidbit the man ranked number three forgot to mention. "Are you sure?"

"Ask anyone. The place erupted in cheers, everyone wanted to buy him a pint."

"The Octopus was outside when Shane declared this?"

"I never saw him again after they dragged him out."

But Rory Mack had seen him after that. Because he and Eamon were the last ones left in the pub. Or is that a lie too?

"Then what?"

Siobhán was starting to think Macdara was like an old record player stuck on those two words, but then again, every time he asked it, Henry Moore came out with something else.

"Shane made the announcement, Clementine called for drinks on them, and the place went sideways. You know yourself."

She did know. A packed pub. Free drinks. Adrenaline. Folks taking their money back from professional poker players. That must have truly enraged the Octopus. Had he taken the rage out on anyone in particular? Could that act have ignited a murderous rage in the target? Had Amanda confronted him? Did he mock her again? Insist he was going to keep her horse? Henry's story was weaving all over the place. Was that just his natural, bumbling way, or was he trying to misdirect their attention?

"What then?"

"I took my daughter home, what do you t'ink?"

"Was she still worked up about the horse?"

Henry's eyes slid over to Siobhán. "No more so than any colleen that age."

"She didn't believe Eamon was going to go along with Shane's proclamation?"

"We've still got the horse, don't we?"

Macdara's mobile buzzed. He took a few steps away, then hung up. "If you think of anything else, give us a call." He touched Siobhán's elbow. "We're needed elsewhere."

Siobhán leaned in so she could whisper. "What about Amanda?"

"I'm afraid it will have to wait."

They said their good-byes to Henry Moore and headed out to the car. Macdara revved the engine and peeled out of the farm. Siobhán clutched the seat. "What's the story?"

"Tom Howell phoned the guards. Celtic Gems has just been robbed."

Siobhán watched her rearview mirror as they pulled out of Henry Moore's farm. Amanda Moore was a solitary figure against the green fields, hair blowing in the wind, eyes fixed straight ahead as if none of her secrets would come out if she could just stand still.

Chapter 22

Tom Howell ushered them into the shop as soon as they arrived. Siobhán was expecting broken glass on the door, or the windows, but everything was intact. Nor did the inside look as if it had been broken into. Macdara followed Tom to the counter. Tom pulled out a tray of diamonds.

Was this a setup? Was Macdara Flannery about to propose? Siobhán had half-a-mind to turn and run. "Oh, my God" tumbled out of her mouth. Macdara turned and gave her a quizzical look. She stood frozen just inside the door. He frowned.

"What's the story?"

"What's going on?" That probably wasn't the best way to handle a surprise proposal, but this wasn't the way she imagined it going down. Near the abbey maybe, at sunset. With champagne and chocolates. Not wearing her garda uniform in the middle of a case, while Tom Howell witnessed it all with his overpowering cologne and slicked-back hair. "What are you doing?" She heard the panic in her own voice.

Macdara's frown deepened. She'd never pegged him as this good of an actor. Did she have the wrong end of the stick again?

"The most expensive diamond ring in me case is missing," Tom said.

Siobhán crept forward. Sure enough, there was an empty spot in the tray. She knew immediately which ring was "missing." The one she pointed out to Shane Ross. Perhaps Macdara thought this was the perfect way to propose. He knew she loved solving mysteries. He wanted to create one for her. "Now how would someone know it was the most expensive? Maybe they just thought it was the prettiest." She couldn't help but laugh.

Tom Howell did a very good job of looking offended.

Macdara turned to her. "What on earth is the matter with you?"

"I can't help it. The two of you!"

"The two of us . . . what?" Macdara said.

Tom pointed to the case. "Do you not see an empty space where a thirty-thousand-euro ring should be?"

Siobhán gasped. "Thirty thousand euro?" She turned to Macdara. "It's too dear. You can't. I won't accept it."

Macdara held his finger up to Tom. "Would you excuse us for a minute." He took Siobhán by the elbow and dragged her outside. "What are you on about?"

Now she wasn't sure again. He was taking it too far. Was this part of the game? He didn't like the fact that she'd copped on. She was ruining his proposal. Emasculating him. "I'm sorry. Let's start over. I have no

idea what I was on about." A grin appeared on her face
without even asking her. She glanced around. "I bet the
light at the abbey is pretty this time of day." Last
night's storm had faded away, and although it was
overcast, the sun was making attempts to peek out.
Perfect weather for a proposal.

Macdara leaned in. "Are you. . . . taking something?"

"What? No." She tried to straighten her lips out, but
they curled right back up again. Now she was excited.
This is exciting. But thirty thousand euro? Macdara
didn't have that kind of money. "It's too dear," she said
again, almost giddy at the thought of it on her finger.
*But really . . . why is he doing this during the middle of
an investigation? Just to throw me off?* Laughter bubbled out of her once more. She hated that she was acting this way, but her body was reacting on its own. She
could feel that ring on her finger like it was a phantom
limb.

Macdara was on high alert. "Are you drunk?"

"Not at all."

"Yes. Let me see your pupils." He edged forward
and stared into her eyes. "Tell me it's not pills you're
taking."

She stood still, waiting for him to show some little
sign that he was messing with her. "I'll behave," she
said. "Can we go back inside now?"

"Not until you tell me what this is all about."

"I will. I swear to you. Let's finish with Tom Howell and then I'll tell you everything."

His eyes focused intently on her before nodding and
gesturing for her to go back inside. She was all mixed
up now, her stomach flopping one way and then the
next as she imagined the ring on her finger. But he
couldn't spend that much, there shouldn't even be a

ring that costs that much. She did have expensive tastes indeed. Wasn't a man supposed to spend the equivalent of a month's pay, not six months'?

"Start from the beginning," Macdara said to Tom.

Tom eyed Siobhán. "Everything sorted?"

"Carry on," Siobhán said, getting a little annoyed they were both dragging this out at her expense.

"I came in and opened the shop as usual. It's been slow since the festival. I was going to head out to our tent this afternoon. I was coming out of the break room"—he gestured to the door at the end of the counter—"when I saw this was open." He pointed at the sliding glass door of the jewelry display case. It was open. "The tray was still inside, although my heart was already thumping, because I never leave it open, never, so I bent down like so, and there it was." He pointed at the empty space again. "The pièce de résistance of my collection." He nodded at Siobhán. "You know the one."

Macdara whirled around. "You do?"

This was all going sideways. "Yes. Shane Ross pointed it out to me this morning."

"I think it was *you* who pointed it out to *him*," Tom said.

"Thank you," Siobhán said, hoping her tone conveyed that she wasn't thanking him at all.

"Why were you in here with Shane Ross?" Macdara sounded browned off.

"He said he was looking for an engagement ring for his girlfriend and he wanted a woman's opinion."

"And she picked the most expensive one," Tom added. "The one that's now missing." He eyed her as though he suspected her of lifting it.

Macdara gave her a look. "I didn't know what it cost," Siobhán said. "Thirty thousand euro is way too expensive for a ring." She looked at Tom. "No offense."

Tom sported a pained smile.

Macdara picked up his mobile. She heard him tell a guard to find Shane Ross and bring him to the station.

Siobhán was starting to think this was not a proposal after all. What an eejit she was.

Macdara turned his back to her and spoke to Tom. "Did you leave your front door unlocked?"

"Of course not."

"Is there a back door?"

Tom nodded, then turned. "I'll show you."

"Hold on," Macdara said. He went to the front door, shut and locked it. "You might want to put your tray back and lock it up first."

"Good idea." Tom followed his advice, and then they followed him to the back door. It was locked and bolted. No broken glass.

"Have you checked your cameras?" Siobhán asked. She assumed Tom would have had them repaired straight away.

Tom hung his head. "I've had no time to get them seen to. If someone hadn't messed with them in the first place they would have went off when Shane was pacing around me shop."

Just like Sharkey's. This is a real robbery. Macdara glanced around. "Nothing else is missing?"

"It's very odd," Tom admitted. "Why didn't they just take the entire tray?"

"Because they were hoping you wouldn't notice right away?" Macdara said. "Buy the thief some time?"

"If it were me I would have taken the tray and replaced them all with cubic zirconium. Buy myself time and get away with the lot," Siobhán mused.

Macdara and Tom stared at her. "We all rest easy that you're on our side of the law," Macdara said at last. He nodded to Tom. "Come to the station and fill out a report."

"You're going to have to call Nathan Doyle to the station too," Siobhán said as they were going out the door. Macdara stopped so abruptly, she barreled into him.

"Ouch!" She stepped back, rubbing her chin. He had a very hard back.

"Why do you say that?" His defenses were up.

She sighed. She'd had enough of these games. "You know why."

"I'm waiting." She'd never heard him sound so cross. Not with her anyway.

"I saw you two in here the other day. Huddled over that same tray of rings, that's why."

His face showed surprise; then she saw him work out her odd behavior right before her very eyes. He stared off into the distance as an awkward silence perched on them like a butterfly. "Why didn't you say anything?"

"I was waiting for you to say something."

"Why?"

"Because it was obvious you were up to something secret. I thought . . ." Oh no! It was bad enough that he knew what she thought. He wasn't going to make her say it out loud, was he?

"You thought?"

He wasn't going to goad her into saying it. She had her pride. Anger settled at her edges. "I thought you'd tell me the next time you saw me. And you didn't."

"Yet, you didn't ask me anything about it. That's not like you."

"It's like me."

"It's not."

"I'm maturing."

"I see no evidence of that."

"I figured you had a good reason."

"You did, did you?"

"Yes. I did."

"You're lying to me, Siobhán O'Sullivan. You know how I know? Your cheeks are as red as your hair."

My hair is auburn. Or dark red. Except in the sun. They were in the sun right now, so she shut her piehole. "Why are we arguing about this? What were you doing in here with Nathan Doyle?"

Macdara's eyes slid away from her. "Are you alright walking back to the festival on your own?"

"Why?" She put her hands on her hips. He was being squirrely again.

"I have to take care of a few things. Meet me at the station in an hour."

That's it? That's all he's going to say? "No problem, *boss,*" Siobhán said. He seemed to clock the bite in her tone. Were they having a row? It felt like they were having a row.

Tom Howell locked up the shop and got into the car with Macdara. They took off, leaving her staring after them.

Bollix. What just happened? It had something to do with Nathan Doyle. Her radar was tweaking. She had to find out what was going on. Maybe it was time she did a little Googling. See what she could dig up on Nathan Doyle. She doubted he had much of a social media presence, but people could surprise you. Tweeting, or Facebooking, or Instagramming, or any of those other time-sucking activities, did not appeal to her. Luckily, she knew just the person to whom those things very much appealed.

* * *

In lieu of a clunky desktop the O'Sullivans had a single laptop that they passed around. The rule was to leave it on the side table in the upstairs hall when not in use, but more often than not, they had to go searching for it. James had his own laptop, and Eoin and Ciarán (thankfully) didn't seem too bothered, so the first place anyone looked was in Ann and Gráinne's room. Since returning from New York, Gráinne typically was the last to use it. Given that Siobhán wanted her help anyway, she waited until her sister retrieved it from under her pillow and brought it downstairs.

"Isn't it time I had me own?" she asked.

"No one is stopping you from buying your own," Siobhán said.

"Can I have a raise?"

"If you go to university I'll buy you a laptop."

"*Uni, uni, uni.* You're a broken record."

"That's the deal."

"Don't rush me."

"Can we please Google Nathan Doyle?"

"You're quite capable of doing it yourself."

"Yes, but you know more sites than I do. It all washes over me."

"That's because you're barely part of the modern age." Gráinne set to typing, her tongue sticking out of the corner of her mouth. It took a couple of tries, as she was like a raccoon, easily distracted by shiny objects. They clicked through every Nathan Doyle that Gráinne could find, and there were a lot. A mechanic in Galway. A racecar-driver-wannabe in Kerry. A musician in Dublin. None of the photos were of their Nathan Doyle. No middle-aged, potbellied researchers randomly volunteering for poker tournaments.

"He's a spy," Gráinne said. She looked as if she wanted to marry him.

Or a killer. "Who doesn't have a social media presence?" Siobhán mused out loud.

Gráinne tilted her head and began counting on her fingers. "Loners, losers, psychopaths, and you."

"Fair play." Kilbane already felt like a fishbowl. Why on earth would she go around posting every little step she took? What she had for brekkie, who she talked to, how many times she gave Trigger a pat on the head? Madness. For some it seemed nothing they did in life counted if they didn't post it for the world to see. Seeking approval like children. *Look at me!* Social media had turned them all into voyeurs, and stalkers, and begrudgers.

That said, Siobhán had caved on one point. Natalie's Bistro had a Book Face page. (She knew it wasn't what the platform was called, but that's what she liked to call it.) There had been no getting around setting one up. Patrons liked interacting with it and it was fun to post pictures of the interior, a roaring fire, brown bread cooling on the racks, a foaming cappuccino. It was somewhat addicting. She could only imagine what her mam and da would think of it. Perhaps they would appreciate it on a business level. Or they would be horrified. Maybe a little of both. But she never shared anything personal. At Templemore Garda College they'd cautioned the students against giving too much away on social media. Nonetheless, it could be a useful tool.

"What about the other players?" Siobhán asked.

Gráinne typed away, her tongue again hanging out of the corner of her mouth. "Clementine Hart and Shane Ross are pretty active. Eamon Foley never posted a thing."

"What about his wife?"

"Who cares about her?"

"At the moment every guard in Kilbane."

"Oh." Gráinne shrugged and typed her name into the laptop.

They found her straightaway: her pretty face, soft brown hair, and those hard, hard eyes. Gráinne clicked on her page. Unlike her husband, Rose Foley was a social media butterfly. "She has way more friends than I do," Gráinne said. She made a finger gun and pointed it at the screen.

"They're not real friends," Siobhán pointed out.

Gráinne rolled her eyes. "You're hopeless."

"Guilty as charged."

"And weird."

"Noted."

"Does Macdara have a page?" Gráinne asked.

Siobhán laughed. "No." *Thank God.*

Gráinne typed in his name, and to Siobhán's utter astonishment, Macdara Flannery had a Book Face page.

Gráinne shook her head. "I would say he's leading a secret life, but it's only secret to those who aren't on it, and that's pretty much all the nuns in the nunnery and you."

"What does he post?" If he had a single cat meme, she was going to break up with him. A person could only take so many surprises.

Gráinne scrolled through it. He had a lot of pictures of craftsman furniture and woodwork. "Aw," Gráinne said. "He doesn't post any photos of himself or you, but he does have a heart emoji next to relationship status."

Siobhán felt a flutter of joy in spite of herself. "Moving on," she said.

"You're *so* going to look at this later."

"Moving on." *I so am.* Siobhán tried not to think of

the diamond rings, the huge, embarrassing mix-up. Now he was thinking that she was thinking that he was going to propose. She had not been thinking that until she saw him looking at rings. What else was she supposed to think? Could she pretend that she wasn't thinking at all?

"Go back to Rose Foley's Book Page," Siobhán said.

Gráinne navigated back to the page. She started scrolling through photos. There were hundreds of them. Many featured her hanging on to her husband. Siobhán was getting dizzy as Gráinne flipped through them. She was going so fast, Siobhán almost missed it. Something flicked by that caught her attention.

"Wait. Stop. Go back."

Gráinne clicked back to the previous photo. Rose Foley and Eamon were standing side by side on Grafton Street in Dublin, grinning in front of a jewelry shop. "I bet he just bought her some bling," Gráinne said with a jealous sigh.

That's not what Siobhán was focused on. In the background, a few feet away from the shop, a familiar face appeared in the crowd. His body was hidden, and the face was thinner, definitely better-looking, but it was him. The man lurking in the background, eyes pinned on the young couple, was the silver fox. Macdara Flannery's new best friend, Nathan Doyle.

Chapter 23

A shudder ran through Siobhán. She pointed at Nathan. "Does Book Face list who this man is?"

"He's not tagged," Gráinne said. *Tagged? Like some kind of wild animal on safari. Or the tag on the end of a cold, dead toe.* "Why? Who is he?"

Gráinne didn't recognize him. At least he hadn't been hanging around her brood. Gráinne probably filtered out any male who wasn't young and hot. The less Gráinne knew, the better. Siobhán didn't answer. *Was Rose Foley in danger, or was she involved with Nathan Doyle? Is that how he got the job? Were they having an affair?* "Check Rose Foley's relationship status."

"Why? We all know she's married."

"Humor me."

Gráinne sighed and clicked to her personal details page. Under RELATIONSHIP the status landed like a slap to the face: *single*. Gráinne gasped. "How did you know?"

"A hunch." Siobhán stared at the word. "Is there any way of telling *when* she changed her status to single?"

Gráinne scrolled through. "Yesterday. So technically she *is* single. But that's cold. Don't you think?"

It was cold, alright. Her husband wasn't even buried. "It's something."

"Do you think she killed him?"

"I don't think she was physically capable of it. But there certainly wasn't any love lost."

"It's not fair. I would have made a good wife."

"You are going to find a much classier man than Eamon Foley."

"I don't want a classy man. I want a hot man."

Siobhán sighed. Gráinne was a work in progress. "Can we print photos from here to our printer?"

"I can," Gráinne said. "I doubt you can."

"Print that photo out for me, please." *Nathan Doyle has been following Rose and Eamon. Is he a stalker? Now Rose is missing. Is she in danger?*

"If this is official business, why not do it at the station?"

Gráinne is sharp. But there was no way Siobhán was going to tell her the real reason why. But she could no longer deny it herself. If she was going to find anything on Nathan Doyle, it wasn't going to be with Macdara's help. She never thought she'd find herself thinking this, but there was no denying it. Macdara and Nathan were getting on like a house on fire. She stopped short of calling it a bromance. Whatever this was, she was going to have to do a little digging before she dropped it on him that his man crush just might be a murderer.

* * *

Clementine Hart and Shane Ross agreed to meet her at Sharkey's. Clementine wandered around the pub, taking in the photos and memorabilia on the walls. The cliché "if these walls could talk" did not apply here, for the walls did speak. Hurling games, and football games, and stained jerseys and trophies, and racehorses, and trad musicians all sang from the walls, along with old advertisements from Guinness with any number of animals drinking pints of the black stuff. Memories gathered like storm clouds, raining down in mismatched frames, marking the craic over the years. *You can take a man out of Ireland, but you can't take him out of the pub.*

Pubs opened and pubs closed over the years. Currently they were on an upswing. There were seventeen pubs going now, each as unique as a fingerprint. If menace was going to happen in any of them, it was somewhat fitting it was Sharkey's. She wondered if somewhere in Donegal, Mikey Finnegan had woken up with an awful twinge. He'd be mortified at what his pub had become and she wished blissful ignorance on him. Or maybe once he left Kilbane, he'd never looked back. Siobhán knew, even if she left one day, she'd always be looking back.

Shane stood in the corner, eyes darting around as if he was a lad in primary school serving out his punishment. The storage room was still cordoned off, but the rest of the pub had been cleared, and soon they'd be setting up for Eamon Foley's wake. Rory Mack was happy to make Shane and Clementine ham-and-cheese toasties and crisps. Siobhán declined lunch, it wasn't a good look to conduct an investigation with your mouth full. It was kind of Rory to offer. But she couldn't help but recall how he'd stormed into O'Rourke's, demanding he get to host the poker games. *Be careful what you wish for.*

They sat at a table in the middle of the pub, and Siobhán purposefully kept the conversation light and not stare at them while the pair of them ate.

"Is there news?" Clementine said when they'd finished and pushed back their plates. "Why are we here?"

"Shane said he saw you with a black marker and a deck of cards Friday evening," Siobhán said. She really wanted to get them talking about Nathan Doyle, but now that they were together, she wanted to see if they would stick to their accusations about each other. Clementine glanced at Shane, who was tracing the tabletop with his index finger. She crossed her arms against her chest.

"It's true," he said.

Clementine pinned Shane with her eyes. "Did you see me blacking out a heart or a mouth?"

"No," Shane said. He shifted in his seat.

Siobhán turned to Clementine. "Why did you have a black marker?"

"To sign autographs," Clementine said. "People ask me to sign cards all the time." That sounded plausible. Suddenly Siobhán wanted one, but it wouldn't be professional to ask. Ciarán would love one too. "What Shane didn't tell you was that we *all* do it. Every single one of the players who are in demand carry a Sharpie and a deck of cards. Himself and Eamon included."

Siobhán stared at Shane. He shrugged. "True." Something about signing autographs rang a bell in Siobhán. She just wasn't sure why . . . "Why didn't you tell me that all of you had markers?"

"Because he was pointing a dirty finger at me," Clementine said.

Shane didn't flinch. "Mine was in my pocket all night. I saw her using hers."

"Because nobody wants the autograph of number three," Clementine shot back.

Shane crossed his arms and stared at the table. "But you draw little pictures with your autographs," he said. "Admit it."

A smile broke out on Clementine's face. "Mustaches mostly. Sometimes horns."

Siobhán decided to skip the scenic route and went for the direct path. "Did you mark the cards found on Eamon Foley?"

"I've already answered that several times. No."

"Let's change the focus for a moment. I want to talk about Nathan Doyle."

Shane raised an eyebrow, but didn't speak.

Clementine blew out air. "That pasty bloke. Finally someone is asking the right questions."

"You said he knows nothing about the game of poker. How did he get this job?"

"It was a bit odd, alright. He shows up and jumps to the front of the line."

"Who made the decision?"

"It came from the top."

"Does 'the top' have a name?"

"If it's important, I can get you a name," Clementine said, tapping her chin, drawing Siobhán's attention to her long red fingernails. They looked like shiny weapons. If she had been the one tugging on Eamon's ropes, there would probably still be fibers underneath those talons. Would she submit to a voluntary examination?

"How long would it take to get me the name?"

Clementine sighed, scrolled through her phone, as if it was a giant bother, and then finally turned the screen.

Anthony Hill. "Give him a ring. He knows everything."

Siobhán jotted down the name and number. "Thank you."

"I thought the tournament had been called off?" Shane said. "Is it rescheduled?"

"No. But whenever it is rescheduled, it won't be held in Kilbane."

"Do you think Nathan Doyle has something to do with Eamon's death?"

"No." *Possibly.* "We're following up on everyone." Did Nathan Doyle *plant* himself on the team, all the while plotting to murder Eamon? If so, what on earth was his motive? Because he was having an affair with Rose? The father of her baby? How would the two even have met? Siobhán said good-bye to the players, her fingers pressing the numbers for Anthony Hill the second she was out of the pub.

Siobhán was walking near the medieval walls, taking in the fresh air and soft green hills, when Anthony Hill picked up the phone. She introduced herself and got straight to business.

"It's funny you mention it," he said. "I had a strange feeling about that one m'self. He was only appointed because of a tragedy."

"What tragedy?"

"The official before him was killed in a motor accident."

"I'm so sorry."

"Aye. Poor lad took a curve too fast on a wet day. You know yourself." Sadly, she did. Irishmen had a tendency to drive recklessly around curves.

"How did Nathan Doyle come into the picture?"

"He must have connections. Higher up the pole than me."

"Why do you say that?"

"I've been in this business a long time. It was my right to hire and fire. I tried to reject him based on his lack of experience, but me boss said I had no choice."

Something odd was going on. She was determined to find out what. "Thanks a million."

"Not a bother. 'Tis a pity what happened to the Octopus. Tell the missus she's in our thoughts."

"Will do." She hung up and took another deep breath. Nathan Doyle had just moved to the top of her suspect list.

Macdara was standing in the doorway to his office when Siobhán walked in, the photo of Nathan Doyle stalking Rose and Eamon clutched in her hand. "Listen to this," she said. "I Googled Nathan Doyle."

"What?" Macdara's face showed something akin to horror.

"He has no social media presence."

"Neither do you."

"Speaking of which . . . nice furniture pics on your Book Page, by the by." Macdara frowned. "And Nathan Doyle knows nothing of the game of poker "

"Hold on—"

"There's more. I just spoke with Anthony Hill, who said he should have had the authority to hire Nathan Doyle—"

"Siobhán—"

"The man who was supposed to officiate the games

had a motor accident just days after he was appointed, and someone higher up—"

"Listen to me—"

"He said he *had no choice* but to hire a man with zero knowledge of the game of poker—"

"Stop!"

What is his problem? "No! Would you shut up and listen to *me*?" She held up the photograph and thrust it at Macdara.

Macdara stepped forward, closing the door to his office halfway. "What's that?"

"That," Siobhán said, pointing to his head in the photo, "is Nathan Doyle lurking behind Eamon and Rose. Stalking them maybe."

"Enough," he said, his voice a harsh whisper.

"What is wrong with you? This is good news. Nathan Doyle may be our man."

"He's our man, alright."

Is he agreeing with me? That's unexpected. "Did you find something on him too?"

"I didn't mean 'he's our man' as in *he's the murderer.*" He put his hands on Siobhán's shoulders. "Nathan Doyle is not our killer."

Siobhán took a step back. "What is going on with you and that man?"

"Pardon?"

"I don't begrudge you a little bromance, but—"

"A bromance?" He sounded a tad outraged.

"The pair of you have been getting on like a house on fire, and I think it's clouding your judgment!" There, she said it.

The door to Macdara's office swung open. There stood Nathan Doyle. His arms were folded against his chest. But instead of a beer belly, his stomach was flat, it was as if he had dropped a stone overnight. He looked startlingly handsome, a right silver fox. But the most mind-bending bit was that he was wearing a gun. And a badge. That's what Macdara meant when he said, "He's our man." Nathan Doyle was a member of *An Garda Síochána*.

Chapter 24

Nathan Doyle grinned, then pointed at her. "You're quite good for one so green."

"I don't understand." Siobhán couldn't stop staring at the gold badge. And the gun. The transformation had her gobsmacked. She should stop staring. She could not stop staring.

"Siobhán O'Sullivan, meet Detective Sergeant Doyle, SSU. He's here undercover."

"SSU?" She knew what the initials meant: Special Surveillance Unit, an elite undercover group headquartered in Dublin. *"Here? In Kilbane?"*

Nathan stepped forward. "Why don't we all sit down." He gestured to Macdara's office like it was his. Macdara didn't hesitate; he entered and sat across from his own desk, allowing D.S. Doyle to take his chair. Siobhán perched on the chair next to Macdara. She felt as if she'd been blindsided.

Nathan Doyle steepled his hands. "I'm here to monitor Shane Ross."

She didn't know what she was expecting to hear, but that wasn't it. "Why?"

"First I need to remind you that what I'm about to tell you is highly confidential."

"Of course."

"I wouldn't be telling you at all, but if you keep on this track, you're going to blow my cover."

"I'm sorry."

"Never apologize. You're sharp. We need guards like you."

"Thank you."

"Operation Diamond Dash," Nathan said. Siobhán repeated it silently, diamonds gathering and swirling in her mind's eye. An image of Shane pacing in front of Celtic Gems rose to mind. Nathan and Macdara bent over, looking at a tray of diamonds. *That's why they were there. Shane lied to me. There was no proposal.* He used her to steal the most expensive ring in the store. She'd have to deal with her humiliation later. "A number of high-end jewelry stores have been robbed in Dublin the past year. We believe Shane Ross is the leader of the pack."

"Are you sure?"

Nathan Doyle nodded. "I've spent a year on his tail."

"My God."

"When we learned *that he'd* lobbied to join this tournament at the last minute, we knew we had to send eyes and ears after him."

"So . . . the other official . . . the motor accident?"

Nathan shook his head. "There was no motor accident. I wanted a way to get closer to the players. The other official is on holiday in Spain. Ibiza. Have you been?"

"No."

"You should. 'Tis lovely."

"Why would you take that position when you don't know beans about the game of poker?"

Macdara kicked her under the table. He had a habit of doing that. She kicked him back. Nathan, to her surprise, threw his head back and laughed.

"I tried. Studied as much as I could at the last minute. Was caught out by Clementine Hart early on. Luckily, her suspicions went the route of thinking I was somehow given the cushy job by a friend high up in the tournament."

"Why the disguise? The fat suit?"

He shrugged. "I thought I'd look more authentic. Have you ever seen those officials?"

Siobhán smiled. "Only on telly."

Nathan grinned in return. "I nailed it, if I do say so m'self."

She still couldn't wrap her head around it. "Shane Ross. A jewel thief." She crossed her arms. "Are you saying he came here just to rob Celtic Gems?" That didn't make any sense. She'd caught him pacing in front of the shop in broad daylight. That didn't sound like the move of a talented thief. That sounded like a foolish way of getting caught.

On the other hand, he may have felt brazen. He had no reason to believe anyone in Kilbane suspected him of being a jewel thief.

"To be fair, he's also a good poker player," Nathan said. "Too bad he didn't just stick to legal gambling."

"How is it that the other players didn't know?" *Or did they?* "Did Eamon find out? Or Clementine?"

"That's the angle we've been trying to follow," Macdara said. "If Eamon found out that Shane Ross was dealing diamonds, he may have been stupid enough to confront him, ask for a piece of the action."

"Forcing Shane to kill him?"

"It's a working theory."

"You've ruled out suicide then?"

Nathan shook his head. "We haven't been able to rule it out. We may be dealing with a situation where Eamon Foley was set up."

"How?"

"Someone created the perfect storm, manipulating Eamon into taking his own life."

"If that's the case, is it then considered murder?"

"If we can prove it beyond a doubt. It's circumstantial. But we very much believe we're dealing with foul play."

"What reason do you have to believe Shane Ross is a diamond thief?"

"Our task force has picked up his name from several of our sources. We tapped his bank records. After each robbery Shane made substantial purchases. A town house in D4. A Mercedes. Several trips to high-end resorts in Spain."

"Ibiza?" Siobhán took a wild guess.

Nathan winked. "Didn't I say she catches on quick?"

"His poker winnings can't explain his trips or purchases?"

"Not when you coordinate the purchases with the robberies. They match."

"Not very smart of him."

"He's arrogant. He thrives on the risk."

That certainly fits the profile of our killer. "Why not

arrest him? Why let him come to our little town and threaten us?" She was suddenly angry. Kilbane didn't deserve this.

"He's never been violent," Nathan said. "In the nearly ten robberies not a soul was hurt. They all took place in the dead of night. If I had any reason to believe he was violent or a threat, I never would have arranged for the tournament to take place here."

"You *arranged* for the tournament to take place here?"

"Kilbane isn't the usual choice for such a prominent poker tournament," Macdara said. "I knew something was funny about that."

"We thought it would be easier to monitor him here. Catch him going after a low-hanging fruit."

"Celtic Gems."

Nathan nodded. "We were watching it closely. Watching him."

"Then why didn't you arrest him when he broke in and took that ring?"

"It's part of the plan," Macdara said.

"Your plan was to let him steal a diamond?"

"It's his signature," Nathan said. "All the stores were robbed twice. The first time was just to test the security, scope out the number of jewel cases, get the layout of the store. Take one item. Something dear enough to be noticed, but sow deep confusion. The managers scratch their heads, wondering why someone would break in for one diamond ring. It made them mental. Then, when the owners were scrambling—not only to report the small theft to the guards, but to convince their insurance company a robber only broke in for one item—the theft ring strikes again. This time they completely wipe them out. A double punch."

"And he's already struck Celtic Gems once," Siobhán said.

"He's going to strike again," Macdara said. "Try to clear out the entire store, including the safe in the back room."

"Are his accomplices with him? Here in Kilbane?"

Nathan sighed. "The crowds have made it difficult for us to positively identify any of the ring. We only have a few definitive profiles, but we're working on it."

"When do you think he'll strike?"

"My guess," Nathan said. "When we're all very, very distracted."

"Eamon Foley's wake," Siobhán said.

Nathan nodded. "Eamon Foley's wake."

Siobhán mulled it over. "There's a problem."

Macdara grinned. "Just one?"

Siobhán made a sarcastic laughing face and then turned back to Nathan. "How can we have a wake without the widow?"

Nathan nodded. "That's why our top priority is to find the widow."

"How are we going to do that?"

Nathan stood and stretched. "We can discuss that and a lot more. But first, I'm starving. Let's continue this over a bite to eat."

Chapter 25

They took their lunch break at O'Rourke's. Declan cleared off the table on the back patio, and after serving them shepherd's pie, along with bacon and cabbage, he let them have their privacy.

"What's the plan?" Siobhán asked when she could stand it no longer.

Nathan took out a small recorder, set it on the table, and pushed RECORD. "First we need to know everything about the encounter you had with Shane Ross at Celtic Gems."

Siobhán thought back to the encounter, feeling like a fool. He'd made up that business about nearly having a fiancée for whom he wanted to buy an engagement ring. Did he even have a girlfriend? That was a fact they could check out. "He told me he planned on proposing to his girlfriend. He wanted my opinion on which was the best ring."

Nathan nodded. "He was probably clocking all the cameras and the security alarm."

"And the ring you picked was the one he stole?" Macdara said.

"The exact one," Siobhán said.

"The most expensive one," Nathan added.

Siobhán felt her cheeks heat up. "I wasn't looking at price tags."

"You just have expensive taste." Nathan winked, then nudged Macdara. "Did you hear that? You should be taking notes, horse." He pounded Macdara on the back.

The tips of Macdara's ears flamed. Siobhán had to change the subject. She thought of the conclusion she'd drawn and then her cheeks started up as well. The pair of them stuck out like glow sticks at an evening concert, and Nathan clocked it all with a lascivious grin.

"I won't say a word," Nathan said with a nod and wink to each. "I've been known to break a few rules m'self. Although I would urge caution."

Siobhán moved to change the subject. "Doesn't it strike you as odd that Shane would be so bold as to steal the very ring I pointed out? I mean, he had to know he'd be the first one we'd suspect."

"Exactly," Nathan said, pointing at her as if she'd just cracked the case. "Shane Ross is a thrill seeker. He thrives on it. And, quite frankly, he's probably underestimating the guards here."

He means me. He's underestimating me. Siobhán turned it over and over in her mind. "If all this is true, then the method of murder doesn't make sense."

Macdara glanced at Nathan. Like a son seeking approval from a father. "How so?"

"The murder was staged to look like a suicide."

"And?"

"That's extremely elaborate and took quite a bit of effort. I can't imagine it would have been easy." She tried and failed to rid her mind of the rope, and the man swinging from it. "Why would a thrill seeker, as you say, go to such lengths to *hide* his crime?"

Nathan nodded. "That's why we don't think Shane *murdered* Eamon. We think he pushed him to it."

"Pardon?" Siobhán's mind was spinning.

"We think he said or did something that drove him to suicide. Even brought the rope to the pub, made sure Eamon was inebriated and suggested he sleep it off in the storage room, then most likely concocted a few lies. One, that he'd spoken to me and I was going to toss Eamon out of the tournament, and two, I think he let Eamon in on the rumor that someone else was the father of Rose's baby—"

"Why is that your theory?"

Macdara leaned in. "There's no evidence that anyone got into that room but Eamon."

Siobhán couldn't see it. "Even if he confronted him with rumors that he wasn't the father of Rose's baby, Eamon seems more the type to murder anyone else before himself." She turned to Macdara. "His own wife told us that."

"Do you trust Rose Foley?"

Macdara had a point. "Not on everything. On that, yes."

"We're waiting for the toxicology report," Nathan said. "Certain drugs mixed with alcohol could tilt the scales toward suicide."

"Couldn't it equally tilt it to murder? Too weak or passed out to realize what was happening to him?"

"Only if there's a way into that room that we haven't sussed out yet," Macdara said.

Back to the darn room.

The three fell into an uneasy silence as all the possibilities floated in front of them.

"Were you really going to kick Eamon out of the tournament?" Siobhán asked Nathan. She was genuinely curious.

"I didn't want to. It complicated our operation, I'll say that. But I reviewed the tapes. They clearly show the blondie waitress with a deck of cards in her hand as she approaches the table. When she leaves, the deck is gone."

"We still haven't found her?"

"She's probably long gone," Nathan said. "Wouldn't you be?"

"Did anyone see her at Sharkey's?"

"Not that we've heard," Macdara said.

"Eamon Foley was the best player. Why would he even need to cheat?"

"Why do these people do anything?" Nathan said. "Because they can. I've studied thrill seekers. It isn't about the prize. It's about getting their adrenaline pumped up when they get away with it."

"Do you honestly think you could prove that Shane drove Eamon to take his own life?"

"I doubt it," Nathan said. "But with his string of thefts, if he goes back to the jewelry store, he'll be arrested and put away for a long time."

"But is that really justice?" She thought of all the ripples of pain caused from a single life being taken. A child growing up without a father.

Nathan studied her. "Justice comes in many forms. We do our best, the rest is out of our hands."

Macdara chimed in. "He'll be off the streets, unable to harm anyone else. That's a form of justice."

"Is it possible that we have two criminals?" Siobhán asked. "Shane, the jewel thief. But someone else murdered Eamon?"

"Anything's possible," Macdara said. "But we're being urged to close this case as soon as possible. Let's at least focus on putting Shane Ross away for good."

"We can't just ignore the fact that there are other viable suspects, can we?"

"List them," Nathan said. "And their motives."

"Amanda Moore."

"Go on."

"She was enraged that her father had gambled away her horse. He's not just an animal to her. He's a member of the family. And she's a strong girl. From carrying pails of water to the barn."

"Strong enough to hang a man?" Nathan said. "Smart enough to think of it?"

"Henry Moore may have helped." Siobhán shuddered at the thought of a father and daughter committing a murder together.

"Next suspect?"

"Clementine Hart. With the Octopus out, she's now number one."

Macdara nodded. "Then there's our runaway widow."

Siobhán remembered the photograph. She brought it out. "Why were you watching them?"

Nathan and Macdara exchanged a look. Macdara nodded. "You can trust her."

Nathan didn't look so sure about that, but he continued to explain. "Here's where my involvement gets a little tricky." He drummed his fingers on the table. "A few weeks ago Shane Ross was in danger of losing his third-place ranking. If he fell below it, he never would have bothered to come to Kilbane. Only the top three stand to win big money." He leaned back and folded his arms. "I saw my chance slipping away. I needed him to maintain his ranking. I did something a little unconventional."

"Go on," Macdara said when Nathan paused. "Siobhán is an unconventional lass herself."

This time she kicked him under the table. "Do go on," she echoed with a smile.

"I asked Eamon Foley to throw a game. There was no way he was going to do that without letting him in on the entire operation. So I did. I told him who I was. I told him what we had on Shane Ross and why we needed him in the tournament."

She didn't know what she was suspecting, but it wasn't that. "That's what Rose meant when she said someone was asking Eamon to do something he didn't want to do."

Nathan nodded. "I'll admit I was worried Eamon had told her everything. But if he did, she's never let on."

"She said Eamon wouldn't tell her much. He just warned her to stay away from Shane Ross."

"I messed up," Nathan said. "If I did anything to cause Eamon's death, I'll turn in my badge. In fact, you're welcome to call my superiors in Dublin and report me."

"Report you?"

"I wasn't authorized to involve Eamon Foley. Now he's dead. That's on me. And I'll take me punishment." He leaned forward. "But first I want to nail the bastard who did this. Pardon my French."

Siobhán waved him away. "I've heard worse."

"She's *said* worse," Macdara said with a wink. "A lot worse."

She kicked him again. "What's the plan?" she asked Nathan. "Is there a plan?"

"I need you and Macdara to watch over the wake. If Shane sneaks out, let him go. I'll be setting up surveillancc at Celtic Gems. Hopefully, we'll finally catch him. Finally close the books on Operation Diamond Dash." He threw his arms open. "And maybe, just maybe, once he's caught, we can get him to confess to the murder. If not, at least he'll be off the streets."

They were just getting up from their lunch when Declan appeared, pulling Siobhán to the side.

"Can I have a moment of your time?" She looked up into a face filled with concern. It wasn't Declan's usual look.

"Of course." She excused herself and followed Declan back inside.

"I know you'll have to bring D.S. Flannery into the loop, but I felt most comfortable leaving this in your hands."

"What's wrong?"

He pointed to the rubbish bin behind the bar. "That." He strode over. Siobhán followed and peered into the bin.

The bin was half-full. Sitting on top was a pair of mirrored sunglasses, a billfold, and keys. "My God."

"Are they . . . his?"

"I think so." She stared. "When did you notice this?"

"Just now."

Did someone sneak in and dump the items while we were lunching on the patio? What nerve . . . exactly the type of move this killer would make. Exactly.

"The bags are always changed at night."

"This was very recent."

Declan folded his arms, glaring at the bag. He nodded. "'Twas."

"How many customers have you had in?"

He rubbed his chin. "Less than a dozen. However . . ."

"Yes?"

"I was recently ferrying back and forth to the patio and . . ."

"And anyone could have slipped in while you were outside."

"Exactly."

"You're going to have to use another bin. Guards are going to have to take this one into evidence." *Rubbish and all. Oh, the glamour.*

Declan placed his hand on Siobhán's shoulder. "Sorry, luv."

"Not your fault." She headed back to the patio to break the fun news to Macdara.

Nathan and Siobhán stood outside taking in Sarsfield Street while Macdara settled the bill. Guards were on their way to retrieve the rubbish bin. Macdara was still steaming at the thought that the killer had been so brazen. Dumping those contents while they were only a few feet away on the patio. This was a killer who truly enjoyed taunting. It was infuriating. It felt like he or she was winning. Time was slipping by, and soon all their suspects would trickle out. The tents were down, cars were back on the road, and most of the tourists were gone. Nathan turned to Siobhán. "You have good instincts. But you're new. Are you open to a few tips?"

"Absolutely." *Tips from a member of the SSU? Yes, please.*

"The day you interviewed Shane Ross. I saw you with your notepad."

Siobhán grinned. "I never go anywhere without

it." At Templemore her instructors had often praised her on her excellent note-taking skills. "Observant O'Sullivan" they'd called her. D.S. Doyle didn't want to know all that. Did he? Was there a way to work it into the conversation without sounding vain?

He shook his head. "Don't write in front of them."

Her ego shrank back into its shell. "Why not?"

"Makes them nervous."

"Isn't it good to make them nervous?"

"Not if you want them to talk. If they think their every word is being written down, they are going to censor themselves big-time."

"Then what do I do?"

He tapped his head. "Use this as your notepad. The minute the witness is out of sight, that's when you write it down."

"Thanks a million." She wrote it down. "What else?"

"Your interrogation rooms? The shade?"

"Yes?"

"It's there for a reason."

"Privacy."

"Not quite."

"I'm not following."

"Did you ever wonder why there was a window between the two interview rooms?"

She felt foolish. She'd never really thought about it. "I'm not sure."

He winked. "There's a reason, alright. Now you lowered the shade *before* you brought Shane in."

Siobhán nodded. "Because Clementine was in IR2."

"Exactly." He waited.

"I'm not following."

"You should have let them get a glimpse of each

other—just a wee glimpse, enough to lock eyes—then fast, pull it down. Not enough time to signal each other, just enough time to panic about what the other might say."

That made total sense. Why else have a window between rooms? How had she not seen it? Why hadn't anyone else mentioned it? "Wow. Thank you."

He nodded. "You show real promise. Ever think about transferring to Dublin?"

She did. Thought about it like a hummingbird, hovering and retreating, never coming to rest for long. She'd imagined what her flat in Dublin would look like, her daily routines, weekends driving home, such a long drive; she had wondered if Ciarán and Ann would cry the whole way; anxiety about Eoin, and James, and Gráinne—technically old enough to be on their own, but would they manage? Would they feel like a family? What would happen to the bistro? She'd have to give Elise her recipe for brown bread. . . .

Never.

Nathan must have sensed her dilemma. "You've got time. Your whole life ahead of you. But if it's a career you want, the rank of detective sergeant someday?"

"Someday. Sure."

He leaned in. "Special Ops?"

Excitement bubbled in her. *Yes, yes, yes.* "Maybe."

"Well, then. You should seriously think about Dublin."

Siobhán had a feeling she was being watched and turned to find Macdara behind them.

Nathan saluted. "I'm off to Celtic Gems. Good luck with finding Rose and with the wake. With any luck we'll get our man tonight."

* * *

As soon as he left, Macdara turned. "Taking you under his wing, is he?"

How much did he hear? "He had some good advice." They began to stroll. Siobhán fixed her gaze on the soft hills in the distance.

"You went from suspecting the guy of all sorts of shenanigans to hanging on to his every word." Macdara's voice was light, but there was a bite underneath.

"Did you verify he is who he says he is?"

Macdara nodded. "The minute he told me who he was, I had Susan call his badge number into the Dublin guards. They confirmed he was one of theirs. I didn't mention Operation Diamond Dash."

That made sense. The SSU would hardly acknowledge an undercover operation. "Why did you keep his identity from me?"

"The less people that know he's undercover, the better."

"Did you like working in Dublin?"

"So-so. I missed home." He stared at her. "Ciarán's only twelve years of age."

"You don't think I know that?"

Macdara stopped, gestured. "There aren't many places left like this in the world."

They took a moment to drink in their village. The wash of colors on the storefronts. Pink and blue, and yellow and greens. The colorful advertisements. The medieval stone walls, and original entrance gates to the town. The town castle. Saint Mary's. The ruined abbey. Kilbane was special. And more than that, there was a *spirit* to their village, even Siobhán couldn't deny that. This would always be home. But did that mean she shouldn't try other places? "We're not some perfect little bubble anymore. We have violent crime now. Drugs. Suicide. Domestics."

"Then why go to Dublin?"

"Were you listening in on our entire conversation?"

"We also have neighbors you can count on. Nearly every one of them would drop everything to help each other out, and you know it."

"Shops are closed up and down Sarsfield."

"People stop and say hello."

"Not when you're a guard. Unless they need you."

"Our job is not to be adored. It's to protect and serve."

"I don't know why you're getting so worked up. Am I not even allowed to *think* about a life elsewhere?"

Macdara focused on something in the distance. She could feel energy radiating off him. Why was he browned off? "Let's be honest," he said. "You've never stopped."

"That's not fair. You've been places. Did anyone try to make you feel rotten about it?"

"I'm settled here. For good. I don't want to be back in a big city."

Did I say anything about you? He wasn't really looking at rings to propose to her. He might never propose to her. Did he just plan on dating her for the rest of her life? "You're about as settled as a game of sticks," she said.

"What's that supposed to mean?"

She started to walk. Macdara followed. "Pull one out and it all comes crashing down," she clarified.

"You'll have to be more concrete."

"No wife. No kids."

"I'm less of a man, then, am I?"

"Of course not. But you certainly can't call yourself settled."

He touched her elbow; she stopped and turned around. He locked eyes with her. "I know what you must have thought. When you saw me looking at diamond rings."

She wanted to deny it. She also wanted to hear what he had to say. "I didn't know what to think."

"I can imagine." He let go of her, looked at his feet. "Is that what you want?"

He was not going to put this on her. Drag out all her hopes, and doubts. Make her the one responsible for what happened when she spoke her answer out loud. "What do you want?"

"Everything is on the table."

She knew it. He was squirming like a puppy wiggling to get down from a child's arms. "Great. Glad we settled that."

He sighed. "We'll talk about this later. We've got a widow to find and a wake to throw."

Thank heavens. She was as bad as he was when it came to this subject. "I'll check in at the bistro, we're catering the food."

"Excellent. I will see you at Sharkey's, if I don't see you before." He leaned in and kissed her.

"Very bold, D.S. Flannery, we're in public."

For a minute they stared at each other. They had never said, "I love you." How ridiculous. She knew he did, and she did too. But she wasn't going to say it first. Why was he so behind when it came to matters of the heart? "Later, boss," he said with a wink.

"Later."

The little banter she and James used to exchange when they were little came floating back to her:

"See you later, alligator."

"Not if the crocodile eats you first."

Chapter 26

Siobhán stood in the kitchen at Naomi's surveying the food. Eoin had overseen the entire operation and he had outdone himself. Shepherd's pie, and finger sandwiches, and toasties, and pasta salads, and bacon and cabbage, and Irish stew, and, of course, brown bread and desserts. Everything was packed up and ready to take to Sharkey's. Siobhán was just about to head there, and then her mobile rang. *Unknown* flashed across the screen. She headed to the back dining room for privacy.

"Hello?"

"Why aren't you investigating Rory Mack?" The voice was low and garbled as if the caller was attempting to disguise his voice.

"What about Rory Mack?" Was it Shane Ross? It could be, but it was hard to tell.

"Friday night. Did you know Rory Mack sat in on a game?"

"Okay."

"He lost."

"Go on."

"He threw his pub in the pot."

"Come again?"

"Eamon Foley won Sharkey's Pub." The phone clicked off. Siobhán stared at it for a long, long time. She took her scooter, her mind flying through the revelation. Losing his pub was just as strong a motive for murder as losing a horse. And Rory Mack didn't bother to mention it. Instead he invited the Octopus to sleep it off in the storage room. It was three hours until the wake. When it was over, everyone would go home. The case might stay open, linger for years, or be closed as a suicide. She had too many questions, too many suspects, and too little time. But there was at least one thing she could do: confront Rory Mack about this whopper of a secret. She was in luck. When she arrived at Sharkey's, Rory was behind the bar replacing stock. "I'm almost ready," he said as Siobhán walked in.

"Did you take part in any of the poker games on Friday night?"

He stopped taking bottles out of cardboard boxes and looked to the ceiling as if the answers were written in the rafters. "I might have done."

"It's a yes-or-no question."

"I believe I sat in on one game. Just for fun." He winked.

"That's a yes." He was being squirrelly, and she was going to force him to admit it.

"Yes, Garda. Am I under arrest?"

"Did you make any bets other than cash?"

"I said it was just for the craic."

"In the spirit of all this craic you were having, did you bet and lose this pub to Eamon Foley?"

"Who?"

"The Octopus." *The man we found hanging in your storage room.*

"Why would I do that?"

"Rory Mack, you had better stop answering every one of my questions with a question. All I want from you is a yes or a no."

He blinked. Then waited.

"Did you bet this pub in a poker game with Eamon Foley?"

He blinked again. "You're constricting my answer."

"How so?"

"Because I'd like to know where on earth did you hear dat?"

"That's not an answer. A witness—let's call him 'Unknown'—has come forward."

"Not a very reliable witness, I'll say dat."

"And yet you haven't answered the question."

"I most certainly did not. I might have made a foolish remark. There was drink involved. You know yourself." He frowned. "I heard dat widow is after Henry Moore's racehorse. Is she the one stirring the pot? Is she after me pub now too?"

Does Rose know about the bet? "Has she been in here to see you?"

Rory's face flushed red. "No!" His anger startled her. He registered her response. "I'm sorry. This murder has me on edge. I've not slept a wink since I heard the news. In me own pub! Well. You know yourself."

She did know herself. And she didn't want to think about that. "It's too bad those cameras weren't working. You'd be able to prove you didn't bet the pub."

"Yes," he said, burying himself in boxes. "'Tis a pity, alright."

She stood there, gaping at him, fury boiling in her veins. "We'll talk to others, see if they remember it the same way."

"'Course you will," he said. "But it will be their word against mine, and everyone was blotto."

She should stop talking. She had nothing else to confront him with but a mysterious caller. None of the other witnesses had reported that Rory Mack bet the pub. Maybe it was said in jest. If it wasn't, they would need solid evidence. It was tough to do your job when so many of your clients were criminals. She headed out of the pub, yearning for fresh air. She'd be stuck in here for the wake, until then she wanted to be anywhere but here.

While Siobhán was weaving her way down Sarsfield Street, someone jostled her from behind. She turned to see Shane Ross twitching in front of her, sweat pouring off him in buckets. "Is it true the diamond I showed you was stolen?"

He was so close to her, they could have been dancing. "Yes," she said. "Who told you?"

"Can I trust you?" His eyes flicked left and then right. "I don't know who to trust."

"You can trust me."

"I think I'm being set up."

"Then you better start talking."

"How? I don't know who to trust!" He started pacing. "This has gone too far. Too far. Way too far!"

"Why don't you give me a try?" She waited. He stopped pacing, but couldn't keep himself from fidgeting. "At least answer some of my questions."

"I was in my room at the inn all day yesterday. I'd had enough of crowds. You can ask the old lady who runs the place."

"I doubt Margaret spent her day keeping track of her guests coming and going." Who was she kidding? That's *exactly* what Margaret spent her days doing.

"I didn't budge from me room all day."

"How did you hear about the break-in?"

"Are they pointing the finger at me?"

"They have to investigate it fully. I had to report the situation."

"Why doesn't a jewelry store have cameras?"

"Apparently, the culprit disabled them."

"How?" He seemed to be genuinely asking.

"Why don't you tell me?"

"I wouldn't know the first thing about *abling* cameras, let alone disabling them!"

"Are you even engaged?"

He looked away. "No."

"Then why did you ask me to look at rings?"

"That sergeant. He asked me to show you the rings. To see which one you liked."

"You're joking me." Now she was browned off. Either Shane Ross was lying, or Macdara was lying. If she wanted to find out, she'd have to ask Macdara again. Which would again bring up the entire subject of marriage. And that went so well the first time. What did she want? She wanted him to make the decision so she didn't have to. *What is so hard about that?*

But this case was more urgent than their romance. One of them was lying. Siobhán would prefer if it wasn't her lover. Shane Ross was the liar. He was playing her. Underestimating her. She would see how he liked deflection when it was used against him. "Do you have any idea how many folks made and lost bets to Eamon that night?"

"You're joking. Almost everyone who was there."

"Big-ticket items. Like the racehorse?"

"I see." He folded his arms across his chest. "I wouldn't t'ink anyone was too worked up about dat. I assured them he wasn't going to follow through on any of those t'ings."

"Wait. You did?"

He nodded. "I told yer man as much. Eamon was too drunk to remember any of those bets anyway."

"Too drunk to remember winning a horse?" *And a pub? And who knows what else?* She highly doubted it. "How much did you lose to him?"

He dropped his arms again. "I knew it. You are pointing the finger at me."

"I have more than one finger to point and this is a murder probe."

"Then why does it feel like a hustle?"

"Perhaps your choice of a career has influenced the way you filter your experiences."

"You're interesting."

"That's one word for me."

"I didn't kill Eamon Foley."

Do you steal diamonds, Shane? Is that why you're really here? There was no way she could ask or even hint. She would be out on her ear if she interfered with an undercover operation.

"Is Clementine going to have to give a statement? Or is she not a suspect because she's a colleen?"

"Both sexes are capable of murder."

"Exactly." Shane glanced up and down the street. "If anything happens to me, I'm blaming yer man."

Macdara? "What are you talking about?"

"I told you. He's the one who asked me to show you the rings. Why is he doing this to me?"

"I have to go. Will I see you at the wake?"

Shane nodded. "I told you. I'll pay me respects to the widow and then I'm gone."

Then you're going to break into the jewelry store when everyone else is still paying their respects. She wished she could be a fly on the wall, see the expression on his face when he was caught. "I will see you later."

He grabbed her elbow, swung her around. "You heard me say it. If anything happens to me, it was him who done it."

Siobhán was passing by the hardware shop when Liam waved frantically at her from the window. She stepped into the shop. Liam waved her up to the counter. "I just remembered something."

"Go on."

"Before I tell you, I must say, I'm sure there's an innocent explanation."

"I'm sure."

"You asked if anyone had come before Saturday to buy rope."

He had her attention now. "Yes, I did."

"I wasn't hiding this from you. It slipped me mind."

"Go on then."

"It was the first day everyone came to town and we were overwhelmed with all the tent poles, and stakes, and O-rings."

"Spit it out."

"Amanda Moore. She came into the shop. And she bought that rope."

"You already told me. They buy it for the horses."

He shook his head. "They do. That's the point. They picked it up earlier in the month. She came in *again*. For more."

"On Friday morning."

"Exactly."

"Early?"

He nodded. "The tents weren't even being set up yet."

"So it was before the players arrived in town."

"Yes."

"*Before* her father bet her prized racehorse in a poker game."

"Exactly." He stopped, thought about it. "Oh." He let out a breath. "Quite innocent then. That's a relief."

"Yes." She let out a breath too. Unless Amanda Moore could predict the future, she might have bought rope Friday morning, but it certainly wasn't to hang a man she'd never met. However . . . it was a chaotic day. Did she buy the rope and then leave it somewhere by accident? Could it be the rope that ended up in Sharkey's Pub? She thanked Liam and headed out, questions gathering in her mind like storm clouds.

Chapter 27

She wasn't two seconds out the door when an orange Mustang zoomed by, engine revving, tires squealing. *Eamon Foley's car.*

She hopped on her scooter, dialing Macdara as she revved it up. She got his voice mail. "Dara. Chasing after Eamon Foley's car leaving Sarsfield." She clicked off, then dialed 999 and gave the operator the same message before pulling out after the car. Although she couldn't match its speed, it was so bright she'd be able to track where it went until the guards could catch up. *Who on earth has possession of his car? Is it Rose?* Whoever it was, he or she was driving it like they stole it. And unless it was Rose Foley, that's exactly what the person was doing.

But why draw so much attention? It was like the person wanted to be chased. The car left the Ballygate entrance. By the time Siobhán was driving under the stone archway, it was just in time to see an orange tail disappear around a curve. Her mobile was ringing. Most likely, Macdara, but she was going too fast to answer safely. The car disappeared around the curve. Still, no sirens behind her. There were more curves ahead of that car. It had better slow down. Siobhán had the scooter at top speed and she wouldn't even take the curves. She slowed down as she neared the first one, actively fighting her own adrenaline. Just as she came around the curve, the excruciating sounds of a crash rang out. Brakes screeching, metal smashing. Black smoke shot into the air. Siobhán cursed. Her instinct was to keep up her speed, but if she did, she, too, would wreck. Seconds later she came out of the curve and spotted the orange car on the side of the road. Its front end was smashed into a tree, crumpled like an accordion. Flames shot from the boot. Was the driver still alive? Sirens sounded, they were on their way, but by the time they arrived, it would be too late. Siobhán had no protective gear, but there was no time to waste. If she had her uniform on, she would at least have her baton. She ran for the driver's-side door. She saw a blond head slumped over the wheel. "Hey. Wake up. Wake up." Siobhán pounded on the window. The driver did not respond.

The smoke was starting to swirl out, angry and dark. Siobhán covered her mouth with her arm and yanked on the door. It wouldn't budge. She yanked again. No movement. She scoured the ground and lunged for the biggest rock she could find. She pulled her sleeve over her fist, and holding the rock she punched the window. On her third try she cracked it, and on the fourth she shattered it enough to stick her hand inside.

Please let the lock be easy to reach. She had to lean against the hot car and bend down until the tips of her fingers touched the handle. She prayed, then shoved her hand farther and grabbed the latch. The flames were too close. She yanked her hand back up, reinforced the sleeve. *Just do it. Fast. Hard.* She shoved her hand in, grabbed the latch and lifted. The door creaked open. *Thank God.* She pried it open as far as it would go. The woman was wearing a seat belt. A petite blonde, face planted into the air bag. *Please let it have saved her life.* There wasn't time for anything, but to get her out. It took three tries, but Siobhán finally released the seat belt, grabbed the woman from behind, and began to pull her out. Guard cars and ambulances were here now, pulling up behind her. "Siobhán!"

It was Macdara, but there was no time to turn around. She began to walk backward, dragging the woman as fast as she could from the flaming car. She was grateful the woman was so petite. By the time Siobhán reached a safe distance from the car and laid the woman down, she had worked out who she was. Their missing waitress.

Siobhán sat on the back of the ambulance with an oxygen mask on her face, watching as another ambulance pulled away with the young woman. She was still breathing, but unconscious. She did indeed appear to be their missing waitress, but they wouldn't be sure until she woke up. *If she woke up.* Siobhán had been praying nonstop. Macdara was pacing in front of her, she'd never seen him so worked up. The fire was out, the volunteer firemen finished reeling in the hose, announcing a tow truck was on its way. They'd take the car to the local mechanic shop and go through every inch of it.

Siobhán removed the oxygen. That was enough, she was fine. "Dara. Please. You're making me dizzy."

"You could have been killed."

"I wasn't."

"You should have waited."

"The car was going to explode."

He turned, stared at her. "Exactly!"

"You would have done the same thing. And you know it."

"Don't talk."

"I'm fine."

"Please, just a little more." He put the oxygen mask back on her.

She hoped he wasn't just trying to shut her up.

"I want you to go home for the rest of the day."

Not a chance. She shook her head.

"We'll cover the wake."

She took the mask off. "Enough. I'm fine." She threw the blanket off and stood. A wave of dizziness hit. She sat back down.

"See?"

"It's all this oxygen. Stood up too fast. I'm *fine.*"

"You need to go to hospital."

"I do not."

"I'm calling James."

"Dara." She touched his arm.

"You're a hero," he said.

"I was just doing my job."

"Please don't ever do it again."

Were those tears in his eyes? She would pretend not to notice them. "How about this. I'll wait at the mechanic's shop to see if there's anything in the car. That will also give me some rest."

"That's your idea of rest?"

"Take it or leave it."

He sighed. "I'll take it."

"And maybe you can send someone to keep me company."

He raised an eyebrow. "Trigger?"

She laughed. "No."

"One of the six?"

"They're busy. I was thinking of Amanda Moore."

"You want to interview her during your 'me time.'"

"We never did get her side of the story. And she was there that evening."

"Fine. I'll see what I can do."

"Any word on the widow?"

He shook his head. "Maybe this waitress knows where she is, or . . ."

Siobhán finished it for him. "Or foul play may have come to Rose Foley."

Siobhán was propped in the waiting room at the mechanic's when Amanda Moore arrived. Siobhán bought them Cokes and crisps from the vending machine. She waited until they were a few sips in to lay the piece of rope on the small coffee table in front of them. As Liam identified, it was the same type of rope they bought, the same rope used to hang the Octopus.

"Recognize this?"

"It's rope," Amanda said. "The kind we buy for our horses."

"When I was out at your farm the other day, you said you hadn't purchased any new rope." Amanda stared into her Coke. "Liam said you bought rope Friday morning before the players came to town."

"It's gone," Amanda said. "I got caught up in the festival after I bought it. I left it at the festival."

"Do you remember where?" Amanda nodded. She wouldn't make eye contact. "Tell me."

Amanda slid something out of her backpack. *Sister Slayer.* "I put it down at Eoin's tent to look at this. It's really good."

Was this another secret Eoin and Ciarán were keeping from her? Did one of them bring the rope to Sharkey's that evening? Or did someone else take it from the table after Amanda left? "And yet you didn't think to tell the guards about this?"

"It's only a rope," Amanda said. "Not diamonds." *Is it just a coincidence she mentioned diamonds? Or is the story out that Tom's shop had been broken into?* "It's that woman. Rose. She probably killed him. Then she has the nerve to try and take my horse. She's evil!"

Amanda Moore was ready to blow. *Normal teenage hormones coupled with the love of a horse? Or is she capable of violence?* "Do you think the rope I bought is the rope that he used?" Siobhán could see true pain in her eyes. That was a good sign.

"I don't know, luv. But if it is . . . it's not your fault."

"But if I hadn't bought it, if I hadn't left it . . ."

"It may have happened some other way, but it still would have happened." She was not going to let this girl blame herself for a grown man's death. *Unless she's the killer . . . But if she isn't the killer, letting a thought like that roll around in her head could damage her forever.* "Look at me." Amanda looked up, her lip quivering. "You bought rope. You left it at a festival. Does that sound that bad?"

Amanda shook her head. "Not when you say it like that."

"Exactly." She patted her on the shoulder. "You're alright, pet." Someone cleared his throat. Siobhán looked up to find the mechanic waiting for her. She thanked Amanda and sent her on her way.

"Did you find anything in the car?"

"Not a thing," he said, wiping grease from his hands with a rag. "But there is news."

"Do tell."

"I know why the car crashed." So did Siobhán. Those deadly curves at top speed. She relayed this. The mechanic shook his head. "That may be so, but it would have happened anyway . . . eventually."

"What makes you say that?"

"The brakes make me say that. The lines were cut."

Chapter 28

"Before you get mad." Chris Gordon stood in front of Siobhán, blocking her path each time she tried to sidestep him. Although he was American, he was considered a local now. He owned Gordon's Comics and rented the flats above through Airbnb.

"What is it?" She wanted to find Macdara and tell him about the brake lines on Eamon Foley's car. She wanted to go back to the bistro, sit in the back garden, where it was quiet, and think about what this meant.

"I didn't know it was her, I swear."

"Chris. You've got three seconds."

"The widow. She's in one of my upstairs flats."

The revelation knocked all other thoughts out of her head. "She's here? In one of *your* rooms?"

"You don't have to say it like that."

"How is that possible?"

He frowned. "What do you mean?"

"First off, she was staying at the Kilbane Inn. And, second, I presume your rooms were booked. Third, we've been on an all-out search for the very pregnant widow for the past twenty-four hours, and what? It just slipped your mind?"

"I asked you not to get mad."

"Tough nuts." She grabbed his elbow and began marching him toward his establishment. "Pray tell, how did this slip your mind?"

"She disguised herself. I thought she was just a fat lady."

"And the matter of the booked rooms?"

"The other day a man up and left. Said I could rent the room. He came for a poker tournament and the star player up and hanged himself. He was out of here. Minutes later . . . in comes this fat chick—"

Siobhán held up her hand. "Do not say 'chick' in my presence."

"Fine. Can I say 'fat'?"

Siobhán sighed. "How did you figure out it was her?"

"I saw the guy. At the festival. Told him I thought he'd gone home. Caught him red-handed. Asked if he had a problem with the room. That's when he told me the widow paid him five hundred euro for it. That's double what he paid me. I thought you could arrest him and give me the money. It's my business."

"I'm in the middle of a murder inquiry and you want me to focus on your lost revenue?"

"Too soon?"

Siobhán gently shoved him against the wall of the hardware shop. "You're going to give me the key to her room. Explain how and when the housekeepers go in, and stay far, far away while we work. Do you understand?"

"And then I'll get my money?"

"No. Then I don't haul you into the station for with-holding pertinent information to an investigation."

Macdara met Siobhán in front of Rose Foley's new room. "Any news on the car?"

"Big news," she said.

Before she could get into it, the door to the flat swung open. Rose Foley stood, suitcase in hand. When she saw them, she slammed the door. "Go away."

Macdara stepped forward. "Police. Open up."

The door flung open. Rose Foley left it that way, then flopped on the bed. She looked bleary-eyed. Red roses sat on the dresser.

"We've been looking for you," Siobhán said.

"Congratulations. You found me."

Siobhán stepped into the room. Macdara hung back in the hall. She maneuvered near the flowers. A dozen roses. She scanned for a card. Saw none. "Who gave you these?"

"A fan of my husband."

"Brilliant. Did you get a name?"

"No."

There was only one flower shop in town. It wasn't unusual that a person would give the widow flowers; in fact, she had a hunch that many had been delivered to the inn. Rory Mack was getting flowers at the pub as a makeshift memorial grew. But red roses? And she could swear there was a hint of cologne in the air. She saw Macdara jot down a note as she headed for the bath-room. Maybe she did have a secret lover. "Why did you leave the Kilbane Inn?"

"I wanted a bit of peace." She rested her hand on her bump. "Is that against the law?"

"We're in the middle of a murder inquiry. We can't be using our resources to search for missing people who aren't really missing."

Rose plopped on the bed. "I'll solve the mystery for ye. My husband did it. He took his own life."

Siobhán was startled by the sudden reversal. "Two days ago you insisted he wouldn't do that."

"It's called denial."

"You insisted."

Rose's eyes flicked to Macdara. "Why is she hovering over there?"

Siobhán ignored her and wandered into the bathroom. On the sink sat men's shaving cream, a razor, and cologne. She popped her head back out and motioned for Macdara. He stepped in and took in the items.

He stepped up to Rose. "Who's been staying in the room with you?"

"What do you mean?"

"There's shaving cream and cologne in the bathroom. And I may not be the most romantic man in the world, but I do know what it means to give a lady a dozen roses."

"Some men are attracted to women in my condition. I can't help it."

"And I suppose the pregnancy hormones are giving you a mustache?" Siobhán piped in.

"They're Eamon's. Happy now? I miss him. I wanted his things near the sink. I bought the roses. Pretended they were from him." Tears filled her eyes. Siobhán felt like an eejit. This was a grieving widow about to give birth. *Possibly a murdering widow, but a widow about to give birth nonetheless.* "I want to go home. I don't want to have my baby in the town where my husband died."

"The wake is in an hour," she said. "It will raise money for Eamon's funeral, and I'm sure there will be enough left over for you and the baby."

Rose wiped her nose with her sleeve. "Not as much as he would have won."

"We have one more question for you," Siobhán said. "Where is Eamon's car?"

Rose's head jerked up. "Why?"

"Answer our question first," Macdara said.

"I don't know."

"Where did he park it when you arrived?"

"We didn't come together. I had a doctor's appointment. I rode with the crew."

"Did you see his car in the parking lot of the inn?"

"Oh, he wouldn't have parked it there. He loved that stupid orange car more than me. He would have parked it far away from other cars." She clenched her fists. "You'd better find it."

"Have you ever met the blond waitress who was accused of slipping your husband a cold deck?"

Rose blinked. Sat there as if she was trying to recall the answer to a question on a test. "I don't recall."

"You don't recall?"

"I meet a lot of people. I believe you're trying to trick me. I don't know who I've met and who I haven't. You know how many of these poker games I've had to endure?"

"We'll let you get changed."

"Changed?"

"Don't you want to wear something a little nicer for your husband's wake?"

"Oh," she said. "All I have is the yellow dress I wore the first night. It wouldn't be proper to wear yellow at a wake."

Siobhán stepped forward. "I'll take you to Ann-marie's shop. I'm sure she has something." Rose glanced at her handbag. "It's on me."

"Thanks a million," Rose said.

A thanks-a-million from Rose Foley. Maybe there is hope for her after all. They were almost out the door when Siobhán excused herself to use the jax. The minute she was in there, she ran the water and removed a handkerchief from her handbag. Using the handker-chief to touch the bottle so that her fingers never did, she dabbed some of the cologne onto the handkerchief. It wasn't to her taste, too cloying, but to each his own. She used the handkerchief to put the cap back on, then tucked the handkerchief back into her handbag.

Siobhán waited until she and Macdara were back on the street to deliver the news. "The mechanic said the brake lines had been cut."

"He was sure?"

"Yes."

"That means . . ." His words wandered off.

"It means if Eamon Foley had survived the tourna-ment, he probably would have been killed on his way home."

"Along with Rose."

"Not necessarily."

"Explain that one."

"They arrived separately. They had separate rooms. Now she has cologne and roses and a Book Face page that says she's single."

"You didn't buy that it was her dead husband's co-logne?"

"I smelled him. He didn't wear cologne." It was brief as he was being dragged from O'Rourke's fighting and screaming. He had been all masculine, with a hint of soap. She didn't need to bog Macdara down in those details, nor did she want to think about the way a dead man used to smell.

"Men can have cologne, but not wear it all the time."

"I know."

"Maybe he just didn't wear it the day you were sniffing him."

"I get it. And I wasn't sniffing him. He just happened to pass by."

"I see. Made an impression though."

"It's not becoming to be jealous of a dead man."

He laughed. "My apologies."

"I just think . . . Rose is lying. I think nearly everything that comes out of her gob is a lie."

"You think she's a black widow?" He folded his arms. "In her condition?"

"Her lover could have helped."

"Shane Ross?"

"He's the most likely. What if the two of them were in on this together?"

"If they fixed the brakes on his car, why the hanging? Do you think Eamon foiled their plan by hanging himself?"

"It would be the ultimate irony," Siobhán said. "And it's quite possible."

If Eamon Foley committed suicide, could Shane and Rose still be charged with premeditated murder? Would it be attempted murder? She sighed. "It only makes sense for them to wait until after the tournament to kill him—*after* he's won all that money."

"That scenario makes sense for Rose. Doesn't make sense for Shane. Not if he really wanted to win."

"Ironic. Maybe the two argued about whether to kill him before or after the tournament."

Macdara nodded. "Diabolical indeed."

"How does he have time to do all this *and* steal diamonds?"

"What are you saying?"

"I'm saying I don't think I understand the full picture yet. Just when one part of it makes sense, the rest of it falls apart. But let's say this. Someone clearly planned on murdering Eamon Foley. Cut his brake lines and assumed he would crash on his drive home. Then this same person—"

"Or persons."

"Or persons make sure Eamon Foley is dealt the Dead Man's Hand. It's a sick foreshadowing of his demise."

"Why?"

"Because we're dealing with a killer who is sadistic. He or she is enjoying the game. First they toyed with the victim, now they are toying with us."

"Say more."

"I don't think the bulletproof vest or the items in his pockets belonged to Eamon at all. The brass knuckles, the marked playing cards—I think the killer placed them there."

"Including the gun?"

"Including the gun. Remember Margaret said Rose was desperate to get into Eamon's room. We thought it was to remove the gun. What if it was to plant it?" She thought of something. "In fact, those were her exact words. 'Someone must have planted it.'"

"But Margaret said she didn't let her into Eamon's room. Do you think our innkeeper is lying?"

"Margaret? Never. Why lie when you don't care what comes out of your mouth?"

"Maybe Rose found another way into the room?"

"Just like a killer may have found a way out of a locked room."

"Exactly." Siobhán thought on it. "Maybe she snuck in when the cleaning lady was there."

"We still have to be able to prove it."

"There's the rub."

"What about the suicide note? It's *his* handwriting."

"That's a piece that still doesn't fit."

"And the locked door."

"That's another."

"Go on."

Siobhán did. "So the murder was planned. But something must have happened at Sharkey's on that Friday evening that sped it up."

"Like what?"

"What if Eamon realized someone was trying to kill him?"

Macdara nodded. "And maybe he confided in the wrong person."

Siobhán shivered. "Amanda Moore said she left the rope at the festival. I believe her. Someone brought it to Sharkey's. Could have been intentional, could have been someone saw free rope and took it on impulse. Once the craziness at Sharkey's started to unfold, the killer—be it someone else or Eamon himself—saw the rope, and saw no other way out . . . and a new plan was hatched."

"So now Eamon did kill himself?"

"I don't know. If this was a work of a murderer, they

were smart. This suicide versus murder business has us all tied up in knots." Siobhán started walking faster as if trying to keep up with her racing thoughts. "In either scenario, how does this waitress fit in?"

"My God, you're right." Macdara stopped, took hold of Siobhán's arm. She turned to face him.

"I am? What did I say?"

"She's a *witness*. She knows who put her up to dropping the cold deck."

"And if we didn't have a murderer running around, the person who put her up to cheating wouldn't go to such lengths to keep her quiet."

"Exactly," Macdara said. "They would try other methods, like paying her off."

"Like with an orange Mustang."

"Like with an orange Mustang."

"Is it possible we're dealing with multiple people? Is it possible she stole the car herself?"

"It's possible," Macdara said. "But didn't we hear that Eamon went to great lengths to hide the car?"

"It's not probable," Siobhán said.

"Not probable. But what we don't know is, did the person who helped our little waitress into the car know the brake line had been cut?"

"Sending her off to her death." Siobhán shuddered.

"And who else had the authority to give away that car besides Rose Foley?"

Siobhán was right with him. "And who says, 'I don't recall' when you ask them if they met a particular person?"

"Someone who doesn't want to answer the question," Macdara finished. *Indeed.*

"Let's pray our waitress survives."

Macdara took out his mobile. "I'll put a guard at her

hospital door." He made the call, then clicked off. "We're running out of time."

"Let's hurry then." She started down the street.

"Where are you going?"

"The flower shop. We can at least find out who those roses are from."

Chapter 29

Jane's Garden was a quaint little shop just past the Kilbane Museum. Jane O'Reilly stood behind the counter elbow-deep in flowers. She was making arrangements for the wake, and when the bell dinged, she looked up in horror. Her eyes flew to the clock. It was four o'clock.

"Don't tell me you're here already. I plan on dropping them off at Sharkey's at half six."

"You're fine, luv," Siobhán said. "We just need to ask you a question."

Her shoulders relaxed. She held up a rose and her clippers. "I hope you don't mind if I work while we talk."

"Not a bother," Macdara said.

"Were you working on Saturday?"

Jane laughed. "I'm always here."

"We need to know who came in to buy a dozen red roses for Rose Foley."

"That's an easy one. They were from the entire poker tournament."

"Who purchased them?"

"The fella himself."

"We'll need you to be more specific."

She sighed, stopped cutting flowers, and turned to her register. She picked up a receipt. "I had him give me his autograph."

She turned it to them: *Thanks for the good deal, Shane Ross.* "Isn't that sweet? A little note with his signature."

"Thanks a million." Siobhán grabbed Macdara's elbow and headed out.

Jane nodded. "Of course." As they headed out, she kept talking. "D.S. Flannery, if there's ever a beautiful woman you want to buy flowers for, do come see me."

The minute they were outside, Siobhán stopped. "Did you just realize what I just realized?"

"That I don't know how long it's been since I bought you flowers?"

"No." *Yes . . .*

"That Shane Ross is our killer?"

"No."

"Spit it out, Siobhán."

"'Can't beat the Dead Man's Hand . . .'"

"I thought about that for a second, but the handwriting is completely different."

"Yes, different because they were written by different men."

Macdara frowned. "Then I'm not following."

"What if the note we found on Eamon wasn't a suicide note? What if it was an autograph for a fan?"

"My God." Macdara began to pace. "If you're right—if that wasn't a suicide note—it's one more check in the column that Eamon Foley did not kill himself."

Haven't I been insisting that all along? "I'm right," she said. "Eamon Foley was murdered."

"It would help if we could confirm he signed that as an autograph to someone. No one has mentioned it so far."

Siobhán was way ahead of him. She plowed forward.

"Where are you going?"

"There's no time to waste. We're going to have to divide and conquer."

One hour until the wake . . . Siobhán was in her best black dress approaching Sharkey's. But before she could reach the door, someone stepped out in front of her. She was shocked to see Greg Cunningham. On second glance she was a tad disappointed that Layla wasn't with him. "Are you here for the wake?"

He shook his head. "I gave me donation though."

"That was so kind of you."

He thrust his hand out. A tiny piece of paper was protruding from his fingers. "Another note from me bird." He turned before she could ask any more questions. She opened it: *Who are you? Eddie*

Eddie Houlihan.

She tucked it in her handbag and headed inside.

Sharkey's had been transformed. Flowers sang from every surface, white lights had been added around the room, candles flickered from tabletops covered in white linen, and it smelled as fresh as the spring air. Rory had a turf fire going, and all the food was waiting on a long banquet table in warmers. A photo of Eamon Foley took center stage. In front of it sat two large donation boxes. By the end of the evening they would be stuffed. There were gorgeous flower arrangements nearly everywhere you looked and a giant wreath in front of the storage room. Volunteers were already here, as well as Father Kearney. It didn't take Siobhán long to spot Eddie Houlihan. He disappeared into a hallway, pushing a mop. She hurried after him.

"Wet floors," Rory Mack yelled as she ran past.

Eddie turned to find her in front of him and visibly jumped.

"Apologies," Siobhán said. She held out the note from the pigeon.

His eyes widened. "You know Layla?"

She smiled. "Yes, we've met."

He grinned, revealing a gap between his teeth. "I love Layla."

"She's a sweetheart."

"She likes me."

"Does she?"

"Yes, she visits me nearly every day."

"Did you send a note with Layla to Greg Cunningham?"

His cheeks brightened. "I just wanted to tell somebody."

"Why him?"

"He's like me."

"Like you?"

"He doesn't have many friends." Her heart gave a squeeze for the lad. He must be so lonely. When this mess was over, she'd have to see about doing something to rectify that. Lonely lads could get themselves into trouble. "I send him a lot of notes."

"That's very kind of you."

"You're not mad?"

"Listen. You're not in trouble. But you must tell me everything. When did you discover Eamon's body?"

"It was half six Saturday morning."

Half six. If Rory's account was correct, and he left at four in the morning, then the killer (if it wasn't Rory) was lying in wait. Most likely, dead soon thereafter.

"How did you discover him?"

"I came early because you wouldn't believe the mess." *I believe it. I saw it.* "I knew I'd need most the day to clean." He gulped. "I noticed the storage room door locked right away, because that's where I'd left the mop."

"We didn't find a mop in the storage room."

"It's where I left it."

"When?"

"Friday evening."

"What time?"

"Before midnight."

She glanced at his mop. "Where did you find it?"

"This isn't it. I had to buy a new one. The old one was disgusting."

Siobhán felt pinpricks on the back of her neck. "Where did you find the old one?"

"Leaning in this back hallway. Filled with gunk."

The killer forgot to take the mop with him. Maybe he heard Eddie coming. She was grateful the lad hadn't walked in at the wrong time, and grateful he didn't seem to realize the danger he could have faced. *"Filled with gunk . . ." Gunk like rope fibers?*

"What did you do with it?" she asked. They'd thoroughly gone through the rubbish and they didn't find a mop.

"I tossed it in the rubbish bins down the street."

"Why?"

He looked away. "Rory would have told me to keep using it. He's like that. But it was disgusting."

"Down the street where?"

He looked shifty again. "In town, actually. I put it in Liam's rubbish." He looked at her, his face pure panic. "Am I in trouble? It really was a dirty mop."

"No, luv." She sighed. All rubbish bins had been collected this morning. It was likely their mop was long gone. But another piece of the puzzle had just clicked. "Did you notice rope in the storage room?"

He shook his head.

"Come on." Siobhán tugged on his sleeve, guiding him out to the patio. It, too, had been transformed. The debris was gone, the cigarette buckets emptied and washed, and a lovely tablecloth covered the picnic table. Flowers had been grouped in pots and set along the edges.

"Tell me how you saw into the storage room." She pointed to the venting window. "When I arrived, there was no ladder. I had to fetch one. So how did you get up there?"

He nodded to the picnic table. "I pulled it over. Then I climbed until I could hang on to the ledge and pulled myself up."

God, it must be nice to be that strong. She was going to have to start lifting weights. Garda college gave her some muscles, but she handn't kept up their rigorous regime. Only so many hours in a day. "Why did you go to all that trouble?" His face turned beet red in a hot second. "Ah," she said. He'd seen the trail of urine. "You were doing a wellness check. Making sure whoever in there was okay?" The nods came rapidly. "Why didn't you call the guards?"

He swallowed. "I'd never seen a dead body before. But on telly they always suspect the person who finds the body. Plus, I even got his autograph."

She patted his hand. "I know what a shock it was. I experienced it m'self."

"I'm sorry. Would he still be alive if I called 999?"

"No, luv. Then what happened?"

"I dragged the picnic table back, and turned to go. Layla was sitting on the picnic table."

"You feed her brekkie, don't you?"

"I save the chips from the night before. How did you know?"

"She's looking a little plump and Greg had thought she'd gone soft in the head because she only flies local. I think she's smarter than he realizes. Who wouldn't give up long-distance flying for free chips?" She finally got him to smile. "Were you here all Friday evening?" A nod. "Did you speak with the Octopus?" A second nod. "That's right. Because you got his autograph. May I see it?"

He pawed the ground. "Someone stole it."

Siobhán's heart thumped. "Did he write you anything special?"

Eddie nodded. Then swallowed. "I thought it was great craic. But now . . . it's not. . . ."

Siobhán knew what the autograph said. "Can't beat the Dead Man's Hand.'"

Eddie gasped. "How did you know?"

She was right. That wasn't a suicide note. "Did you see or hear anything suspicious?" He shook his head. "Did you mop the storage room?"

"When?" he asked.

"Friday evening or Saturday morning?"

"I mopped it Friday morning. I shouldn't have bothered."

"Why?"

"It was a mess. This entire place. Took me ages to clean. At least I didn't have to do the storage room."

A professional cleaning company had taken care of the crime scene. Not a job anyone would envy. "Do you know any way in or out of that storage room besides the main door?" Eddie shook his head again. "Did you see anyone marking playing cards with a black marker?" Another shake. *He's not a chatterbox.* "Just one more question, luv, you're doing great. Did you tell anyone you lost the autograph?" He shook his head. "Okay, luv." She patted his hand. "Let's keep this little talk to ourselves."

Chapter 30

By the time she went back inside, there were twice as many people roaming about. The drunken toasts had begun and they filtered through the room. "Four blessings upon you. Older whiskey. Younger women. Faster horses. More money."

"Sláinte!" Pint glasses clinked.

A drunken male voice called out. "Let's drink to California, way out by the sea, where a woman's ass, and a whiskey glass, made a horse's ass out of me."

"Hear! Hear!"

"Merry met and merry part, I drink to thee with all my heart."

Siobhán was wondering if things were getting a bit too rowdy, but then she noticed Rose's face lit up like a firecracker. She was enjoying the banter. Siobhán sighed. It was best to let them at it. Death had a funny

way of making you long for any distractions—even, or
especially, if it was a tad crass. She was saved the trouble when the band started playing "Danny Boy" and
everyone joined in.

"Oh, Danny Boy, the pipes, the pipes, are calling. . . ."

She passed Margaret standing in a clump with Liam
and Mike.

"How's that electric heater working out?" Liam said
as Siobhán walked by. Siobhán stopped, turned.

"I hate it," Margaret said. "It makes a clicking
sound. *Click, click, click.*"

"Sorry there, Margaret. You should have brought it
back to me."

Margaret shrugged. "Beats all that firewood."

Shane Ross lied. Again. He had to be their man. The
stolen diamonds. The gloves. The markers. He's the
one who bought the flowers for Rose. Two questions
remained: Was the widow in on it? Or was he a lone
dark horse and she was one of his victims?

She approached Rose, looking down as she did,
fumbling in her handbag, digging out the handkerchief. She came up from behind.

"There you are." Rose turned, as if expecting someone else, then blinked. "Oh. It's you."

Siobhán took her hands. "I just wanted to say how
sorry I am for your loss."

"Thank you."

Siobhán hurried off, feeling Rose's hard eyes on her
back. Next she got a pint of Guinness from Rory and
hurried over to Nathan Doyle. He was standing in the
middle of the room, his eyes glued to Shane Ross. Just
as she reached them, her drink spilled. "Clumsy me!"
Ale sloshed on the floor. She touched Nathan's arm.

"Do you mind running for the mop? We wouldn't want the widow to slip."

"It's no bother," Nathan said. She watched as he headed off. He returned moments later with Eddie Houlihan trailing after him.

"Thank you, Eddie," Siobhán said.

"Not a bother." When he was finished cleaning, Siobhán followed Eddie Houlihan back to the hallway for another little chat.

Macdara arrived, looking devastatingly handsome in his dark suit. She had to resist the urge to kiss him. Siobhán quickly filled him in on her conversation with Eddie and the bit she overheard from Margaret about her new electric fireplace. "It really looks like Shane Ross is our guy. Do we really have to let him leave to break into Celtic Gems?"

"We don't have enough to arrest him."

"What if we get Rose to flip?"

"That's assuming Rose is in on it."

"She is if Shane Ross is the father of her baby."

"I'll have to alert Nathan," Macdara said. "Although I don't think he needs more convincing, he's been the one trying to convince me how dangerous Shane Ross is."

"Trying to convince?"

"It was my fault. I didn't have that feeling around Shane. He's very good at hiding his true nature."

She knew what he meant. Shane was edgy, but likable nonetheless. With his slim build and floppy hair, he just didn't paint a menacing portrait.

More trad musicians had arrived and were setting up in the corner. Rose Foley walked by. Her black dress barely covered her knees. She was wearing a sweeping black hat with a veil and three-inch heels.

Hardly looking like Shane's victim.

Shane, Clementine, and Nathan, all wearing black, gathered in a clump. Clementine's dress was modest, the most subdued outfit Siobhán had seen her in so far. The donation boxes were already getting fed. It wouldn't be long before everyone, including their suspects, would be gone. Siobhán found herself staring at Shane Ross, tracking his every move.

She began to think back to her last encounter with Shane at the jewelry store. Was Rose the woman he was going to propose to?

Macdara was in her ear. "I see those wheels in that big brain spinning. What are you thinking?"

"Shane told me you were the one who put him up to asking me to look at rings."

Macdara bowed his head. "I'm very sorry about that."

"I know." (*"That sergeant. He asked me to show you the rings. To see which one you liked,"* Shane had said—something was bothering her. Why couldn't she put her finger on it?)

"We know why he was lying. He couldn't exactly admit he was casing the joint."

"Did you get any report on him from Dublin?"

"They're not going to hand over files on an undercover operation."

"All of this rests on believing every word we've been told about Shane Ross. We've observed nothing sordid from him ourselves."

"Casing the jewelry shop?"

"What if he was thinking of proposing to his girlfriend?"

"We've caught him in a ton of lies. Where is this coming from?"

"*You*. You stopped trusting your gut when it came to how you felt about Shane Ross. I have the same feeling, Dara. I still feel like we're all being played."

"He's the third-ranked poker player. If anyone's capable of playing us, it's him."

He was right. But then why did she have this relentless, nagging doubt? "In order for Shane Ross to be our killer, he has to know how to disable security cameras. Figure out a way out of a locked room. Know how to cut brake lines—"

"He's a cat burglar, Siobhán. Sounds like it would fit his skill set to me."

"But what if he isn't a cat burglar? Do we still see him with that skill set?"

"I need a pint, you're wrecking my head." He took her hand, squeezed it, then dropped it.

She couldn't blame him. She was wrecking her own head. One minute she was convinced Shane Ross was their man, and the next a little voice inside her warned she was off the mark.

Macdara touched her shoulder. "Don't forget we're here to pay our respects." Siobhán thought the best way to pay her respects to the dead man—and that was the individual she worked for, no matter what—was to find out who killed him. "I know what it is. We've been handed the killer with a neat little bow. Is it possible you're still spinning because you didn't figure this one out?"

Siobhán took a deep breath before responding and forced a smile. "Anything is possible, Dara." *It's just not probable.*

He placed his hand on the small of her back. "We'll know soon. If Shane Ross tries to break into Celtic Gems, then he's our man."

If Shane was their man, then Macdara was right. But if he wasn't, waiting could turn out to be the most dangerous game of all.

Chapter 31

They were an hour into the memorial when Siobhán stepped onto the back patio. There she found a few young ones playing with sticks. Before they spotted her, the tallest one whirled around with his stick, catching Siobhán's handbag and nearly yanking her arm off with it. They were all squeals and apologies as the lad swiped it from the ground to hand it to her as if he hadn't been the cause of the trouble.

After a gentle reprimand a strange feeling came over her. She was close to figuring something out. It hovered at the edges of her mind. But before she could work through it, her mobile rang. The conversation was quick. It was a nurse from the hospital. The waitress was awake and only wanted to speak to the redheaded woman who had saved her life. Siobhán checked her watch. Nathan predicted that Shane would sneak around after two or three. If Siobhán wanted to hear what the waitress had to say, she'd better slip out now. She called a taxicab, asking it to wait down the street.

Her name was Emily and she was in Room 301. Siobhán entered to find her sitting up in her hospital bed, face cleared of makeup, eyes pinned on the door as if she'd been holding her breath waiting for her visitor. She looked so young. Siobhán's heart went out to the girl, regardless of what she was wrapped up in. "Good to see you alert."

"Thank you," she squeaked. "You saved me life."

"You remember?"

Emily shook her head. "But everyone is talking about it. They say you dragged me out of the car."

"Anyone would have done the same."

"I don't know about that."

Siobhán pulled a chair up near the bed. Emily wrung her hands. Siobhán looked toward the empty hallway. "I thought there was supposed to be a guard at your door?"

Emily nodded. "I think he's on break." She straightened her sheets. "Am I in trouble?"

"We've been wanting to speak with you. I won't be able to promise anything until I know the facts. But I do know that you can never run from the things you've done. They'll follow you. Even if the authorities never catch you, lies have a way of eating you up."

Tears filled the girl's eyes. "I brought Eamon Foley the cold deck."

"You wanted to help him cheat?"

"No. He knew nothing about it." She sniffed. "Is that why he did it? Because of what I did?"

"I think it's more complicated than that. But you can

help us get to the bottom of this. Who asked you to bring him the Dead Man's Hand?"

"I didn't bring him the Dead Man's Hand. The dealer did that. The deck was just a distraction. The dealer switched the hand when I brought the water. Then I dropped the deck on his chair."

"Who asked you to do this?"

Emily pointed to her bedside table where her handbag sat. Siobhán handed it to her. She pulled out a piece of stationery. She handed it to Siobhán. On it a single phrase was written: *I'm an undercover operator for the SSU.*

Nathan Doyle . . . something didn't fit. "He *told* you he was undercover?" How many people had he dragged into this operation?

She nodded. "He came to one of my shows. In Dublin."

"One of your shows?"

Her face lit up. "I'm a magician's assistant."

"I see."

"The dealer who switched the hand is the magician." She leaned in and whispered, "He's my boyfriend."

"Where is your boyfriend?" *How ironic, the magician made himself disappear.*

"He left Friday night. I wanted to stay." She sighed. "Big mistake."

"Did he show you his badge?"

"My boyfriend?"

"Sorry. The undercover guard."

"Shane Ross has a badge? He's a guard?" She frowned. "I thought he was more like an informant."

Siobhán started. "Shane Ross?"

The girl frowned. "Shane Ross."

Siobhán felt like she was caught in the middle of one of those confusing comedy routines. "Shane Ross told you he was an undercover operator?"

"Yes. I *just* told you he came to my show. I showed you his note!" She rolled her eyes. "You'd think you were the one who had been in a car wreck."

Siobhán let the dig go. She had bigger things to worry about: *What does this all mean? Does Shane Ross know about our investigation into him? Why is he still in Kilbane? Does he know we're expecting him to attempt another break-in? Should I call Macdara? I should tell Nathan Doyle . . .*

"Have you ever spoken to Nathan Doyle?"

"Who?"

"The coordinator who announced all the games?"

She frowned, then shook her head. "Only Shane Ross."

"How long ago did he find you?"

"Let's see." She pulled out her mobile and opened a calendar app. "My show a fortnight ago. He was waiting for me after."

Siobhán tried not to show too much alarm, she had more questions for her and didn't want to startle her. Premeditated was right. Eamon Foley's murder had been in the works for at least two weeks, probably a lot longer. If Siobhán had to guess, she had a pretty good idea that this murder had been planned since Rose found out she was pregnant. "You didn't think to tell us what you knew earlier?"

Emily placed her hand over her heart. "I figured Shane would take care of it. He's the undercover one. Not me. I was just honored to help." She bit her lip. "But *did* I help? I would have never gotten involved if I knew Eamon was going to do *that* to himself. Did they drive him to it?"

Siobhán wasn't going to answer the unanswerable. "How did you end up in Eamon Foley's car?"

She pulled her knees up, the blanket tenting, making her seem like a child. "I was tricked."

"Tricked?"

"She set me up!"

"Who?"

"Rose." She clamped her lips. "She said she didn't want it. Sold it to me for ten euro."

"She knew you delivered a cold deck to her husband and she sold you his car for ten euro?" *The widow certainly acted upset about the car being stolen. Which one is the liar?*

Emily reclined. "I need to sleep."

"This is important. She told you to take the car. The brakes failed. You could have been killed."

"Are you saying she knew? She . . . wanted *me* to die?"

"You set her husband up as a cheat. Didn't it give you pause that she was selling a sporty little car for ten euro?" Siobhán's empathy was draining. A little common sense was in order.

Emily chewed on her lip. "I didn't think she knew who I was."

"How did you find out it was for sale?"

Emily looked away. "She ran into me. Asked if I knew anyone who was interested." Before Siobhán could chastise her a second time, Emily crossed her arms and glared. "I get it. I was played." Siobhán sighed. Some people were their own worst enemies. "Are you going to arrest her?"

"We need to gather all the facts. If we can prove she knew the brakes would fail, then yes. We will arrest her."

"But she might get away with it?" Emily's eyes danced with anger.

"Let me worry about that. Get some rest."

Emily reached out, grabbed Siobhán's hand, and squeezed. "Thanks a million." Siobhán started to leave. Emily yanked her back, her grip surprisingly strong. "I'm sorry."

"For what?"

"That."

Before Siobhán could ask anything more, she felt a presence behind her. It was too late to even turn around. Something was shoved over her head. A pillowcase. It tightened. She struggled and landed a kick to the person holding her. A male voice groaned. "Try that again and you won't be able to breathe." She didn't recognize his voice. The pillowcase tightened even more.

"Stop struggling." It was Emily. "We're not going to hurt you. You just need to let us get away."

So the magician boyfriend hasn't disappeared after all. Siobhán had a strong feeling that's who had a hold on her.

The person behind her began to move Siobhán backward. They walked a few feet, as she continued to kick—and every time she did, the pillowcase tightened. If she didn't stop, he might accidentally asphyxiate her. They stumbled a few more feet.

"In there," she heard Emily say.

Siobhán heard the creak of a door. Next she was shoved from behind. She lost her balance and hit her chin on a hard surface as she heard a door slam behind her. She whipped off the pillowcase. She was in the bathroom. She lunged at the door. Something was lodged on the other side, trapping her inside. *Eejits.* She reached for her mobile. *Amateurs.* She'd be out of

here soon. The bigger questions were: Who else
wanted her out of the way? And what were they planning?

By the time a nurse let her out, Emily and her boyfriend were gone. Siobhán called the station and dis-
patched guards to find them. The great thing about
having a walled town was there were only a few places
to exit. Siobhán had a feeling the little duo wouldn't
get far. She called a taxi and directed it to take her directly to the station. She snuck in, relieved that all the
top-tier guards were at the memorial or out looking for
their escapees. It would make what she had to do that
much easier. She was going around Macdara, and if
her hunch was wrong, she'd have to face him—and
even if her hunch was right, she would still have to
face him, but this had to be done. *When you have to lie,
stick as close as possible to the truth.* She was relieved
to find Susan at the counter. "I need to check on a call
Macdara had you make to the Dublin guards."

"Which call?"

Susan knew very well which call. She was stalling.
"He had you call the Dublin guards to confirm that
Nathan Doyle was a member of AGS. Remember?"

She waited while Susan eyed her, not sure how to
process her request. "Why aren't you getting this directly from D.S. Flannery?"

"If you want to give him a bell, I'll wait. He's at the
memorial."

Susan chewed on her lip. "Why doesn't he just tell
you himself?"

"He couldn't remember the exact quote. We think it
might make a difference."

She sighed again, then thumbed through her notes.

She pulled out a piece of paper. "I called the Dublin Guards on Saturday. Spoke to Detective Sergeant Flannery. Here it is."

Siobhán read the message. "That's it?"

"That's it."

"Did you change the wording?"

Susan's eyebrow went up. "Pardon?"

"Did you write down an exact quote or an approximation?"

Susan pushed her glasses up. "I am always precise with my dictation." She appeared to be doing her best not to look offended.

Thank God. Siobhán nodded. "Sometimes the tiniest words matter." She looked at the message again: *Yes, Nathan Doyle was a Dublin guard.*

Siobhán let out a sigh of relief. It was just as she thought. She had to make sure before she accused the wrong man. "I need you to call Dublin again. Here's what I need to know." She jotted it down.

Susan eyed the request, then Siobhán. "It takes forever to get a real person."

"I know. That's why you have to start now. Keep calling them. As soon as you get a human being that can talk to us, patch them directly to my mobile." Siobhán leaned in. "And not a word. To anyone."

"Including anyone here?"

"Including *anyone* here."

"Okay. If you're sure?"

"I'm sure." Siobhán was about to leave when she saw a stack of flyers on the desk. The words "bingo" and "fund-raiser" caught her eye. "Are these your missing bingo flyers?"

Susan nodded. "I had to print them up again. Poor trees."

Siobhán stopped. Stared. Her thought processes locked

up like stuck gears. She picked it up. She stared at it. Her pulse quickened. Her heart began tap-dancing. "It can't be."

"What can't?"

"This is the original?"

"Yes."

"These used to be sitting here? Right here?"

"Yes. Until someone swiped them."

"I see." Her body began to pump adrenaline. She wouldn't need the phone call from Dublin now, although it might help convince Macdara.

"What's the story?" Susan said. "You don't like them?"

"I like them," Siobhán said. She grabbed several and stuck them in her handbag. "One might even say they're a lifesaver."

She hurried out as Susan stared at her, confusion stamped on her face.

Siobhán stopped next at Liam's hardware store, got what she needed from the befuddled man, then texted Macdara.

Don't let any of them leave Sharkey's. Especially Shane Ross.

What? Where are you?

I'm begging you. Keep all of your guards there and keep our suspects there.

Shane has to be allowed to leave.

BEGGING. Keep Shane there!

Siobhán stopped texting. He would either listen or he wouldn't. She had no time to waste. She got back to Sharkey's and hid her purchases on the patio. Luckily,

Rory Mack's truck was still parked in the lot. She removed the ladder and took it back to the patio. She entered Sharkey's and found Shane Ross pacing, and Nathan Doyle eyeing him from the corner. Macdara was on her right away. "What's going on?"

"Is Nathan Doyle armed?"

"I would say so. They're waiting for Shane's break-in attempt."

"It won't be safe to have anyone armed."

"Why?"

"We need to empty this pub of everyone but guards and our suspects. And no firearms."

"You're interfering with an undercover operation?"

Nathan Doyle was making his way toward them. "Please. Dara. There's no time. *Please.*"

As Nathan approached, she saw the anxiety swimming in Macdara's eyes. She'd put him in a horrible position. She had no choice. *Please let him trust me.*

"I expect Shane will be sneaking out any minute now." Nathan clapped Macdara on the back.

"I just came from the hospital," Siobhán said.

"Oh?" Nathan raised an eyebrow. "Are you ill?"

"No, no. There was a car accident. The girl who allegedly planted the cold deck on Eamon Foley was nearly killed today."

"She's still here?" Nathan sounded as if this was the first he'd heard of it. Siobhán knew the guests at the wake were whispering about it.

"She was speeding away in Eamon's car. The brakes failed."

"Speeding away in his car? She was stealing it?"

"Did you have her on your radar?"

Nathan frowned. "We wanted to speak with her after Friday evening's fiasco. Is that what you mean?"

"Did you recruit her back in Dublin?" Emily hadn't pointed the finger at Nathan Doyle, but Siobhán had to be sure.

"Why would I need to recruit a waitress?"

"I thought you'd been casing Shane for a long time."

"We have." He was defensive now.

"She's not in your file?"

"Garda O'Sullivan, you're obviously chewing on something big. Why don't you spit it out?"

"Shane Ross met Emily two weeks ago. After one of her shows." She turned to Nathan. "He told her he was working undercover for the SSU."

"He told her?" Nathan looked outraged. "I had no idea. I should have known he'd go rogue."

"Her shows?" Macdara asked.

"She's a magician's assistant."

"Were they dating? Did Shane get her to set Eamon up?" Nathan looked as if he wanted to storm out of the pub and confront Emily in the hospital. "I feel sorry for her." His eyes swept through the crowd and landed on Shane Ross. "What is he still doing here?"

"I think it's best that everyone stays," Siobhán said.

Nathan pointed at her. "There it is again, an insinuation in your voice. Just what have you learned?"

"I'm about to tell you," Siobhán said. "I'm about to tell everyone."

Chapter 32

Siobhán stood on the little stage and surveyed their suspects while she waited for the pub to quiet down. Sharkey's was empty of everyone but the people Siobhán needed to be there. Rose Foley leaned on a table, drink in hand, heels off. Once more, Siobhán felt for the unborn baby. She could only hope the wee thing had a team of angels ready to look after him or her.

Shane Ross and Clementine Hart were huddled together in the back corner of the pub. Shane looking twitchy; Clementine as cool as usual. Rory Mack watched her from behind the counter. Amanda and Henry Moore stood stiffly near the front of the stage. Jeanie Brady was perched on a stool, eyes on Siobhán. Macdara looked the most uneasy, he had no idea what pieces of the puzzle had finally clicked for Siobhán and what she was about to say. Eddie Houlihan peered out from the shadows in the back.

Siobhán cleared her throat. "There are many ways to honor a man's memory. The best, in my humble opinion, is to find out who killed him."

"This again?" Rose cried out. "At his memorial? My husband took his own life." She looked around as if searching for reinforcements.

"Funny. In the very beginning you *insisted* he didn't."

"I was grieving."

Macdara stepped forward and placed a hand on Rose's shoulder. "Let her talk."

Siobhán gave him a nod before continuing. "At first this case seemed too complicated to solve. Starting with, was it even murder? We had a locked room. A supposed suicide note signed by the deceased, and plausible reasons why Eamon Foley would have taken his own life." She looked around the room. "Unfortunately, many people in this room played a role in what transpired here Friday night and early Saturday morning." Siobhán pointed. "Let's start with Clementine Hart."

Clementine stepped forward. "*Me?* You're starting with me?" She tossed her head as if she'd just won a prize. "Is that good or is that bad?"

"You riled up Eamon that evening by spreading the rumor that he wasn't the father of Rose's baby."

"It's a little more than a rumor," Clementine said. "Started by none other than Eamon himself."

"Outrageous!" Rose stormed forward. "Of course, he was the father."

"That's not what he told us," Shane said. "He said the doc told him his swimmers were quitters."

Rose rubbed her belly. "It's our miracle baby."

Clementine pointed at Rose. "You might have convinced Eamon of that, but not us. Drop the pious act."

Rose blinked rapidly.

Siobhán wasn't done with Clementine Hart. "You also marred the playing cards." Clementine stared. "You will all do yourself a favor by telling the absolute truth right here, and right now. The killer will continue to lie of course. And that will be very helpful."

Clementine sighed and relaxed her posture. "Fine. I marked the cards. Just doodling. Eamon told me I had a black heart, so I found myself scribbling. Shane was running his mouth in the background, so I did his next."

"Where did you leave the cards?"

"On my table. I don't know how they ended up in Eamon's pockets."

"The killer placed them there. The killer had to improvise when you stirred Eamon up about his paternity."

"I don't understand."

"Eamon Foley was going to die all along. He just wasn't supposed to die until *after* he won the tournament, collected a quarter of a million in winnings, and hopped into his orange Mustang."

The group was on full alert. "The one that crashed?" someone called out.

"Yes. The one whose brake lines had been cut."

A gasp rippled through Sharkey's.

"Try proving all that," Jeanie Brady said.

"I'm going to do just that." Siobhán found her next suspect in the crowd. "Amanda Moore."

Amanda stepped up. "I didn't kill him. I wanted to. But I didn't."

"But you did buy the rope, and then you left it at the festival?" Amanda stared. "Only the killer needs to fear the truth. No one else does."

Amanda burst into tears. "Okay, okay. I didn't leave it at the festival. I left it here. But I didn't bring it to kill anyone! I was planning on going for a ride when Da was here playing cards. He keeps the ropes in a cabinet in the barn, so I needed my own."

The crowd murmured.

Siobhán turned to Henry Moore. "It was such a foolish thing to do, betting your racehorse."

"I know." Henry Moore hung his head. "I'm a flawed man. But I'm no killer."

"No. I don't think you are. It's a relief, I might add." She stared at Rory Mack. "You as well."

"Me?"

"Insisting the games be played here. Betting your own pub!"

"I've learned me lesson. No more gambling in Sharkey's!"

Yeah, right. "I knew something specific must have happened Friday evening to force the killer to reimagine his murderous plan. And I was right. Eamon Foley was waiting for a return call from his doctor. He was very close to finding out he wasn't about to be a father. He confessed this to the wrong person. He confessed this to his killer."

"Somebody stop her. Make her stop!" Rose was in hysterics.

"So reimagine it, the killer did. Saw the rope. The shape Eamon was in. Found the playing cards on the table, decided that would throw suspicion on others. Threw in a few more props from his or her arsenal. Brass knuckles. A bulletproof vest. And then the killer stole an autograph."

She held up the evidence baggie:

CAN'T BEAT THE DEAD MAN'S HAND
Eamon Foley

"Eddie," Siobhán called out. Heads swiveled to Eddie Houlihan, who stood in the back, slouched, hands shoved in his denim pockets. "Is this the autograph Eamon signed to you?"

"'Tis," Eddie said, straightening up at the sight of it. "Here's my book to prove it." He held up a notebook turned to a torn page.

"It wasn't a suicide note at all," Jeanie Brady murmured. "Well played."

"I'm leaving," Rose said. But she remained where she was standing.

"There were many signs you had a lover. The roses. The cologne. The shaving kit. Separate rooms at the inn. Your social media pages."

"I explained all that."

"Lies," Siobhán said. "More lies." She turned to Shane. "Shane Ross bought you the roses. Didn't you, Shane?"

"Not just from me," Shane said. "Official ones. From all of us."

"You were also the one who brought Emily here."

"Emily?" Macdara said.

"The blond waitress who slipped Eamon a cold deck while her boyfriend, the magician, dealt him the Dead Man's Hand."

"You don't understand," Shane said. "You've got this all wrong."

"You also paid multiple visits to Celtic Gems."

"Now you're going to blame me for that missing ring?" He had started to sweat. "I told you. I think I'm being set up!"

"All those lies, Shane. They didn't help."

"What lies?"

"The gloves? Margaret switched to an electric fireplace earlier."

"It makes a clicking noise," Margaret said. "I don't like that."

"I got those gloves for someone else. It's not me!"

"Everywhere I looked, Shane Ross, there you were. And you've spent a lot of time around Mrs. Foley, haven't you?"

Rose thrust up her chin. "That's Widow Foley to you."

Shane Ross looked ready to bolt out the door. Siobhán had to keep going. "Motive is huge here. This killer wanted to protect an unborn baby." She eyed Shane. "I assume you'd submit to a DNA swab?"

Shane stepped forward. "Of course. Swab me cheek right now!"

"Enough." Jeanie Brady hopped off her stool. "I don't want to hear another crazy theory until you tell me how the killer got in and out of the room with a dead bolt."

Siobhán nodded. "The killer had to be someone smart. He or she needed the skills to disable cameras, change plans when the original one didn't work out, stage a suicide. I'll admit, the locked room had me at first." Siobhán found her sister in the crowd. "Gráinne, will you please go into the storage room and slide the dead bolt?"

"My pleasure." Gráinne walked over to the storage room and entered. They could clearly hear the dead bolt sliding into place. "It's locked."

"James. Would you please try the door?"

James walked up to the storage room door and pulled. "It's locked."

Siobhán nodded to Eoin. He headed for the patio. "You can stay in here as I narrate, or you can follow Eoin out to the patio. We all know that Eamon Foley spent the night in the storage room. Most likely, fell asleep in a chair. Right now, my brother Eoin is climbing a ladder up to the venting window. A ladder that, according to Eddie Houlihan, was in the storage room Friday day, along with a mop and a bucket."

"They were," Eddie said. "I swear."

"I know, luv." Siobhán smiled at Eddie. "As Eoin is climbing the ladder, in his hand is one of these." Siobhán leaned down and picked up the tent pole she'd placed near the stage. It had an O-ring attached to the end. "It's approximately ten feet from the window to the door. I believe a tent pole like this was used to catch the bolt and slide it in place."

"My God." Jeanie Brady sounded both disgusted and impressed.

"Several times I saw people playing with these tent poles and catch on things. Still, it took me a while to put it together," Siobhán explained.

"But you did," Macdara said.

"Let's see."

"Rory Mack, didn't you say you used your truck to deliver tent poles Friday morning?"

Heads turned to Rory. "I did indeed."

"You must have missed one. The killer found it in the back of your truck. Which was parked where on Friday evening?"

He nodded. "Right out front."

The door to the storage room swung open, and Eoin stood, tent pole held aloft. "It worked." The crowd murmured.

Jeanie Brady shot out of her chair. "My God!"

"How's that for proof?" Admiration shone from Macdara's voice.

"That'll do," Jeanie said. "I can officially rule his death a homicide."

"But who is the killer?" Clementine couldn't help herself.

"Garda O'Sullivan, I need you to stop talking." The order came from Nathan Doyle.

"Best of luck with that," Macdara replied with a wink.

She'd deal with him later. Siobhán turned to Nathan. "You especially are going to want to hear this."

"D.S. Flannery?" Nathan turned to Macdara. "Deal with her or I will."

"Dealer's choice," Siobhán said. She smiled at Nathan. Macdara shifted. "I want to hear what she has to say."

"So do I," Clementine said. "This is riveting."

Nathan didn't like taking no for an answer. "I order you to stand down."

"I would try that if I were you too," Siobhán said. "But you can't order anyone, anymore, can you? Seeing as how you're retired."

"He's retired?" Macdara said. He shook his head. "He has his badge and gun. I had one of my clerks call Dublin. He checked out."

Nathan stood like a statue.

"He didn't *return* his gun or badge. My guess is, he also had the vest and brass knuckles from his time on the force. Someone in Dublin will have to answer for that. And you misunderstood the message out of Dublin. I just checked with the clerk." It was obvious from his expression that Macdara was taken aback.

"How did I misunderstand?"

She pulled the phone message out of her handbag. "The guard in Dublin said this, 'Yes, Nathan Doyle was a Dublin guard.' You took this to mean present tense. But Dublin meant it as in past tense. He *was* a

guard. As opposed to, He *is* a guard. A simple miscom-
munication."

"Doublespeak! What is this nonsense?" Nathan Doyle
was unraveling. *Good.*

"Siobhán?" Macdara was pleading with her. He
stared at Nathan. "Are you retired?"

Nathan stared without replying.

"I bet if we checked into travel records, we'll find a
plane ticket for you. Ibiza, maybe?"

He glared at her. "You think you're such a clever
girl, don't you?"

"No," she said. "I think I'm such a clever *garda.*"

"This isn't possible," Shane said. He pointed. "I was
working undercover for him. He had me buy the
gloves. He told me he was casing Eamon Foley for illegal gambling."

"If only you knew what he was saying about you,"
Sibohan said.

"This is enough," Nathan said. "You're ruining a
very sensitive investigation."

"Shut up," Macdara said. He nodded to Siobhán.
"Continue."

She turned back to Shane. "When I met you outside
the jewelry shop, I had already received a complaint
from Tom Howell that someone was casing his store."

"Casing?" Shane said. "Me?"

"You were told that someone was going to propose
to me. This person asked for your help in getting me to
pick out a ring I liked."

Shane nodded.

"When I asked you, who put you up to it, you said,
'yer man,' and 'that detective.' " Siobhán took a deep
breath. "I thought at first Shane was referring to Macdara Flannery." She glanced at Dara. His handsome
face looked pained. "But you weren't. Were you? You

were talking about *that* one. The undercover one." She pointed at Nathan Doyle.

"Undercover," Clementine muttered. "No wonder the bloke didn't know two figs about poker."

Rose paled, and did not say a word. Her hand went to her stomach. Siobhán had to keep going.

"O'Sullivan, I warned you. He's a master manipulator." Nathan jerked his head to Shane Ross.

Shane whirled around. "Me? I am?" His confusion was too good to be an act. "It's you. You're the one!"

"Supposedly, you're also a diamond thief," Siobhán said. "A very notorious one back in Dublin."

Shane threw his head back and laughed. He stopped when he realized he was the only one. "You're joking me?"

"Step down, now." Nathan moved to the stage. Macdara stepped in front of him. "You're going to stay here and let her finish. I have guards surrounding this place."

Nathan stood his ground. "That's why you wanted my weapon." He pointed at Siobhán. "She is off the mark."

"So far, she's hitting it pretty good as far as I can see."

Siobhán held up the photo Gráinne had printed off Rose's social media page. "Stick as close as possible to the truth. Isn't that the way, Detective Sergeant Doyle?"

Nathan began to scan the room as if looking for an escape. "You're making a fool out of yourself."

"Here's a truth. Before you retired, you were assigned to Eamon Foley. That's when he met and fell in love with Rose Foley."

"Liar!" Rose was coming unglued. She looked liked a trapped rat.

Siobhán pulled the handkerchief out of her handbag. "When I dabbed some of the cologne from your bathroom at the inn on my handkerchief, and then came up behind you, you thought I was Nathan, didn't you?"

"That's hardly evidence of anything," Rose scoffed.

"And when I asked Nathan to fetch a mop for my spilled pint"—she made eye contact with Nathan—"you headed directly for the back hallway."

"So?"

"Why did you think the mop would be there?"

"You're being ridiculous."

"Eddie kept the mop in the storage room. The killer used it on the floor after he hanged Eamon. Not only to get rid of his footprints, but also to hide the rope fibers."

"Prove it!"

"Then you left the mop in the hallway. In the exact spot where you went to fetch it again."

"Circumstantial!"

She nodded to Eddie. "Eddie will confirm that."

"This is ridiculous," Nathan sputtered.

"Speaking of ridiculous . . ." Siobhán plucked the flyer from the garda station out of her handbag. She held it up. "These had been sitting in the station for days. Until somebody stole them. If only I had seen it first." She turned the flyer toward the crowd. Everyone stared at it, but Nathan Doyle.

BINGO FUND-RAISER
OPERATION DIAMOND DASH

Macdara came closer. "What is this?"

"A bingo game," Siobhán said. "The winner gets a pair of diamond earrings." She handed the flyer to Macdara.

"My God." Macdara stared at Nathan. "You made it all up?"

"Not a poker player," Siobhán said. "But a master at distraction nonetheless."

"How could you?" Real hurt rang from Macdara's voice. "How could you betray the shield?"

Nathan moved toward Macdara. "I didn't have a choice. Eamon Foley was scum. I wasn't going to let him hurt her anymore. Or our baby."

"Leave us alone," Rose said. "We've overcome too much!"

"She had nothing to do with this," Nathan said. "It was all me."

"She had nothing to do with the hanging," Siobhán said. "But she had everything to do with the tampered brakes. That's why she sent the waitress to her death. Or thought she did."

"It's a pity no one will ever know for sure," Rose said.

"You didn't hear? Emily survived the crash. She and the boyfriend tried to make a run for it, but I just got a text that they've been apprehended. They're at the station giving their statements as we speak. You sold her Eamon Foley's car for ten euro."

Nathan bent down. When he came up again, he was holding a gun. "Everyone get down." People screamed and hit the floor. Nathan nodded at Macdara. "Always check for a second gun, horse." Siobhán, Macdara, and Rose were the only ones who remained standing.

"It's over," Macdara said. "Put that down."

"I don't want to use it. I did like you two. A little naive, but likable. I'm going to take my love and we're going to leave." Nathan took Rose by the arm and began to haul her to the door. No one moved, but

Nathan whirled on them anyway, waving the gun. "If you try and stop me, I'll use the gun. You know I will."

Rose bent over and screamed. "My water," she said. "The baby is coming!"

"Not now!" Nathan's voice rang with pain.

"Don't you tell me, 'Not now.'" Rose shoved Nathan. "Tell the baby!" She screamed and bent over. "Oh, God!"

One look was all it took to see it wasn't a ruse. Water puddled beneath her. "Call an ambulance," Macdara said as he rushed to her side.

Nathan threw a desperate look to the door. Rose caught it. She grabbed Nathan. "Don't you even *think* of leaving me."

"I'll be arrested." He tried to tug away. Rose held tight.

Siobhán stepped forward, speaking only to Nathan. "You have a choice. Flee now and be caught down the road, or surrender to us and we'll make sure you get to see your child come into this world."

"You don't have that authority." Nathan sounded as if he wanted to take the deal.

"I do," Macdara said. "I'll allow it. You'll get a chance—maybe the only one—to hold your newborn."

"Then I'll be arrested."

He was close. Siobhán took another step. "There aren't many experiences in life that you can't replicate in books or on telly. The birth of your child is one of them."

"If you don't stay, I'll kill you!" Rose clung to him.

Nathan's gun hand went slack. Macdara swiped it away.

Nathan whirled. "Okay, okay. I'll make a full con-fession. Just let me see my baby born. Let me hold him or her. Just once."

Macdara nodded. He was a man of his word. "A full confession on the way to hospital. And we'll have guards on you the whole time."

Nathan nodded. "Yes, yes." Sweat dripped from his brow. "Thank you." He turned to Siobhán and shook his head as he wiped the sweat from his brow. "I didn't lie about everything. You're going to make a fantastic detective sergeant one day."

"It's too bad I can't trust a word you say."

Nathan's face softened and for a moment she didn't see the face of a killer. She saw the face of a man who had taken too many wrong turns. "Stick as closely as possible to the truth, O'Sullivan. Remember?" Sirens wailed nearby. The ambulance was almost here. Nathan wagged a finger at Siobhán as Rose was escorted out. "And you of all people know the truth when you hear it."

Chapter 33

⤜✕⤛

The lads were playing cards in the back room of the bistro. The fire was going. It was a warm spring evening, so Siobhán had the door to the back garden open. She stood with a mug of tea, drinking in all the flowers. They all needed healthy distractions. She was already plotting different universities where Eoin could go to develop his artistic schools. And Gráinne remained a challenge, but Siobhán vowed to help her sister tame a bit of her wandering spirit. Maybe she would like to become a stylist or fashion designer. Either way it was a relief to have the poker tournament and festival behind them, to get on with the rhythm of life, and with a little luck have a string of quiet months at work, filling out forms for property disputes or petty shenanigans.

The front door opened and the bell dinged. Siobhán smiled as the butterflies swarmed her stomach. "How

ya?" she heard Macdara call to her brood. She turned
to make him a cup of tea, when he took her hand. "Go
for a walk with me?"

"Sure." She ruffled Ciarán's hair on the way out.

They walked down Sarsfield Street, nodding hello
to neighbors, and taking in the warm evening.

"The baby will be placed with Rose's sister."

"I hope Rose gets out in time to be a mother."

Macdara nodded. She'd given birth to a beautiful
baby boy. Before he was arrested, Nathan Doyle had
been there to hold his son. He had a longer road ahead
of him, with charges both in County Cork and Dublin.
It was hard to see that kind of ending for one of their
own. But justice had been done. Rose Foley and the
baby would remain together in custody until the baby
could be placed with her sister. Rose would do time for
the attempted murder of Eamon Foley and the cover-
up, not to mention cutting the brakes in the Mustang,
and setting Emily up to die. Sadly, evil seemed to be
like a cancer. Once a person committed one evil act, it
seemed the impulse multiplied, making it easier to do
again, and again. Making the job of the guards vital to
society. The ultimate goal would be to stop a person
before they crossed that line, if only they all had crystal balls.

Without discussing it, they headed for the abbey as
the sun began to set, spreading red and orange streaks
across the sky. They crossed the bridge over the little
river, and headed down the gravel path to the ruined
structure. Once inside, they continued to the stairs
leading to the bell tower. The top was their favorite
place to sit, looking out over Kilbane. The silence between them was filled with anticipation. Macdara had

something on his mind. They sat on the top steps, continuing the silence for a little more.

"That was excellent work," Macdara said. His voice was thick.

"Thank you."

"He was right about one thing. You would do well in Dublin. You will make a fantastic detective sergeant one day."

She nodded, feeling her heart tap dance in her chest. Macdara looked out over the walls, over the gentle hills. "This is it for me. This is home."

"I know." It was her home too. Why did she feel a stab of pain?

"I don't want to be the person that holds you back."

"I don't see it that way." But sometimes she did. Sometimes she wished he longed for something, somewhere, beyond these walls.

"When you thought I was going to propose . . ."

Here it was. They were going to talk about it. She wanted to, and she didn't want to. "Yes?"

"Did you . . . want me to?"

This isn't fair. All on me to answer. "I was trying to figure that out myself," she said. "A part of me felt excited. A part of me worried. I'm only months into this job."

"Exactly," he said.

What did that mean? Did he want or not want to marry her? She knew him better than anyone outside of her siblings, yet there were still parts of Macdara Flannery that were closed to her. What did he want? Why wasn't he already married with kids? "I have a pretty full house too."

"You do."

He was being cautious, parsing his words. So was

she. "But it wasn't horrible to imagine." *There. Take that.*

He chuckled, startling her. "I see."

She clenched her fist. Impossible man. "Is it . . . something you've ever imagined?"

"Given your tastes in rings, it would take me a while to save up."

"That's not fair. I was set up. He wanted to know what my favorite was—if money was no object. And I wasn't looking at price tags."

That chuckle again.

She'd had enough. Stood. "I'm glad you find this so funny." She started down the stairs.

"Siobhán." He took the stairs faster, headed her off. He took her hands.

Was this it? What Shane had meant? After Nathan and Rose were taken away in the ambulance, Shane Ross had come up to her in the parking lot of Sharkey's.

"You're good," Shane said. "But you had me sweating."

She smiled. "I'm sorry. I was waiting for backup to arrive. I had to stall before revealing the true killer."

A grin spread across Shane's face. "There is one little thing you got wrong."

"What's that?"

He shook his head. "It's not my secret to tell. But I hope you find out someday."

Siobhán forced herself back to the present. Macdara cleared his throat. "Nathan Doyle didn't send Shane to look at rings with you. I did."

Siobhán had never heard thunder roll on a cloudless spring night, so it must have come from somewhere inside her. "Why?" she squeaked.

"Why? Because I love you, you eejit."

She blinked. Tears filled her eyes. She shoved him. "I love you too. *Eejit.*" She gave him a little shove. He laughed and pulled her into him. "Just tell me you didn't buy that ring."

"Here she goes again. Can't stand secrets, can you?"

"It's not like you to use a suspect like that."

Macdara nodded. "I told myself it was all about the case. But it was also an opportunity to gain a little insight." He chuckled. "Didn't know you were going to pick the most expensive one."

"Wait. If Shane wasn't a diamond thief . . . then the ring isn't really missing."

Macdara winked. "Tom Howell did a good job, didn't he?"

She nodded. "So it's still there. Right? The ring? At the shop?" He just stared at her. "Macdara."

"Would you please shut up and let me get through this?"

She stood still. So did all of the birds in the trees, and blades of grass, and the ancient stones in the walls. Macdara sank to his knees on the stone steps. He reached into his pocket. Her hands flew over his mouth. "This doesn't have to change anything."

"Yes."

"We can be engaged forever."

"Yes."

"If you want to go to Dublin, we'll go to Dublin. Or China. Anywhere you want. Or just stay here."

"Yes."

He removed a box.

"You didn't."

"Shut up."

She did.

He opened the box. There it was. The ring she picked out. She shook her head. "I can't."

"You can."

"It's too dear."

"Tom might have exaggerated the price for dramatic effect."

"By a lot?"

Macdara chuckled. "What does a bachelor like me need a nest egg for?"

"Dara."

He reached for her hand and slipped on the ring. The emerald sitting up high. Diamonds forming a Celtic cross around it. The most gorgeous thing she'd ever seen, placed on her finger by the man that made her heart skip beats. This imperfect, lopsided, handsome man. She looked up. The skies were full-on red, with orange and purple tints. Gorgeous. It caught the emeralds and diamonds and they twinkled. Fat tears rolled down her cheeks. "You are the most beautiful woman in the world. You know that, don't you, Siobhán O'Sullivan?"

"Dara."

"Not just beautiful. Inside and out. You're whip smart. You're funny. You're kind. I might be an eejit, but I'm no fool. And only a fool wouldn't want to marry a woman like you." She wanted to reply, but her heart was in her throat. "Siobhán O'Sullivan . . . will you—someday—marry me?"

"Yes. Yes, I will someday marry you." She launched into his arms before he could change his mind, almost knocking him down the steps. She ended up in his lap. He leaned in and kissed her. When they finally broke away, he took her hand, hauled her to her feet, and grinned. "Curried chips? Maybe a little champagne?"

"Absolutely." This time his chuckle didn't annoy her. This time she joined in. Hand in hand, they maneuvered through the remains of the abbey out to the path, heading for the little bridge, and the river where the monks used to brew beer. She imagined them stopping to congratulate them. So much history, so much character. *Home.* She wanted to shout it to the world. "I'm engaged to Macdara Flannery!"

She paused. She liked her surname better. He wasn't going to make her become a Flannery, was he? *Someday* . . . She had time to deal with that. She couldn't imagine not having the last name O'Sullivan. . . .

Now wasn't the moment for negotiations, now was that glorious time to feel the joy. And her heart was bursting with it. Somewhere up in the heavens she was sure her mam and da were looking down, sending Irish blessings, and welcoming the messy-haired man with the deadly blue eyes and lopsided grin to the family.

Someday.

And that was soon enough for her.

In a remote—and superstitious—village in County Cork, Ireland, Garda Siobhán O'Sullivan must solve a murder where the prime suspects are fairies . . .

Family is everything to Siobhán: her five siblings; her dear departed mother for whom the family business, Naomi's Bistro, is named; and now her fiancé, Macdara Flannery. So precious is her engagement that Siobhán wants to keep it just between the two of them for a little longer.

But Macdara is her family, which is why when his cousin Susan frantically calls for his help, Siobhán is at his side as the two garda rush from Kilbane to the rural village where Susan and her mother have recently moved. Unfortunately, tragedy awaits them. They find Susan, who is blind, outside the cottage, in a state. Inside, Aunt Ellen lies on her bed in a fancy red dress, no longer breathing. A pillow on the floor and a nearby teacup suggest the mode of death to their trained eyes: the woman has been poisoned and smothered. Someone wanted to make sure she was dead. But who?

Devout believers in Irish folklore, the villagers insist the cottage is cursed—built on a fairy path. It turns out Ellen Delaney was not the first to die mysteriously in this cottage. Although the townsfolk blame malevolent fairies, Siobhán and Macdara must follow the path of a murderer all too human—but just as evil . . .

Please turn the page for an exciting sneak peek of Carlene O'Connor's next Irish Village mystery MURDER IN AN IRISH COTTAGE coming soon wherever print and e-books are sold!

Chapter 1

Ellen Delaney sunk the last spoke into the soft earth, then worked her way around the tent's circumference, tying off the stakes and giving it a good shake, making every effort to see that it would stand whatever curse might befall a lone soul under the solstice moon. It had been some years since she'd gone camping, but she could still pitch a tent. When it was solid she counted off ten paces to the hawthorn tree. At the height of bloom, its gorgeous white flowers were a stark contradiction to the mythology embedded deeply into the gnarled tree, right down to its tangled roots. Just beyond it, popping out of the grass, like an image in 3-D, one could see a distinct ring, which from above would look like a giant O. *A fairy tree and a fairy ring.*

The ring in the grass was made up of wild mushrooms, yet like the tree, the circle was endowed by some—mostly the older folks in this village—with mythological properties, and it came with dire warnings. It was the domain of fairies. Cunning, playful, and vindictive creatures who could bestow riches with one hand while striking them down with the other. The tales of their mirth and feisty deeds were as long and dark as the Irish night sky.

Nonsense, of course, and it would soon be put to rest. And it wasn't as if anyone was asking for them to be taken down. Live and let live, leave well enough alone. She and her grown daughter had recently moved to Ballysiogdun, and their stone cottage, visible in the distance, was said to be in the middle of a fairy path. Typical that no one deemed to mention it until *after* they'd moved in. It was true that on the other side of the cottage, if one continued in a straight path, one would soon come upon *another* fairy tree, and another fairy ring, placing her cottage squarely in jeopardy. Structures built in the middle of fairy paths did not bode well. And apparently, the fairies wanted it gone.

Rubbish. If the cottage posed such a danger, then why hadn't the councilman ordered it bulldozed before she and her daughter moved in? This was Aiden Cunningham's fight, not theirs. He was a coward, that's why, already bending from the backlash of the villagers. Perhaps *one* villager in particular.

If the villagers wanted to point the finger at someone, it should be each other. With their lies, and cheats, and schemes. Maybe she should start outing their secrets, let them have a go at each other. If there was one thing Ellen Delaney had learned, it was that a woman her age was often completely overlooked. Perhaps a more delicate type would be hurt by this fact, this surreal invisibility. But it had served Ellen well. She knew so many dirty little secrets, and she wasn't afraid to expose them. If tonight didn't do the trick, she was going to do exactly that.

Sinners were calling for the destruction of her home, not fairies, or shape-shifters, or piseog, one of the many Irish words that referred to the supernatural. Such tales belonged in the pages of a book. Ellen groaned at the thought of the professor's book. Dylan Kelly. He was also behind this. Riling everyone up with the promise of wild tales. Enough. She didn't want to think about them anymore. Ellen Delaney dove into the tent and rifled through her bag for her bottle of Powers whiskey. This nonsense would end tonight. She had made a bet. In her quieter moments, she called it a "Deal with the Devil," but she would see to it that the terms were honored. As she sipped on the whiskey and looked out over the soft green hills, kissed by the lingering sun, the conversation played in her mind, like background music:

"If you're so sure fairies don't exist, spend the night near the fairy ring."

"I will, so."

"Sundown to sunrise."

"Not a bother."

"Alone."

"If I do, what's in it for me?"

They opened the calendar to study the cycles of the moon. The twenty-first of June, the summer solstice. Ellen's daughter was leaving for a conference in Dublin just at the right time. Ellen had no intention of forcing Jane to camp overnight with her; she wasn't built for it. Legally blind, her daughter startled easily. With Jane gone, it was the perfect weekend to do it. She said as much, and the next thing she knew the date was set. Friday evening, sundown. An official agreement between villagers. The contract had been drawn up, witnessed, notarized, and signed.

Streaks of red and orange in the sky promised a remarkable sunset, and soon a full, honey-colored moon would send sweet light shining down on her. Ellen continued to gaze out over the meadow as she supped her whiskey. Sixty-four years of age and she never failed to be awestruck by the landscape. One didn't have to profess a belief in fairies to cherish the trees, and the rolling green hills, and the cragged rocks. *Preserve away, just don't get carried away!* Stories had their place, and their place was on the lips of seanchaíthe—professional storytellers enthralling folks gathered around a roaring turf fire.

Yes, she respected storytellers, with the exception of Eddie Doolan (don't get her started), who could be seen spouting off everywhere she looked, draped in theatrical garb and stuttering around pretty women. He was giving professional storytellers a bad name, had no right to call himself a seanchaí.

Speaking of fools, in the distance a clump of color soon turned out to be her fellow art students, hiding behind their easels. Annabel's evening painting class. She'd forgotten all about it. Was Mary Madigan among them, Annabel's prize student? They would capture the setting sun, and the full moon, and then be gone. She prayed her tent would go unnoticed, relieved that the brown material blended in with the night and no one would think to look for it. She thought of making a fire but didn't want to draw any unnecessary attention to herself.

When the sun finally dipped below the horizon, the art students packed up and disappeared. The moon did not disappoint—a fat orb pulsing with life. So palpable was its glow, Ellen could almost feel a magnetic pull, igniting the first prickle of fear. *Nonsense.*

She crawled into the tent lest her imagination get the best of her. Moments later she opened the flap and peered out at the hawthorn tree. She had to admit, against the amber sky the gnarled branches were ethereal and downright witchy. She took a last gulp of whiskey, noting with some shock the dent she'd put in it, as the nibbles of worry turned into vicious little bites. Would their deal be honored? How could anyone prove she'd actually spent the night? It dawned on her now, how foolish she'd been not to ask. Was she being watched? Once the thought hit, it took root, digging deep into her psyche. Someone, somewhere, was watching. Maybe several someones.

Let them.

There was a slight chill to the air and she snuggled farther into her sleeping bag. Fairies! Those tales were for fools. What time was it? Had she been here an hour or four?

They put a stray on you. If a fairy put a stray on you, you could be standing in your own yard and nothing would look familiar. What felt like days might only be hours. Was this what was happening to her?

Stop it. Stop it right now. Shame on her, a schoolteacher. She knew where she was. She knew who she was. A right fool. All to prove to an even bigger fool that no fairies meant her harm.

She just needed to fall asleep, that was the key to surviving this night. She'd been forbidden to bring her sleeping tablets. *Cheating.* At least the whiskey went unchallenged. She'd gotten the short stick, she saw that now. What was to stop a person from creeping up on her, pretending to be a fairy? She would not be fooled, or frightened. There was no need to jump at the crack of every little twig. She set her head back in her sleeping bag, pulled it up to her face, and closed her eyes. Outside there was a faint whistling of the wind, and her limbs began to relax as she listened to nature's tunes. How sweet. It sounded like flutes.

Flutes! Someone was playing music nearby, trying to make her think it was fairy music.

She shot up, wishing she had brought a weapon. A knife from the kitchen at the least. She pawed her side for her torch. If anyone tried anything, she could strike them with it, and run. She found it, gripped it, then relaxed again once it was securely by her side. The wind was louder now, more of a roar than a whisper. She attempted to soothe herself by imagining cheerful fairies, dancing around the ring. Nothing to fear as long as you stayed out of their way.

The cottage was in their way. Why else had all the poor souls who lived there before her come to such misfortune? Just say it . . .

They died.

She sat bolt upright, for the voice had sounded real, not in her head, but like someone whispering the words directly into her tent. *They died, they died, they died.* A chorus of whispers now. How could that be? How could anyone know what she was thinking and finish her sentence out loud?

She reached for her torch but felt only the soft ground underneath the tent. It had been right there, right by her side. She was being tricked. Set up. She pawed the ground on both sides, all around the tent. Her torch was gone!

The sound of giggling, like children, filtered into the tent, making her blood run cold. "Who's there?" She sounded terrified, which infuriated her. Another twig snapped. She sat hunched over inside her tent, eyes squeezed shut, livid at the tricks that were being played on her.

Malevolent.

The word came into her mind, and she felt little pin-pricks all over her body. What if this wasn't a simple prank; what if someone meant her real harm?

Run.

A dark shadow fell over the tent, and she squeezed her eyes and scrunched her body up in a ball, and that's when she felt it. The tip of a bony finger touching her face, tracing her jawline. Her hands automatically tried to slap it away and met with nothing but air. Her eyes flew open. She saw nothing but the black of night. And yet someone was there. *A creeper creeping.*

Stories she'd heard over the years settled around her neck and squeezed like a pair of old hands. The farmer whose head was severed while trying to pull a fairy tree out of the ground with his tractor; the woman who had the gift of sight, only to have dozens of black beetles crawl out of her eyes the moment she died; cattle that were seemingly healthy one day struck dead in farmers' fields the next. No one spared. Not even children. Sickened in their cribs, their souls snatched and switched. She shivered. She was hallucinating. Hearing things, seeing things, feelings things. Her limbs were tingling. Would they shut off that music? She clasped her hands over her ears as colored lights danced in her mind. Something strange was going on. This wasn't worth it. *They died, died, died.* She had better do something before she was next. *Dead.* She scrambled out of the tent, set her sights on her cottage, and ran.

Connect with Us

Visit us online at
KensingtonBooks.com
to read more from your favorite authors, see books
by series, view reading group guides, and more.

Join us on social media

for sneak peeks, chances to win books and prize packs,
and to share your thoughts with other readers.

facebook.com/kensingtonpublishing
twitter.com/kensingtonbooks

Tell us what you think!

To share your thoughts, submit a review,
or sign up for our eNewsletters, please visit:
KensingtonBooks.com/TellUs.